MOTHER OF CHAOS

JOHN PATRICK KENNEDY

2017

Deep into that darkness peering, long I stood there, wondering, fearing,
Doubting, dreaming dreams no mortal ever dared to dream before.
— *Edgar Allan Poe, "The Raven"*

CHAPTER
ONE

PISA, ITALY, 1730

"You want to summon a fallen angel." Ruxandra managed to keep her composure right up to the word *angel.* Then it left her entirely. *"Are you insane?"*

When Kade showed up out of nowhere after 120 years apart, suddenly there outside her favorite café, she had run from him, overwhelmed by memory and emotion. But as she crossed the rooftops of Pisa, the beautiful and faded Italian city that had become her newest home, the lit buildings smears of gold against the night sky, the peaceful views had calmed her and she'd stopped, letting him catch up. She was a vampire, not a victim. And he was not her worst enemy. But what he wanted shattered her facade.

"No," Kade said. "Though I nearly became so, traveling with Elizabeth."

"To hell with Elizabeth! You can't summon a fallen angel, Kade. A fallen angel created me!"

"I know."

"You know because I just told you." Ruxandra snarled the words. "Because you certainly didn't know before you came here."

"I did, actually."

"How?" Ruxandra demanded. "By the time I remembered it, things were already out of hand in Vienna. I never told any of you."

"She is still the same, you know," Kade said, moving a little closer to her on the roof where they stood, overlooking the Arno. His presence shone to all her senses, bright as a star, more vivid than any human's. "Elizabeth, I mean. She murders with impunity. She tortures girls and young women whenever she wants. She bathes in their blood because she enjoys the feel of it."

Elizabeth Bathory had been a monster *before* she met Ruxandra. She tortured and murdered girls in a desperate quest to maintain her youth and power. She sent men to track Ruxandra, daughter of Vlad Dracula, and bring her out of the wilderness. Ruxandra had been a mindless Beast, living on the blood of animals. Elizabeth helped her regain her intelligence and strength. She also manipulated Ruxandra to her own advantage.

Ruxandra made Elizabeth a vampire, thinking they would travel the world together.

Instead Elizabeth showed her true colors, returning to her castle and going on a rampage of torture and murder. Ruxandra stopped her, but not before Elizabeth turned her servant Dorotyas into a slave vampire and vilely abused both the girls and

Ruxandra. During the fight that ended Elizabeth's reign of terror, Kade drank Elizabeth's blood, becoming a vampire.

One hundred twenty years ago and he's trying to change the subject.

"God dammit, Kade—"

"Whereas you"—Kade spread his hands wide, taking in Ruxandra's outfit and sword—"have changed immensely."

Ruxandra looked down. She wore a blue coat of proper knee length and tight black breeches over a white shirt with a short, plain collar. Her red hair hung down her back in a ponytail, held in place with a strip of leather. A long cloth tied down her breasts to help her disguise. Her boots and stockings currently sat on a rooftop a half mile away, thanks to the chase Kade had led her on.

"I dress as a man for simplicity's sake," Ruxandra said. "Women cannot roam the streets at night." *But someday I shall*, she thought. *As a woman. The world has to change eventually.*

"You are at the height of fashion."

"And you are fifty years out of date and changing the subject."

He wore a hip-length coat that clung tight to his body, with puffed sleeves. His trousers hung loose on his legs, and his cape and boots were both too short and unfashionable. His beard was gone, his skin now as pale and smooth as Ruxandra's own. He was beautiful in a way he had never been, though easily recognizable as the same man.

"I do not think of my wardrobe," Kade admitted. "I'm not seen by many, and those who see me do not care about clothes or fashions."

"Dressing out of date makes you stand out, which we cannot afford. The angel, Kade. Why?"

"It only makes one stand out if one is noticed, which I am not."

He leaped to the ground, the edges of his body shimmering in the darkness. All vampires could go unnoticed. This was not invisibility, but a persistent ability to be ignored by any human, even those who stood mere inches from one's face. Only other vampires saw through it. She followed, also unnoticed, though there were few around to see at this hour. Kade held out his arm. "Shall we talk as we walk?"

Ruxandra stared at his arm as if it were a foreign object. "You are joking."

"Is there something wrong?"

"You show up out of nowhere, follow me, and then tell me you want to summon a fallen angel? *Of course* something is wrong! I don't even *trust* you; I'm certainly not going to walk arm in arm with you."

Kade's eyebrows rose. "You don't trust me?"

"You made me a *prisoner*, Kade." Ruxandra growled the words. "You made it so I couldn't leave Elizabeth. I could have been stuck with that sadistic monster forever."

"Elizabeth made you a prisoner," Kade corrected. "Yes, I cast the spell that kept you by her side, but it wasn't done willingly."

"You still did it!"

"She would have tortured me for weeks." The calm demeanor he'd been wearing to that point vanished, replaced by a dark intensity. "Killed me in as horrendous a manner as she could conceive. You know what she could do."

"So you let her torture me instead? You let her torture those girls?" Ruxandra turned her back on him. "Coward."

She stalked away from him. In truth, she did not know how brave or cowardly she'd have been if she'd been allowed to grow up, if she'd been a man like Kade with independence and choices.

Perhaps those very privileges made it harder to give up life. But she would never know who she could have been, how she might have lived—only that she felt an overwhelming loss when she remembered the girl who had not yet been turned vampire, not yet killed.

She shoved down the feeling. Killing was something she'd had to come to terms with, and she had. Right now she wanted to get her boots, kill Pasquale—the bullying rapist she'd been on her way to dispatch before Kade showed up—and go to bed. She wasn't in the mood to talk anymore.

"Ruxandra, please." The tapping of Kade's boots on the cobblestones echoed off the wall, so noisy compared to Ruxandra's bare feet. "A hundred years have passed. More, in fact."

Ruxandra didn't look back. "I know how many years have passed. I've been enjoying them all." Not entirely, of course, but certainly they'd been better than the time spent with Elizabeth and the hundred years before. She had love, art, music, and freedom. She had seen high places and low, watched and listened to the talk in cafés and noble houses, marketplaces and bedrooms—not always with the knowledge of those she was observing. She'd read and learned.

"You were not a person when I cast that spell." Kade caught up to her. "You were an animal and a danger to everyone around you."

Ruxandra stopped walking. "That had nothing to do with it, and you know it. She bound me to her so she could manipulate me, and she used you so she could keep manipulating me when I turned her into a vampire."

"I know." Kade's tone softened. "That is why I didn't cast a spell that protected Elizabeth from you. I thought that if worse came to worst, you could kill her and escape." His voice was low and seductive, and she shivered. *If only I had.*

"Why didn't you tell me?"

"Why do you think?" He stepped in front of her, his eyes blazing. "You are immortal, Ruxandra. Elizabeth is immortal. I wanted immortality. If I had told you how to escape, we would not be standing here, one hundred twenty years later, having this argument. I would be dead and moldering in the ground while you wandered the world."

He took one of her hands in his. "I only wanted to be like the two of you. Supernatural creatures with all the freedom in the world, able to see and learn! Is that so wrong?"

Hating that his mention of learning echoed her thought, Ruxandra extended the talons in her fingertips. Kade pulled his hand away before they dug into his flesh.

"I know you were angry," Kade said. "I hoped time would make it less painful."

"Do you know what she did to me?" Ruxandra kept her tone even to hide her pain at the memory. "Her and Dorotyas?"

"No." Kade's voice was gentle. "You never told me."

"They tortured me," Ruxandra said. "Dorotyas stomped on me like she was killing a rat. Elizabeth whipped me for hours. I had to let them or they would have murdered all the girls in Elizabeth's *gymnaesium*."

"Given how you hurt Elizabeth and Dorotyas after, I think that score was settled."

"That's not the point!" Ruxandra drove a finger into his chest hard enough to make him grunt and take a step back. "You're the reason it all happened. *You* trapped me! I wanted to see the world but *your* magic dragged me back."

"I know."

"So what made you think I would *ever* forgive you?"

He looked at her for a moment, his eyes unreadable. "Time."

"Time?" Ruxandra scoffed. "Time means nothing to me, Kade. I remember everything that happened at the castle."

"So do I." Kade opened his hands. "I remember the agony of transforming into a vampire. I remember how I slaughtered those men to feed. I remember how the sunlight trapped me inside the castle. I hunted the hallways, mad with hunger, until night fell. Then I went to the woods and found a cabin. A man, his wife, and his three children. The youngest was five."

Ruxandra looked away.

"I remember what each of them tasted like, Ruxandra. I remember waking up surrounded by their corpses and thinking, *I am a monster.*"

"You *chose* to be a monster. You and Elizabeth."

"Yes, I did." Kade's shoulders slumped, his head coming down. "I didn't know what it meant. I didn't realize how little control I would have at the beginning or how it would feel to be the author of atrocities rather than the witness. I'd grown insensitive to others' pain, I admit. I assumed that would continue to be the case. And then there I was, committing murders myself and fully aware of the horror."

Both fell silent. Ruxandra remembered when she had changed. She'd slaughtered her father and six men the first night, then other innocents until she'd run off to live in the woods like an animal.

"It is a dreadful thing to acquire a conscience just as one can no longer make use of it. Or so it seemed to me at first. So I denied it. I quashed it and traveled with the other monsters. For fifty years I stayed with Elizabeth and Dorotyas. I watched Elizabeth torture a thousand girls before drinking their blood, and torture a thousand more for the fun of it. I watched Dorotyas use a thousand men for her pleasure and kill them all. And I helped them. I joined in their games, and I *reveled* in it."

"So now what?" Sarcasm filled Ruxandra's voice. "You've reformed? You've stopped drinking blood?"

"I stopped doing it for fun," Kade said, his voice firm. "One night, in Chartres, I watched Elizabeth torture a fourteen-year-old girl. Just another girl, just another victim. No one important. Elizabeth had gagged her so no one would hear her scream. She did worse things to that child than anything I saw when I was a *fiscal* in the Inquisition."

Ruxandra's eyes went wide. "You? You're a sorcerer. What were you doing in the Inquisition?"

"There is no better place to hide than in the enemy's ranks. And no better way to make money than by extorting the guilty."

"Noble of you."

"I have *never* been noble." Dark, bitter anger filled his voice. "I was born the son of a farmer and a hedge-witch. A nobleman murdered them both because my mother helped his wife end her twelfth pregnancy."

And that was your excuse for torturing others? Ruxandra didn't say it. She wanted to find out why Kade left Elizabeth, not start another fight.

Kade took a deep breath. When he spoke, he sounded calm once more. "I may have deserved pity once but certainly not anymore. I *know* that, Ruxandra. I know I could have walked away from Elizabeth at the very beginning. I chose not to. But when I was watching Elizabeth and this screaming child, it suddenly struck me how utterly pointless it all was. I was living a life without purpose, without reason. I didn't want that. Even when I was human, I never wanted that. So I left and searched for a purpose."

Ruxandra's eyes went to the night sky. In the east the stars were fading, and a line of dark blue edged up against the darkness. She felt tired and weighted down by the past in a way she had not felt for more than a hundred years. Elizabeth was a nightmare—her nightmare. She had made her.

"And that's why you want to summon a fallen angel?" Ruxandra asked. "To give you purpose?"

"Yes."

"Then why drag me into it?" Ruxandra's shout echoed off the buildings around them. "Why not just do it and leave me alone?"

"Because immortality is *lonely!*" Kade's voice, much quieter than hers, held no less passion. "I have friends, scholars I work with, but no one who understands the past. Not the way you and I understand it. None of them have lived there. So I spent months tracking you through Italy, just to speak to someone who has. I want to hear what happened after you left the castle. I want to know if you saw Venice during the Cretan War. I want to know if you read Galileo's treatise on the moons of Jupiter. I want to hear about what you saw and heard, learn what you experienced, and share what I experienced with you."

Ruxandra hesitated, just for a moment. It *had* been difficult, these many years, to talk as though she had only the eighteen years she appeared to have lived. Ruxandra had seen and done more than any woman alive, but she could not share it with anyone. She was always curbing her speech, thinking through every comment, playing a part.

But just that he's lonely is no excuse . . .

"Meet with me tomorrow," Kade said. "I will tell you all I know about the angel."

Ruxandra's eyes narrowed. "Fine. Tomorrow after the sun goes down, at the Aquila Café."

"Thank you," Kade said. "I look forward to it. Now, where is this place?"

"You're the one who is always learning." Ruxandra jumped in the air, landing on the tile roof some twenty feet above. "Figure it out yourself."

When she reached the Aquila Café, Kade was already there. He sat alone at a small table, an empty chair opposite him, a cup of coffee cradled in his hands. The men at the other tables—a dozen in all—were having lively discussions on everything from politics to animal husbandry. Kade didn't seem to hear them. He sat still, eyes closed, inhaling the coffee's aroma with a smile on his face. He opened them, saw Ruxandra, and waved her over.

"I forgot how wonderful coffee smells," Kade said.

Ruxandra sank into the chair opposite him. "Elizabeth did not allow it?"

One of his eyebrows rose at the sarcasm in her voice. "Neither she nor Dorotyas partakes of anything except blood. They said that now they have . . . risen to a higher level of existence, to use Elizabeth's turn of phrase."

Ruxandra shook her head. "Still fixated on being Blood Royal."

"Of course. I, on the other hand, find I enjoy the taste of tea and wine and spirits. And coffee, which I have not drunk for twenty years." He signaled the waiter to bring another cup, then sipped his own.

"Why not?"

"Because coffee has not reached the place where I was." He took another sip and set it aside. "Now tell me, Ruxandra, why is it we exist?"

T HE DEMON LIFTED *her hand to her mouth and ran the end of one finger over the tip of one of her teeth. The skin split open, and silver blood welled up on her fingertip. She lowered the finger to Ruxandra's lips. "Open your mouth."*

Ruxandra wanted to protest, to beg for God's forgiveness and the creature's mercy, to run screaming from the cave, but she couldn't find words or strength in her limbs. She could do nothing but cry as the fallen angel parted her lips.

"I send you out instead, my child," the fallen angel said, "to sow chaos and fear, to make humans kneel in terror, and to ravage the world where I cannot."

"Ruxandra?"

Ruxandra blinked, and the fallen angel's image faded away. Kade still watched her, waiting for an answer.

"Think, Ruxandra." Kade put his coffee on the table. "All creatures on earth have a purpose, from the smallest gnat to the largest elephant. We must have a purpose as well."

"God's creatures have a purpose," Ruxandra said. "We're not God's creatures."

Kade smiled. "I know."

Ruxandra's eyes narrowed. "*How* did you know?"

Kade took another sip of his coffee. "Did I ever tell you that I was one of the last sorcerers left in Europe, before I went to Elizabeth?"

"Kade . . ."

Kade ignored the impatience in her tone. "The Inquisition rooted out so many of them that the rest fled, or turned from the path to become monks. I was one of the fortunate few who escaped to the East before they came. Even then, I had to leave most of what I had behind."

"I'm sure. *How did you know?*"

"Almost all the sorcerers' writings were burned. After I left Elizabeth, I searched the offices of all the inquisitors in Spain. I even searched the Vatican, but there was nothing left. Certainly nothing about vampires. So I went further afield."

He wants to play games? Fine.

Ruxandra sat back in her chair, crossed her arms, and glared at him with the same look she'd once used to stare down a bear. Kade put on a smug little smile and took another sip of his coffee.

"I went east of the Holy Roman Empire," he said. "I searched through Brandenburg, through Prussia, Poland, Lithuania, Livonia, Estonia. I searched for thirty years. I found folktales everywhere, but no hint of anything more. Not until I went to Russia."

Kade took another sip of his coffee. The waiter brought another and set it in front of Ruxandra. The steam from it drifted up, filling her nose with its warm, savory, slightly bitter fragrance. Ruxandra left it alone and glared.

Kade put his cup down. "You're not going to ask me what happened next?"

Ruxandra narrowed her eyes and tightened her lips.

Kade took another sip of his coffee. He waved the cup in her direction. "Your coffee will grow cold if you don't drink it."

Kade finished his coffee in slow sips, taking time between each mouthful to look out the window as if the people passing were the most interesting thing he had ever seen.

"How long," he asked at last, "can you sit without moving?"

"Five days before the hunger becomes too much."

"I see. Does the Beast still break free?"

"Not often anymore. Though I'm getting tempted right about now."

The Beast—Ruxandra's animal self that had manifested during her hundred years in the woods and now lived separately within her mind—growled at the mention of its name. It had taken her years to fully regain control, and even now it still lurked, ready to take over, growing more powerful as Ruxandra grew hungry.

Kade smiled. "I suppose I should tell you about your fallen angel, then."

"Yes," Ruxandra said through clenched teeth. "You should."

He sipped his coffee. "In Russia, where the Inquisition never ventured, I discovered a very interesting group of people: one that studies both the natural world and the occult. And their library, oh . . ."

His gaze left Ruxandra and went far away, as if he were seeing the library in front of him. "It is huge. Stored deep underground.

They have books there in languages that no one speaks anymore. I had to learn a whole new alphabet, a whole new way of thinking before I could read them. It was there that I learned the origins of vampires, and the origin of you. The tablet said nothing of angels, though. Do you know the goddess Ishtar?"

Ruxandra shook her head.

"She was a goddess from the ancient world known in Babylon and Assyria and even Phoenicia. A goddess of war, of sex, of love and power. The tablet said that a great king asked her to grant him immortality. She did, but at a terrible price. He could no longer stand in the sun, nor partake of food. He was doomed to spend eternity roaming the night, able to take sustenance only from blood. Anyone who drank his blood became as he and was doomed alongside him."

Just like us. Ruxandra frowned and looked away. The last of the sun's light was fading from the sky, leaving the world in darkness.

"The cult of Ishtar vanished with the coming of Christianity," Kade said. "A later book in the magicians' collection said that the knights of the Christ chased down the unholy offspring of the vampire king, dragging them into the sun and burning them alive. Apparently it took five hundred years, and the king was killed in Russia."

"And in *that* book were explicit instructions for summoning a fallen angel. A woman of great size with black wings, just as the tablet described Ishtar. A creature of great power who destroys any who summon her without care and for any purpose not to her liking."

Like my father and his men.

"And it was then I realized *how* you must have been turned. Nothing else explains how completely ignorant you were about what a vampire was. Another vampire could not have created you. You had to have been created by the goddess herself."

"Renaldo!" called a man by the door. "There you are!"

A short, wide man in a bright red coat stood in the door, a smile on his face almost as large as his belly.

"Everyone wants to drink your health before the duel!"

"A duel?" Kade choked back a laugh.

"Yes," Ruxandra said sourly. "Before I ran into you last night I was on my way to meet Pasquale—a rapist and a murderer. Elizabeth would love him. But since you interrupted me, I have to meet him this morning."

"Ah. Now what will you do?"

"Drink all night," Ruxandra said. "Kill him in the morning."

"Isn't dueling illegal?"

"Doesn't stop anyone." She stood up. "Right, to the tavern!"

Kade caught her sleeve. "Do you need a second?"

Ruxandra stopped, surprised. "I hadn't thought about it. I suppose so."

"Then allow me. As a way of making amends for what has gone before," Kade said. "Besides, I still need your answer."

"My answer?"

"If you're coming to Russia."

Ruxandra shook her head and went to the bravos at the door. They cheered and led her off to the nearest tavern.

Seven hours and eight jugs of wine later, Ruxandra waited in a glade outside the city, under a pale predawn sky. She had put on a fresh shirt and jacket over clean breeches. She looked every inch the young bravo, down to the sword at her waist.

"What's his name?" Kade asked.

"Pasquale." Ruxandra's eyes went to the eastern horizon, watching it grow brighter by the minute.

"So you said. Last name?"

"No idea."

Kade shook his head. "Bad form, that."

Ruxandra shrugged. "So is being late. And if he's much later he can wait until another day."

"Have no fear of that," Pasquale said as he stepped into the glade. He had a pistol in each hand, the flint hammers cocked back, the barrels pointed skyward.

"About time," Ruxandra said. "Let's get this over with."

"Such a hurry to die," Pasquale said. "Foolish."

"Where is your second?" Kade asked.

"Second?" Pasquale smiled. "I didn't bring a second. I brought friends."

Ruxandra extended her mind out to the area around them. She could not read minds, but she could sense emotions, which was quite handy for finding prey.

Or, in this case, Pasquale's four friends hiding among the trees, anger and anticipation burning red inside them.

"Four of them," Kade said.

Ruxandra frowned. "How did you know?" she asked, voice pitched low.

"I sensed them," he said, speaking just as quietly.

"I didn't teach anyone that," Ruxandra said.

"Elizabeth discovered it," Kade said. "After all, it only takes the desire to know what the other person is feeling. Can you imagine Elizabeth *not* wanting to know how much a victim is hurting? Pity one can't actually read their thoughts."

"True." Ruxandra turned her attention to Pasquale and raised her voice. "You aren't wearing a sword. Are you not planning to duel?"

"I am planning on seeing you beaten and shamed." Pasquale smiled. "After I have my way with you, of course. Or did you think me as stupid as the others?"

Ruxandra's eyebrows rose. "I thought you far stupider than the others, but I didn't know you liked men."

Pasquale swaggered closer. "You are no man. Which is why I am not dueling you. Instead I will shoot your second, and my friends and I will have you in every hole until night falls. After which I will hang you naked by your ankles in the square as a warning to other sluts."

Ruxandra sighed and looked at Kade. "You see why I wanted to kill this *pezzo di merda*?"

Kade nodded. "We have to kill his friends, too, I suppose."

"I would rather not." Ruxandra pitched her voice to the shrubbery. "My quarrel is with Pasquale, not with any of you. If you leave, you live."

Pasquale laughed. "They will not listen to you, *putana*."

Ruxandra put her hand on her sword's grip and walked toward him. She felt something dark and animal stirring inside her.

"A sword will do you no good whatsoever," Pasquale said. "I am an excellent shot."

"The duel begins when I count three," Ruxandra said, keeping her voice loud. "Your pistols against my sword."

He laughed loudly. "Oh, you stupid little girl."

"One."

"I'll enjoy ripping you open," Pasquale said.

"Two."

Pasquale pointed one pistol at Kade and pulled the trigger. A blast of smoke and flame and noise lurched out from the barrel. It cleared a moment later. Kade remained standing. Pasquale's mouth fell open in surprise.

"Three."

Ruxandra had drawn her sword and run three steps forward in the second before Pasquale turned back to face her. She leaped forward into a graceful lunge, driving her sword fully through his body. His pistol, halfway along its trajectory to aim at her head, fell from nerveless fingers. Ruxandra stood up and let his body slide off her blade. His fingers closed over the hole in his chest.

Ruxandra looked to the woods, a small smile on her lips. "Run."

She heard scurrying as the men abandoned their hiding spots and ran.

Kade stepped up beside her. "Not much of a challenge, was he?"

"They never are." Ruxandra knelt and put her mouth over the hole in Pasquale's chest. He gasped in pain as she began sucking the blood out of his body. He tried to struggle but had no strength. Five seconds later he died.

Ruxandra stood up and wiped her mouth. "You want to know why we exist?"

Kade blinked. "Pardon?"

"We exist because a fallen angel wanted to spit in the face of God." She kicked Pasquale's body. "We exist because she wants us to roam the world and cause terror and chaos in her place. That's what she said when she made me."

"It was Ishtar, then?"

"She didn't give her name." Ruxandra remembered the giant phallus the creature had produced when offered Ruxandra's body. "She said she was an angel that fell with Lucifer."

"Fascinating."

"Not fascinating, *frightening*." *But not only that, either.* Ruxandra remembered how safe she had felt in the beautiful angel's arms, how warm her skin felt. The fallen angel had acted as if she cared about her.

She couldn't, or she wouldn't have done this to me. How is this anything but the most evil punishment?

Though another voice in her mind quietly disagreed, reminding her of the art, the music, the love, the freedom, the everlasting youth.

But those are side effects and choices. They are not what she cared about.

"Don't you want to meet her?" Kade crossed the glade to stand before Ruxandra. "Don't you want to ask her why you?"

"Why me?" Bitterness filled Ruxandra's voice. "Because I was there, so why not? If she went up against the will of heaven, she's probably insane enough to make vampires for the fun of it."

Not that the idea hasn't tempted me. My favorite artists, writers, musicians, lovers . . . But I didn't do it again after Elizabeth. Who would choose this?

"That is possible." Kade rubbed his chin and frowned. "Do you think it's possible that her creation of you was also the will of heaven?"

"*How?* How can *I* be the will of heaven?" She kicked Pasquale's body again. "How can *this* be the will of heaven? Just because

God made the world doesn't mean he has a plan for it. Or that he's always paying attention."

"But if he *is* paying attention, what then?" His eyes burned with excitement. "You can't imagine that you and I know all there is to know about God or his angels? What our purpose is, what the purpose of life is? This is an opportunity, Ruxandra. A chance to learn more about ourselves than was ever possible before."

"I don't care. I don't want to meet her. I don't want her walking the earth ever again."

Kade nodded. "Well. I respect your feelings, my dear. But you need to come to Russia."

"I said—"

"Because they will summon her, with or without me, at the winter solstice."

"What?"

"I had hoped that you would help," Kade said. "And I hope I can still convince you to help. But whether I can or not, they will summon her anyway."

THREE

*G*OD *DAMMIT.*

"We should probably leave," he said. "Before others arrive."

"Why would you let them?"

"I cannot stop people from coming here."

"You know what I mean, God damn you." Ruxandra squatted and wiped her sword on Pasquale's coat. "Why would you let the magicians summon the angel without you?"

"How could I stop them," Kade asked, "short of killing them all?"

"And you don't believe in killing?"

"I am not the person I was," he said in a low voice. "I don't kill without reason. But in this case it's simpler than that—I don't kill my friends."

Kade has friends.

"So you came to me, knowing I would come."

"I came to convince you to come," Kade said. "I came hoping your curiosity would bring you. I did not mean to present an ultimatum."

"But you did anyway." Ruxandra closed the distance between them. "You did the same thing back in Castle Csejte. You made it sound like I had a choice when you knew damn well that I didn't!"

Kade didn't back up. "As I recall, you managed to come up with another option."

"Yes." Ruxandra walked past him. "I did."

Kade fell in beside her. "Perhaps you will come up with another option this time as well."

"Perhaps I'll kill them all and burn the library."

"Perhaps," Kade said, and Ruxandra heard the happiness in his voice. "But I doubt it. You will like the magicians, Ruxandra. And there are things in that library that very few people have seen. Wouldn't you like to know about them?"

For a moment Ruxandra wondered at what, exactly, the library contained. *The vampire king . . . did he create a family? A court? What would that be like, a society of vampires?* She shoved the thought away. "Not as much as I'd like to stop *her* from coming back."

"And the only way you can is to come to Moscow with me." He smiled and held out his arm for her to take. "Shall we walk together?"

For a reply Ruxandra drove half the length of her sword through his body.

Kade yelled in pain and fell to his knees, hands scrabbling at the blade.

"Stop whining," Ruxandra said.

Kade grabbed the blade, trying to pull it out, gasping. "*Why?*"

"Because you made a prisoner of me in Castle Csejte," Ruxandra snarled. "Because you came here *knowing* that I would go with you. Also, because you *deserve* it."

"Knowing . . ." Kade winced and grabbed the blade. "Does this mean you'll come?"

"Three conditions." Ruxandra knocked his hand away from the blade. "First, you tell me everything you know about vampirism and the dark angel, and I mean *everything*, from every book you've read."

"Done."

"Second." Ruxandra grabbed the sword's grip and shoved the full length of the blade into Kade's body. He screamed. Ruxandra twisted it and pulled it out. "I need my sword."

Kade collapsed again. Ruxandra wiped the blade on his shirt, leaving trails of silver across the gray fabric.

Kade watched her cleaning his silver blood from the blade. The blade shone.

"And third?" Kade asked, warily.

"Third," Ruxandra said. "Buy some new clothes by tomorrow night. I don't want to be seen with you looking like this. After all, I *am* the height of fashion. See you at the café at sunset."

Ruxandra turned her back and started walking.

"Wait!" Kade called. "Am I forgiven?"

Her scornful laughter echoed in the alley. "Not even close."

Ruxandra spent the day clearing out her apartment. There was very little furniture: a chair to sit in, another for a guest, a wine rack and wines, a comfortable bed with linens, and a set of three-layer-thick curtains that blocked out the sunlight. She had a stack of books—novels and poetry—in Italian, another in Hungarian, and a third in Latin.

Then there were the clothes.

Ruxandra stared at the cupboard and sighed. She loved the fashions of this time. She loved the knee-length coats the men wore and the many colors fabric came in. She loved the way the dresses flared out at the hips to create a wide, elegant line. She owned a dozen dresses and six men's outfits, as well as gorgeous shoes in silk and leather with buckles, embroidery, paste jewels, and real pearls, and she didn't want to leave any of them behind.

I can't carry them all, so there is no sense crying over it.

She picked a plain, dark coat with matching pants and a white shirt to travel in. She had learned long ago that plain clothes were best for travel—they didn't get as dirty and didn't go out of fashion so readily. Especially among the poorer classes, where Ruxandra often fed. She packed a second of everything into a bag she slung over her shoulder. Then she packed her plainest dress—for when she could act like a woman again—a pair of shoes to match, a warm shawl, and all the underclothes she needed.

She hiked the bag over her shoulder, took one last look at her apartment, and then closed the door behind her.

Maybe Moscow will be pretty.

She went to the café, took a table, had a coffee, and waited. Kade didn't appear for the better part of two hours. When he arrived, though, he looked far better than the night before.

He'd found new clothes—a knee-length black coat with silver buttons, dark-blue trousers, and knee-high boots. He wore a new white shirt, and his hair was pulled back into a ponytail, much like Ruxandra's. He also carried a bag over his shoulder. The angles of his face caught the candlelight and caused more than one head to turn in his direction.

"I must have done well," Kade said as he sat down beside her. "You're staring."

"In surprise," Ruxandra said, ignoring the heat that she felt low in her belly. *Just because it's been a while is no reason to act like a cat in heat.*

She preferred women, though it had taken her ten years after Elizabeth before she'd been willing to trust anyone enough to have sex with them. Elizabeth had used Ruxandra to become a vampire. Then she'd assaulted her and laughed at her pain.

It had taken even longer before she'd gone with a man.

A hundred years before Elizabeth, she'd met Neculai. He was strong and handsome, and she was newly turned and alone. He became her lover in the same moment that she became his murderer. And far worse than that. She'd drunk him, but couldn't let his soul go. He turned first into an undead slave; then, when she fed him her own blood, into a mindless vampire. She'd had to hack him to pieces and leave him in the sun to die. It had frightened her so much that she'd gone deep into the woods, living like a Beast for a hundred years.

It was a beautiful, dark-skinned, dark-haired courtesan in Venice who had convinced Ruxandra to try the joys of the flesh again. Donatella, she of the laughing mouth and inventive endearments. Ruxandra had made certain to be sated with blood before she went to the woman, and it had been very pleasant indeed.

Another woman—a Roman matron with blonde hair and a taste for both men and women, preferably both at once—had reintroduced Ruxandra to men. The results had been worth waiting for, a feast of charm and desire. The big bedroom lit with dozens of candles, carafes of wine, and the men so young their flesh was like apple blossoms. Of course, they thought she was young, too . . .

She hadn't had a lover in a year, since she'd come to Pisa. She'd played both man and woman but hadn't wanted anyone to get too close, lest they find out what she was doing. She'd settle in as a woman for a while soon, find a girlfriend, but it was hard to let go of the freedom of the streets.

She preferred girls, but the way Kade looked now . . .

No. Never. Not as long as my fingers still work.

"Better?" Kade asked, one eyebrow rising.

"It's an improvement." Ruxandra kept her voice neutral. "At least you don't stand out like a pig in church."

"Thank you," Kade said drily. "Now, shall we be on our way? We have a long way to go."

"How far?"

"Nineteen hundred miles, more or less."

Ruxandra blinked. Kade smiled.

"How are we getting there?" Ruxandra asked. "Running?"

"I thought of hiring a carriage and driver."

"We can cover two hundred miles in a night, running, assuming there's a road. I doubt you'll find a carriage driver willing to try the same."

Kade's eyes widened. "Two hundred miles running. Truly?"

"You've never tried?" Ruxandra shook her head. "What have you been doing?"

"Wealthy people don't need to run." Kade signaled for a cup of coffee. "A carriage takes only a month."

"We're in a hurry."

The waiter brought two cups of coffee and set them down in front of them. Kade picked his up and blew on it.

"We can run to Moscow in twelve days," Ruxandra said, "if we stop every third day to eat. Which we'll need to do if we run like that. It makes you hungry fast."

"How on earth did you find this out?"

"I heard that Louis XIV ordered a remount of Lully's *Atys* two weeks before the performance opened. So I ran there. Made it in nine days."

Kade sipped at his coffee again. "How was it?"

"Mediocre. Louis loved it. And the dresses were splendid."

"I see."

"So let us run." She looked at his boots. "I suggest taking those off."

Kade's face fell. "Do you know how long it took me to find someone the right size?"

"Take them with you," Ruxandra said. "Just don't wear them while we run. The heels will wear out and trip you up after a few dozen miles."

"As opposed to rocks in my feet?"

"You don't feel those after the first mile."

"Wonderful."

Ruxandra stood up. "Now, shall we?"

"Finish your coffee first," Kade said, taking another sip. "There's none of that in Moscow unless you're in the palace."

They made it to the Venetian Lagoon the first night. Ruxandra stood on the shore, looking at the city. The sky was growing light now, and in the distance she saw the church spires, the buildings, both medieval and new, and the grand canals. It made her smile.

"How long did you live here?" Kade asked.

"Fifteen years. I attended every ball, every dance, and every concert in the city." She sighed. "It was glorious."

Kade nodded. "Why did you leave?"

Ruxandra shrugged. "I'd met everyone, seen everyone, and no one who was anyone didn't know my face. They all started commenting on how well preserved I looked and wondering aloud if I'd sold my soul to maintain my youth. So I left."

"You should go back. They are all dead now."

"I know." The sunlight grew brighter, the sun closer to the horizon. "We stay in Mestre for the day. Then tomorrow night we go on."

Two nights later, in Maribor, they hunted.

They became unnoticed to slip across the long stone bridge over the Drava River. The water rushed past beneath them, the soft sound of it rubbing past the bridge supports acting as counterpoint to the near-silent padding of their bare feet on the stone walkway.

Ruxandra jumped to the top of the city wall, landing without a sound. The guard, twenty feet away, didn't notice. Kade jumped and landed clumsily on the parapet beside her. The guard heard him hit and looked. His eyes slid past the vampires. After a moment he went back to looking out over the water. Ruxandra wondered that Kade hadn't learned to use his marvelous body as well as she had hers. It was one of the greatest pleasures of being a vampire, this speed and strength and precision, what even the Olympic athletes of ancient Greece could only dream of.

"So now what?" Kade asked, his voice loud in the silence.

Idiot! Ruxandra spun, talons out, ready to fight the guard.

The man hadn't moved. He stared out over the water, not paying attention. Ruxandra spun back, her mouth open.

"Don't speak." Kade put his finger against her lips. Ruxandra glared at him but said nothing. "In one book I learned that vampires could talk in a way that no one hears but other vampires. I can scream in a room full of humans, and not a single one will hear me. But I have not had the opportunity to see if other vampires could hear it until now."

Ruxandra glared harder, then turned away. *Well, I guess I deserved that. Thinking he hasn't been using his body.*

Kade smiled. "I'll teach you how after we hunt."

And with that he jumped down off the wall and into the city.

Show-off. Ruxandra raised her eyes to the heavens for patience and jumped down after.

Kade hunted with a ruthless efficiency that surprised Ruxandra. She liked to search for her prey, to hunt the alleys and streets and find the other predators. Sometimes they fought back. Sometimes they begged. It didn't matter to her.

Kade, by comparison, walked down the middle of the street, scanning each building as he passed. He stopped and pointed. "There."

"What?" Ruxandra looked, saw nothing, and reached out with her mind. Inside she sensed four people, all sad and angry, and three of them in great pain. "Them?"

"They are dying," Kade said. "I am sure of it."

He walked to the door, knocked, and waited. After his second knock, a young woman opened the door. Her eyes shone, the thin moonlight reflecting off the tears floating there. Dark circles surrounded them, and the face they sat in looked wan and exhausted.

"Let us in," Kade commanded.

Ruxandra had discovered that trick in Vienna. A *command* from a vampire made a person do almost anything the vampire desired, for a while, at least.

The woman stepped aside, and Kade went in. Ruxandra followed on his heels. He led them upstairs to a bedroom. Three cots lay side by side. In them two men and a woman lay, their breath coming in ragged gasps, their eyes squeezed tight shut with pain.

One man was older, with gray in his hair and a wrinkled face. His arm was missing, the stump covered in bloody red bandages. The woman also had gray hair and was missing a leg. The second man was younger, his body strong and his hair deep brown. His chest was misshapen, the ribs beneath the skin bent wrong and poking at the skin.

"My father and mother and brother," the young woman whispered. "They were visiting the church, and men were doing work on the wall and the stones tipped over and . . ."

"We will end their pain," Kade said. "All of them. Then you can rest. *Go downstairs, make tea, and drink it.*"

She obeyed his command and walked out. Kade turned to Ruxandra. "Which one do you want?"

Ruxandra looked across the three. "It doesn't matter."

"Then if you'll excuse me." Kade knelt down beside the older man and opened his mouth. The fangs hidden in his gums emerged, long and razor sharp and pointed like needles. He leaned close and drove them through the flesh in the man's neck.

The older man gasped with shock, his eyes flying open. He cried out once. Then Kade's hand pressed down on his mouth, silencing him until the last of his life was gone.

The woman opened her eyes as Kade raised his head, the man's blood still on his lips. She gasped in a breath.

Ruxandra crouched over her, hand covering the woman's mouth, teeth sinking deep in her throat before the woman exhaled. The woman's blood exploded in her mouth, drowning Ruxandra in ecstasy even as the woman's body bucked under her hand. She drank deep and fast, pulling the blood from her until not even a drop remained.

In the midst of it, the woman died.

Ruxandra raised her head. Kade was kneeling beside the younger man's cot. His eyes were wide open, too, but he didn't make a sound. He stared up at Kade, his breath quickening, his eyes never leaving the vampires.

At last the young man whispered, "You said . . . all of us. Please."

Kade smiled. He put his hand over the boy's mouth and nose, holding them tight. The boy shook, and for a time struggled. Then all movement stopped, and his eyes stared sightlessly at the ceiling.

Kade stood. "Come. We must find a different place to rest before sunrise."

Ruxandra commanded the young woman not to remember them and not to be afraid of the dead upstairs. *They died of their wounds.* Then they left.

In the darkness of a cellar, far from the house, Ruxandra lay back against the stone floor and sighed. She pulled her cloak tight around her body, making a cocoon of it. Across the room she made out Kade's form in the darkness.

He hunts well. And chooses his victims well. Maybe he isn't like Elizabeth.

The thought gave her some comfort as she drifted off to sleep.

As they went farther east, Kade insisted on stopping in the cities rather than small towns. It lengthened the journey, but the time wasn't unpleasant. Kade taught her how to use the vampire voice by pitching her voice at several frequencies at once, none of which the human ear heard. It was fun to sit in cafés and hold conversations without having to lower her voice.

In the early mornings, before they lay down to sleep, Kade taught her Russian. Ruxandra had discovered when she first arrived in Italy that she could learn a language just from hearing it spoken—she learned Italian in three weeks. However, having someone say something in the new language and then repeat the words in a language she knew doubled how fast she learned.

He also told her about the magicians.

"Six of them," Kade said one morning in a cellar outside of Bratislava. "Michael, Sasha, Victor, Derek, Dimitri, and, of course, the Alchemist."

"The who?"

"The Alchemist. The only woman sorcerer I have met since the Inquisition. A brilliant mind and a great magician. She is certain that within the library is the formula to turn lead into gold, and she is determined to find it."

Ruxandra's eyebrow went up. "You like this woman."

"You will, too," Kade said. "She is . . . a force of personality. But she is brilliant. It was her idea to call the fallen angel."

"Ah."

"Don't kill her out of hand," Kade said. "Please."

"I won't kill her out of hand." *Though that doesn't mean not at all.*

"We also have two librarians: Kurkov and Eduard. Neither can use magic, but they love the books. When I left, Kurkov was translating five volumes into Russian—all in different languages. He was the one who found the spell to call the fallen angel. Be careful. He is a charmer."

She gave him an incredulous look. "Do not concern yourself. So are any of them boring?"

"Derek," Kade said without hesitating. "Loves nothing but his dinner and magic. An enormous bore on the subject of sturgeon, sour cream, apple pancakes, gingerbread from some provincial city, et cetera. And he is most incensed when his magic doesn't work."

Ruxandra frowned. "Why would it not work?"

"Human magic is a stitched-together cloth of lies, myths, and half-truths. Very little of it has an effect on people. He is fortunate to be in the library, where most of the spells actually work."

"Then how do you know if the spell to summon the angel is real?"

"We don't. But we also don't know that it isn't. And given that much of the magic in the library works, we have high hopes."

He leaned back against the wall. "I suspect that most human magic was never meant to work on humans."

Ruxandra felt confused. "Then whom does it work on?"

"Us, of course. As I discovered at Elizabeth's castle, human magic works extraordinarily well against vampires. It is almost as if that's why it exists."

Which makes sense, because they can't beat us physically. Ruxandra thought about it. It was fair, she supposed, but a bit unnerving. "How many spells against vampires did you find in the magicians' archives?"

"Very few. Some basic warding spells, which they tested on me. They work. A few protection spells, similar to the ones I used in Castle Csejte. Nothing other than that."

Odd. Ruxandra lay back on the floor and put her hands behind her head. *You'd think a place with so much vampire lore would have more spells against us.*

In Kraków they talked about vampires.

"The library keeps the myths and legends in one place," Kade said. "And in addition to the first history, which I told you, they have several other stories of different places our kind rose up and were destroyed."

"Like where?"

"Greece, in the times of the ancients. A vampire stalked the streets of Sparta until they hunted it down. In Egypt a vampire threatened to kill the pharaoh if he did not give her tribute. His magicians murdered her. And there are many, many stories of vampires in other times."

"What about our powers?" Ruxandra asked. "You said you were learning them?"

Kade sighed. "That is an entirely different matter. I found six books, in a language that no one knew. After a year of study to translate a few words, I realized that it must be a written language of the vampires themselves. It took years of work to translate the section that taught me how to use our voice. I expect to learn the rest faster, now that I managed that much, but it will still take a great deal of time."

"Time we don't have," Ruxandra said.

"We have forever."

"Not before they summon the fallen angel."

Kade smiled. "We will have all the time in the world after that."

Perhaps. What if she decides to unmake us? Would that be so bad?

"I'm going to sleep. We still have three days to Moscow."

"Good night, my dear."

Her dreams were a confusion of blood, screams, and a beautiful, unearthly woman gazing into her face with a look of unbounded delight. She woke up hungry.

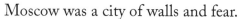

Moscow was a city of walls and fear.

Unlike the cities of Europe, Moscow had not overflowed its walls. Rather, the walls had expanded to encompass the city and part of the countryside beyond as if trying to hide what prosperity lay inside. A few farmhouses lay scattered over the landscape on the approach to the city, each with its own wooden walls, high enough to be difficult for any human to jump over.

The outer, wooden wall had sheltered slits for archers or rifle-men dotting the length of it and wooden towers every twenty yards or so. The wall and the deep ditch in front of it went for miles, encircling the outer city, and even stretching across the rivers—the Moskva and the Yauza, Kade told Ruxandra—that flowed through the city.

Men in uniform peered through the slits in the walls, some glaring out at whatever enemies might attack, others looking glazed with boredom. Kade went unnoticed and jumped onto the wall with ease. Ruxandra did the same and landed beside him. All the running had tuned his prowess, she decided. Perhaps after Moscow they could take a long lap around the huge country, see what was happening in Russia's other cities. It was good to have a companion. She switched her voice to vampire frequencies. "My, they do like their walls, don't they?"

Inside the outer wall lay farms, and beyond them a second wall surrounded the city proper. And beyond that, rising higher than the rest of the city, stood yet another set of walls, made of gleaming white stone.

"They have reason to," Kade said. "The Crimean Tatars attack the city regularly, taking slaves and burning down the buildings."

He pointed to a wall gleaming white in the distance. "The last time they burned everything but the buildings inside the Kremlin. Now everything is walled, in the hopes of keeping them out."

"Does it work?"

"No. But they hope. This way."

Kade let her to the city proper, and when they jumped the wall, Ruxandra discovered that smaller walls surrounded each neigh-borhood, connecting the houses and churches. The buildings were wood, save for a few stone churches. Paint covered everything, giving life to otherwise drab boards. Onion-shaped towers rose above the churches, looking down on the houses like benevolent parents gazing at their children.

They jumped off the wall into the city proper. Kade led her down one fence line, then through a tall gate. That opened onto a series of small, fenced-in farms. Some held cabbages ready to be picked; others held trees, the last summer fruit still dangling from the branches. Others contained drowsy cattle sleeping where they stood. Kade led her between them to a small cluster of buildings. She saw houses with a few chicken coops and a single field. In the middle of these buildings, standing higher than the others, rose a three-story house with a high-peaked, wooden-shingled roof. Red shutters closed the windows, and curlicues decorated the gables.

"This is it," Kade said. "The magicians live here."

Ruxandra, curious, reached out with her mind. She stopped walking.

"What?" Kade said. "Surely you're not shy of meeting a few old magicians?"

"There's no one inside," Ruxandra said. "Check."

Kade stared at the building, his eyes growing wider every second. He took off at a run, rounding the building.

The front door lay open. Nothing stirred inside.

FOUR

K ADE STEPPED INSIDE, Ruxandra at his heels. The house
was well appointed, with thick, colorful tapestries on
the walls to keep in the warmth. The furniture looked
decent, though not rich—it lacked the excessive ornamenta-
tion so popular in Italy. But the house was a mess. The chairs lay
overturned on the floor, and a table in one room lay on its top.
Bloodstains, dry and dark, splattered the floor.

"I don't understand." Kade stalked from room to room, taking
in the scene. "They were safe when I left. No one felt concerned
about anything. They had no reason to vanish."

"They didn't vanish," Ruxandra said, looking at the mess.
"They were taken."

Kade nodded. "I know. But by whom?"

Ruxandra crouched and lowered her nose to the floor. She
sniffed deep, but the scents were old and faded.

"I don't understand how you can do that," Kade said. "I can
smell a hundred smells in a room, but to differentiate them, or
follow them . . ."

"Practice," Ruxandra said. "I recommend having to hunt your food for a hundred years. It does wonders."

"I'm sure," Kade said. "What do you smell?"

Ruxandra shrugged. "I can't tell. There's no scent here less than a month old. Even if I knew whom I was tracking, it would barely help. Any scents outside vanished weeks ago. Right now I just want to learn the smells, in case I run into them again."

Kade growled in frustration. "Follow me."

He headed through the house, passing a parlor, a dining room, and a smaller, cozier room with comfortable chairs and a fire-place. He stopped in a doorway.

"Derr`mo," he snarled. "They didn't."

Ruxandra looked past him and saw a small room with dead plants on a table near a wide window. In the center of the floor sat an open trap door. Before she could ask if it led to the library, Kade was already half out of sight down the stairs. Ruxandra followed.

The stairs went down deep, hemmed in first by wooden planks that held back the packed earth, then by natural stone walls. The air grew stale and musty, and the darkness closed in on them as the light from above faded.

When Ruxandra was first made a vampire, she'd learned that all things gave off their own light, even stones, walls, and old wooden stairs. After all this time, she had stopped noticing it, except in moments like these, when a human would have needed a lantern. It was a thin, gray light, but enough for them both to see by as they descended deeper into the earth.

The stairs ended, and the walls opened up. They stood in a cavern at least as large as the house above. Dozens of shelves lined the walls, stretching the length of the cavern and down the middle of the floor.

All stood empty.

Kade turned in a slow circle, his eyes wide. If the empty house had surprised him, the empty basement practically sent him into shock. Ruxandra watched as disbelief, grief, and fury all took turns on his face. Fury won out, blazing. Ruxandra kept a wary eye on him, not sure what he would do.

"All this way." Anger made the words sound like a growl. "All this time spent traveling, and *this* is what I come back to?"

Ruxandra said nothing.

"I will find them," Kade said. "I will find who came to this house, then I will destroy them all."

"Who would do it?" Ruxandra asked. "The church? The empress?"

Kade shook his head. "Not the church. They would tie the men to the bookshelves and burn them with their books. The empress . . . maybe. But why?"

Kade headed back up. "We go ask the neighbors before the sun comes up. They saw something, I am certain."

The nearest neighbor, an old woman, did not at all like being disturbed. Kade and the woman spoke rapid-fire Russian at one another. The woman spoke loudly and shrilly at first, but Kade hissed a command in Russian, and she quieted. Ruxandra recognized the irritation in the woman's tone, though not much else at first. But with every word spoken she began to understand more.

"One day" was followed by a string of words Ruxandra didn't understand. Then, "not my"—more words—"to know."

Kade's reply was unintelligible, except the ending words, "My friends."

"Those were friends?" The old woman scoffed and then spoke at length in words Ruxandra didn't understand.

"Go back inside," Kade commanded. The woman went in, and Kade shook his head in disgust and switched back to Italian. "The woman knows nothing. Worse, she made sure to know nothing. She said she heard a ruckus before they all went away, with lots of shouting and horsemen."

The next two neighbors were just as helpful, saying only that they'd heard horsemen and fighting. The fourth neighbor, two houses away, owner of a snug little cottage with a well-tended fence and barn, had seen everything. He was more than happy to tell them once Kade stopped his complaints about the early hour.

"They were in black," he began, and Ruxandra understood that much. He went into a long-winded explanation that Ruxandra barely understood. She caught "horses," "fighting," "books," "taken to the palace" and a few other random words and phrases. Kade looked grimmer as the man went on. When he finished, Kade thanked him and commanded him back to bed.

"Are your friends still alive, then?" Part of Ruxandra fervidly hoped not. The rest of her realized that, if these people didn't summon the dark angel, whoever had taken the books would. Power called to power, and what power greater than a dark angel?

Assuming it doesn't kill them.

"I don't know," Kade said. "I think so. The night is drawing to a close. We should rest."

"Where?" Ruxandra asked. "Down below?"

Kade shook his head. "They know of that place. I would hate to be caught below with an army above, especially one armed with oil and fire."

"True. Do you have another place?"

"Two," Kade said. "One is known to everyone. The other is known only to me."

"A bolt-hole?"

Kade nodded. "Moscow is not always safe or stable. It is good to have a place to run. This way."

Someone followed them.

At first Ruxandra wasn't sure. She couldn't see anything, couldn't hear anything, but something made the hair on the back of her neck stand up. She reached out with her mind but felt only the people in their houses, most of them asleep. She looked behind her, scanning the ground and the buildings, searching for . . .

For what? What am I sensing?

She switched her voice to vampire frequencies. "I think we're being followed."

Kade didn't change his pace or turn around but answered in his own vampire voice. "I don't sense anyone near. Are you sure?"

"No." Ruxandra's frustration came out in her tone. Kade looked back at her, eyebrows raised. "There's no sight or sound of anyone, but . . ."

"You *think* we're being followed."

"Yes."

"Shall we speed up?"

"Not until we get around the corner." Ruxandra pushed her chin toward the next building. "No sense letting them know we spotted them."

Kade went around the corner and sped up, going unnoticed at the same time. Ruxandra followed a second later, also disappearing from notice. Unlike Kade, whose footfalls she heard as he ran, Ruxandra moved silently. Instead of following him, she circled the building to come up behind whoever followed.

She saw no one.

There's someone here. I'm sure of it.

The ground was hard and dry, but she saw scuff marks where people and animals walked during the day. She spotted Kade's footprints and her own, but didn't see anyone else's. Ruxandra sniffed deep, searching for the scent of man. Many men were nearby, but inside the houses. Outside she smelled no one.

They're gone.

If anyone was here to begin with.

She had been a hunter for more than a hundred years. She knew what it meant to stalk prey and to be stalked. Once she'd led a mountain lion on a three-day chase through the woods before taking it from above. Every instinct she possessed told her that someone followed.

There's still no one here.

She began walking in a widening spiral across the road, searching for a whiff of someone—or something—different from what she saw.

There.

A fresh boot print, barely visible in the dust of the road. She knelt down, caught the scent of leather first, then the sweat of the man wearing the boot. She smelled fear in that sweat, and excitement. She wondered if whoever followed knew what he pursued. She breathed deep again, then reached out with her mind and found Kade. She ran and caught up with him.

"Did you find them?" Kade asked, still using the vampire voice.

"No," Ruxandra answered, speaking in the same tones. "I found a boot print, and I smelled someone, but I didn't see anyone or anything."

Kade frowned. "That is . . . disconcerting."

"Yes." Ruxandra spread her mind wide. Still she sensed no one outside. "He's human, though."

"A human you cannot see, hear, or sense?" Kade's eyebrows went up. "A magician?"

"One of yours?"

"They would not hide from me." Kade frowned at the street, then at the lightening sky above. "We should get under cover. This way."

Ruxandra followed him through the city. She sensed no more pursuers, but her mind raced the entire time they went to Kade's other house.

If it is a human who knows how to hide from vampires, how did he know that vampires would come?

Kade's house lay across the river. They ran the entire distance, silent and unnoticed, seeing only tired guards who turned away from them as they went by. They slowed down when they reached the yard, and even then Ruxandra looped back in a slow spiral search in case someone still followed them. This time there wasn't even a footprint in sight.

The house stood only one story high, with wooden walls and shingles and three rooms. The first held the fireplace, a large table with chairs, and a kettle and teacups. A shelf along the wall held twenty different blends of tea, the sharp scents of each forming a symphony of smells in Ruxandra's nose. The second room had a bed, the coverlet dusty from disuse. Beyond it was a small room with a thick door that could be barred. A pair of shutters hung on the inside of the window, thick nails driven into the window frame securing them closed. A pair of tapestries hung above, ready to drop down and cover the window. A chest large enough for a man to lie in stretched the length of one wall. Kade opened it to reveal a mattress with a thick blanket and pillows.

"I'll take the bed," Ruxandra said. The idea of lying closed in the chest all day made her stomach crawl and reminded her too much of when she'd tried to kill herself. She had woken under the earth and panicked, tearing at the ground until she broke free.

"As you wish."

"May I make tea?"

"Of course," Kade said. "There's a tinderbox and kindling in the box beside the fireplace."

"Good. Teach me more Russian while we wait."

It took time for Ruxandra to get the fire, longer still for the water to boil and the tea to steep. Kade joined her at the table, sitting across from her and speaking in Russian and Italian, expanding Ruxandra's vocabulary.

Ruxandra picked a fragrant tea to drink, and the two sipped it until the sky grew light and the sun stood just below the horizon, ready to break free from the earth. Ruxandra doused the fire and went to the small room.

"In all the rush, I completely forgot that I could wear boots again," Kade said as he slipped into his chest and lay down. "I can't tell you how much I am looking forward to that."

Ruxandra chuckled. "Fair enough. I'm looking forward to putting on a dress."

"I am sure you will be lovely in it," Kade said. He yawned.

Ruxandra smiled and lay back on the bed. "Kade?"

"Yes?"

"What if we don't find your friends?"

"We will," Kade said. "Not all of them lived in that house, and the ones that didn't may still be free."

"So where do we look for them?"

Kade chuckled. "The place where one looks for all great Russian visionaries. The *kabak*."

It was not a word that Kade had taught her, and Ruxandra puzzled over what it meant until sleep took her.

When the sun slipped behind the horizon, Kade led Ruxandra back across the city. Both went unnoticeable before leaving the house and stayed that way. Ruxandra kept eyes, ears, nose, and mind all wide open, searching for the one who'd followed them the night before. She detected nothing.

This early in the evening the entire neighborhood was out and about. Old women gossiped over their back fences, men talked and argued cheerfully in the street, and children dashed in and out among adults. Kade wove through them with ease, going to a long, low-slung building with a wide-open door and much noise coming out of it.

"The kabak," Kade said, using his vampire voice, "is where everyone gathers to drink. If any of my friends survive, they will certainly visit one."

He led her inside. The noise grew five times louder the moment they stepped through the door. Men and women shouted at one another, laughed, and sang. Two men danced in one corner, singing at the top of their lungs, while two others engaged in an arm-wrestling match.

"Is it this lively every night?" Ruxandra asked, also in vampire voice.

Kade looked around and shrugged. "Tonight is calmer than most."

He slipped through the crowd. The people moved out of his way, even though they couldn't see him. Ruxandra followed in his wake. He rounded the bar and stepped into the back room. He stepped back out, noticeable, and shouted to the barman in Russian. The man put a cup on the bar and poured a generous amount of vodka into it. Kade thanked the man and then commanded him in Russian. Ruxandra caught every third word. She sighed, wishing her Russian would improve faster, and turned to survey the crowd.

Then she noticed the empty space.

So many people crowded the bar that the walls threatened to burst. Yet against one wall, amid a crowd of people talking and laughing together, she saw an empty space. Ruxandra turned away, watching it out of her peripheral vision. Kade still questioned the man at the bar. Ruxandra extended her mind to the empty space, but felt nothing. She inhaled, long and deep, learning the scents of the room. By the second breath, she had identified every alcohol the men drank. By the fifth, she knew each person's scent.

By the sixth, she knew the man standing in the empty spot, a different man from the last time. He smelled of steel and leather and silver and sweat.

"Come," Kade said. "Time to go."

He pushed his way through the crowd. Ruxandra followed after, still keeping the spot in the corner of her eye. The man there didn't move to follow them.

Once they were outside, Kade led her at a rapid pace away from the tavern. His boots struck the ground with unnecessary force, and he made no attempt to go unnoticed.

"They have not been there in a month," he said, agitation filling his voice. "None of them. Not the magicians, not the librarians. All are missing."

"It is very bad," Ruxandra said. "We were followed again. Or they were waiting for us."

"What?" Kade stopped and turned on his heel. His eyes scanned the streets around them. He frowned, and Ruxandra could tell he did the same with his mind. "There's no one here."

"There is." Ruxandra tapped her nose. "It's not the one from last night, but someone is definitely there."

"Magicians." Kade rubbed his chin, almost as if running his fingers through a beard that wasn't there anymore. "Or men using magic. What are they?"

"Human," Ruxandra said. "Other than that, I have no idea. But I think other humans can see them. Where I thought one was in the tavern, there was room for him. No one tried to move into his space."

"No one moves into our spaces when we are unnoticeable. It may be the same thing."

"Should we try to capture him?"

"Not yet. First we learn who took the magicians and if we can get them back. Then we go after them." Kade turned unnoticeable. "We should hurry."

He broke into a run, and Ruxandra followed. They left the neighborhood and went to another one nearby. They went into a second kabak, then a third. Each time Kade held a long conversation with the barman, and each time he came away with nothing.

Both times Ruxandra watched the bar, looking for empty spaces that should be full. In the second kabak, a chair sat unused near the door. In the third, a spot of wall amid the crowd near the fireplace made a gap like a pulled tooth. The human in each space smelled different from the others.

"Found them," Kade said in her ear. "This way."

He led her out of the kabak, unnoticed and moving too fast for human pursuit, across the River Moskva to a two-story kabak near the banks. The crowd inside was older and talked more quietly. Kade made himself noticeable before he stepped inside. Ruxandra stayed unseen. He crossed the floor.

"Where," he commanded the barman, *"is Lyosha Kurkov?"*

"Upstairs," said the barman, "but he is busy right now."

"Not so busy as that." Kade walked past the bar and mounted the stairs two at a time. Ruxandra stayed close behind. She heard the sounds of pleasure—most faked—coming from a half dozen small rooms. Kade paused a moment, listening, then went to one at the end. He pushed it open. Ruxandra, right behind him, caught a glimpse of an older man's bare, wrinkled backside ramming forward hard and fast. A much younger man, bent over the bed in front of him, groaned in pleasure.

"Kurkov, you old sodomite," Kade growled. "Where are the rest of us?"

The older man whipped around so fast Ruxandra heard the sound of him escaping his partner's body. The younger man cried out in pain and surprise and jumped across the bed.

"Kade!" Kurkov's next words were in Russian, but Ruxandra knew enough to understand them. "Thank God you are returned. They've taken them all!"

CHAPTER
FIVE

"WHO?" KADE'S VOICE turned cold. "Who took them?"

"We don't know who," Kurkov said. "Just that they were taken."

He turned away from the bed and reached for a towel, putting his body on full display. Ruxandra's eyebrows went up, but she didn't say anything. He was impressively hung, but no more so than several of the men she'd known in Rome. Tall and wiry, with thick graying brown hair and sharp gray eyes, he looked as a magician should look, she thought. Both scholarly and assertive, with an indefinable quality of secrecy or difference, yet still clearly human. Even his cock had an elegant curve to it, going in its own direction. She smirked.

Both men got dressed and sat down on the bed.

"Tell me what happened," Kade said. "In Italian so my friend can understand."

"Of course," Kurkov said, switching languages with ease. "We do not know much. We went home. We came back the next morning.

The house was in shambles and there was not sign of anyone. We did not know what happened. They may have been there and been taken. They may have been at home, drinking vodka and wondering how deep they could penetrate their wives or donkeys or whatever it is they fuck."

He laughed then, a high, hard laugh filled with more anger than amusement. Kade watched in silence as the laugh went on longer than was reasonable. The younger man, blond and slight, with a melancholy, intelligent face, put his hand on Kurkov's shoulder. The old man threw it off, shoving the hand away as if the very touch were burning him.

"What happened?" Kade asked again.

"I don't know!" Kurkov spat out the words. "They're gone. Either drowned in the Moskva or buried in the sewage pit or hiding like rats in the walls of their outhouses for all I know. We visited their houses, talked to their wives and donkeys, and none said they have been fucked recently."

"Lyosha," Eduard began, but Kurkov kept going.

"None of them *looked* like they have been fucked recently, either. Except one donkey, who I suspect, from its eyes and gait, met with an amorous stallion and will no doubt produce a fine young mule in the near future."

"Kurkov." Kade's voice was calm. "You did nothing wrong."

Kurkov's face twisted. Tears began pouring out of his eyes. "Of course I did nothing wrong. I wasn't even there. They were my friends, every one of them, and I was not there."

Kurkov crumpled in on himself, his face falling into his hands and his shoulders shaking with silent sobs.

"I was not, either," Kade's voice stayed calm. "I was not even in the city. How long ago was this?"

"Last month," Eduard said. "Twenty-two days."

"No one returned since?"

Eduard shook his head. "We searched the city, spoke to their family and friends. No one saw anyone."

"Their families are terrified," Kurkov said. He sat up, rubbed his face, and managed a small smile. "Even the donkeys."

Kade leaned against the wall and rubbed the beard that wasn't on his chin anymore. "Do you think it was someone inside the city?"

Kurkov shrugged, a larger motion than the Italian shrug, and just as expressive. "There was no sound of alarm, no disturbance at the watchtowers, so it wasn't an attacker. But then, who attacks a city and steals a bunch of old men and a crazy woman? It's not like they make good toys for the Taters like our daughters."

Bitterness, corrosive as acid, spilled out of his mouth with the last words.

"Who inside would want them?" Kade asked. "The church?"

"The Metropolitan takes a dim view of magic," Eduard said. "He would take them, but I don't believe he would leave them alive afterward."

"Or that he would do it without making a show," Kurkov said. "He would burn them all in the square. After breaking them on the wheel."

"Excuse me," Ruxandra said. "Who is the Metropolitan?"

"The leader of the Church of Moscow," Eduard said.

"And before we answer any more questions," Kurkov said, his eyes narrowing, "you must introduce your companion, Kade. Is he to be trusted?"

"*She,*" Kade said, "is to be trusted more than anyone else who walks the earth. Eduard, Kurkov, I present to you Ruxandra Dracula."

"Ruxandra?" Eduard stood up. "The woman you told us about?"

"The very one," Kade said.

"You idiot!" Kurkov jumped to his feet. "You fool! How could you?"

"How could I what?" Kade asked, frowning.

"How could you let a woman in here when I am balls deep in Eduard!" He swung a hand in Eduard's direction. "And then to let me stand with my prick pointing at the ceiling and waving in the breeze? Idiot!"

Ruxandra managed to get her hand over her mouth to cover her smile at the bemused expression on Kade's face. Kurkov turned his back on Kade and bowed.

"I ask your forgiveness," he said. He reached out and captured her hand. "Truly, our dear friend Kade lacks manners. Otherwise he would not let a woman witness such a spectacle. I hope you forgive my nakedness, and that you are not offended by the nature of my relationship with Eduard."

"I am not sure," Ruxandra said, doing her best to sound disapproving. "I mean, he is so much younger than you."

Kurkov's mouth fell open. He blinked several times, and his lips moved without sound. Then he brayed with laughter. On the bed Eduard blushed and looked away.

"It is true!" Kurkov wheezed. "It is very true! But love knows no age, and this young man happened to fall for my brilliance, and so how could I deny him?"

"I did," Eduard admitted. "And he has other attributes."

"I noticed," Ruxandra said, her voice bland.

"Ah! You make me blush again!" Kurkov grabbed his coat. "Enough. This place is costing me money, so let us go from here and walk."

They walked out together into the darkness. Kurkov led them toward the Kremlin but stayed away from the gates. Instead he took them to the riverbank, and they walked along it. The stench of raw sewage, dumped into the river, filled the air.

"The beautiful Neglinka," Kurkov said, pointing at the river. "Protector of the Kremlin, carrier of our shit."

He raised his finger to point at the northern end of the inner wall then ran it backward, tracing the line of battlements. "That is the enclave of the of the rich. The government men and the nobles who must be protected from us hoi polloi."

His finger shifted down the length of the Neglinka River to the southernmost part of the wall. "That is the Kremlin. Home to the Metropolitan, the government, and our most holy empress, Anna. It is, needless to say, heavily fortified. If any of our friends still live, we may find them there."

"Unless they were taken by someone else," Eduard said. "In which case we will never find them at all."

"Never say never," Kurkov said. "Our Kade has returned, and if there is something he cannot find, then it does not exist in this world."

"You are too kind," Kade said. "But Ruxandra is the one who will find them. She is a true hunter. I am merely a scholar."

"Who works only at night," Kurkov said, drily. "Yes, he is only a scholar. And a disgrace to his kind, I might add, given to hunting the easiest prey, and only when it doesn't discommode him from his reading."

He paused and looked to Ruxandra. "You do know what kind he is, yes?"

The same as me. Ruxandra stopped before the words came out.

"You should know not to be alone with him," Kurkov said. "Rather, come and stay with me. Eduard is a fine man, but even I need the touch of a woman once in a while."

"Enough of that, you old wolf," Kade scolded, though he was smiling. "You will eat her up before a single day passes."

"How can I resist?" Kurkov said. "She is so young, and so beautiful. And a hunter, you say. What could be more exciting, more rousing? Now tell me, who is hunting you?"

With the words, the facade of the perverted old man dropped. Curiosity filled his face, and his eyes peered deep into Ruxandra's.

"You see," he continued, his voice far quieter than before, "since we first laid eyes on you, you appear distracted. Even when I turn my not-inconsiderable charms on you, you only half pay attention. Your eyes are always moving, and your nose flares as if you are sniffing for someone. Tell me, does whoever follows smell so bad that you can detect them that way?"

"Say rather that my nose is strong enough to detect them," Ruxandra said. "No matter how good or bad they smell."

Kurkov's eyes left Ruxandra and went to Kade for a moment. When they returned, he looked her up and down. "Ah. I am an old fool. Of course you are safe from Kade's thirst, if not from his rather boring company."

"I beg your pardon," Kade said. "I am hardly boring."

Kurkov took Ruxandra's hand. There was no flirtation in the movement, no sense of teasing or laughter in his face.

"Please," he said. "If you are a hunter, if you are good as Kade says, please find them."

"I will," Ruxandra said. "If I can."

He nodded and let go of her hand. "Then we bid you good night. For we are day creatures, and tired. See you tomorrow night, if you think it wise?"

He directed the last words at Kade, who shook his head.

"I think not," Kade said. "Rather, we will spend tomorrow night searching and see you the night after."

"As you wish." Kurkov bowed to them both. "Now, let us go, Eduard. I feel the need for sleep."

The older man slung a companionable arm around the young man's slim shoulders, and the two walked off into the night. Ruxandra watched them go.

"Kurkov is not what he appears," she said as the two men disappeared into the mess of houses of the nearest neighborhood.

"No, he is exactly what he appears," Kade said. "He is also the smartest man I know. He understands things that most men cannot even dream of learning."

"You never told them what I am?"

"No." Kade shook his head. "I didn't even tell them what I am. The Alchemist figured it out first but told only me. Then Kurkov figured it out and promptly told the rest of them. Fortunately, they found me too interesting to fight or drive off."

Ruxandra turned in a slow circle, sniffing the air. "Do you think they told whoever caught them?"

"It is possible, if they were tortured."

Which is why we're being followed.

"She is a brilliant woman, the Alchemist." He sighed, and in his breath Ruxandra felt the weight of his friends' loss bearing down on him. "I think you will like her, assuming she lives."

"She lives," Ruxandra said, though she knew it was probably a lie. She linked an arm through his, squeezing his shoulder. "We will find them."

Kade looked down at his arm. "This is not Italy. Here they believe a woman should not take a man's arm unless they are relatives or in love."

"Then I'll make sure I'm not seen." Ruxandra turned unnoticed. "Now come, take me back to your house."

"Immodest woman," Kade growled, but he patted her hand, vanished from notice, and led her into the night.

They stayed up late that day, talking while the sun beat down on the roof until they came up with a plan. Ruxandra burrowed under the covers of her bed, and Kade went into his trunk. Both slept until the day passed.

◆ ◆ ◆ ◆ ◆

When night fell, Ruxandra rose and stripped off her clothing. She would not search just as a vampire this night, not when those who followed them could see through her magic. She would hunt like the animal she had been in the forest, swift, silent, and unhindered. She folded her clothes, laid them on the bed, and stepped out into the next room.

Inside her, the Beast growled.

It was a quiet growl, a faint warning that she was growing hungry. It would not be enough to cause a problem. She could wait to hunt until the next night and be perfectly fine.

She hadn't had a slipup with the Beast in years.

A quick intake of breath behind her told her that Kade was awake.

For no good reason, Ruxandra found her hands moving to cover her breasts and sex as she turned around. If she had been capable of blushing, she suspected her face would be bright red.

"Avert your gaze, please," she said.

"I had forgotten how beautiful your body is." Kade turned his back. "I will not turn back around until you leave."

How can the man make this more awkward even as he stops looking? "I'm going inside the Kremlin. I shall return in a few hours."

"You will not," Kade said. "The Kremlin is vast, and it will take more than one night to search it."

She nodded. "I'll search as many buildings as I can tonight, and go back again tomorrow, if necessary."

"Excellent. I will visit the wealthy ones I know in the enclave to see what assistance they can offer."

"I will see you in a few hours," Ruxandra said. "Where shall we meet? Here?"

"I imagine you will want to dress first. So let us meet at the kabak where we met Kurkov. Try the vodka. It is . . . quite stimulating."

"I'm sure."

"Not that I need any more stimulation," Kade teased.

Ruxandra raised two fingers in insult at his back, turned unnoticed, and stepped outside.

An orchard stood near the southernmost bridge to the Kremlin, and Ruxandra went there first, fading into the shadows of the trees even though no one could see her. Years of hunting had ingrained in her the need for cover when she hunted. She went to the orchard's edge and examined the walls across the river and, beyond them, the construction scaffolds that rose around a dozen buildings inside

It's not like I wasn't naked the first time he saw me.

And he's not unhandsome.

And why in the name of God am I thinking of this right now? Was it seeing the old man and his lover? Not just sex but friendship?

She slipped across the bridge, gliding between the sentries on either side. A small stone guardhouse stood on the far end of the bridge, twenty feet away from the gatehouse in the wall. A pair of men sat on the guardhouse steps, smoking pipes and talking to each other. She stood beside them, listening for a time, hoping to gain more Russian words from their conversation. One was talking about his desire to buy a farm, she thought, and the other was wishing that drinking were allowed on duty.

She walked to the wall and looked up. Unlike the rough wooden walls of the city, these were smooth stone and twenty feet high. Ruxandra looked for a place with no sentry, bent her knees, and jumped, clearing the wall with ease.

She smacked into something hard and fell as heavily as a dropped stone.

The men at the guardhouse jumped up at the sound of her body hitting the earth. The fall surprised Ruxandra so much that she barely remembered to stay unnoticeable. Her head rang from the impact. She shook it, trying to clear her mind.

The guardsmen, muskets in hand, walked toward her. They peered suspiciously at the empty ground. Ruxandra rolled onto her hands and knees and crawled away from them, even though they could not see her. The pain faded fast, as always, and she stood up. She walked as far down the wall as the small strip of land allowed. She glared up at the air above it, looking for some sign of what she had hit. She saw nothing.

She went to the gatehouse and looked at the join between the tower and the wall. Silent and slow, she put one hand and foot on the wall, another on the tower, and began climbing. No one looked her way, not even the sentry standing twenty feet away. She reached the top and grabbed for the parapet with one hand.

Something threw her down again, just as hard as the last time.

Ruxandra was ready for it now, or at least as ready as she could be for a shove from an unknown something that she couldn't see, hear, or smell. She landed on all fours and glared up at the wall.

It's not a person or animal. Being angry is stupid.

She marched to the guardhouse, ready to command one of the men to get her inside.

Then she caught a new scent.

It was the man from the first kabak they had visited—the man she couldn't see, though she'd known he was there. He was nearby. Ruxandra turned a slow circle, watching and waiting. No one looked in her direction, no one moved. The guards stayed on their feet, their eyes fixed on the bridge.

They're looking at someone.

But there's no one there.

No one I can see.

Ruxandra advanced on the bridge, nostrils flaring as she took in the man's scent. The guards both started and turned away from the bridge to stare at the fortress. Sweat glowed suddenly from each man's brow.

Someone gave them an order.

The one on the bridge.

Can he see me?

The last thought disconcerted her, and not because she was naked. No human had ever seen her when she had chosen to be unnoticed, not for 130 years.

Which means what? He isn't human? He smells human.

Ruxandra closed her eyes and breathed deep, pinpointing the place where the man stood. She opened her mouth wide, letting her fangs come down, and raised her hands, her talons ripping out of her flesh. She charged the bridge, running blind, listening for the man to scramble out of her way.

Then the scent was behind her, though it hadn't moved. Ruxandra swore silently and spun around. She charged again, her eyes open this time.

Again she went past him.

I know he's there. I should have caught him. How could I miss him?

She walked toward him this time, all her senses alert. And this time she felt the push that changed her direction. A subtle pressure that refused to let her touch him, no matter how hard she tried.

Human magic. She took off at a run, fear twisting her stomach. *I must tell Kade.*

CHAPTER
SIX

RUXANDRA DIDN'T RETURN to the house or go into the kabak. Instead, she crouched on the roof of a house across the street from the kabak, hidden in the shadow of the chimney. Her eyes searched the street, her nose twitching with every breath, trying to sniff out the man from the bridge, or any of the men from the kabaks they had visited.

None were nearby.

Ruxandra watched for places where no one stood or walked. She looked for where the shadows fell wrong or the dogs avoided walking.

There was nothing.

She wished she were back in Italy—Venice. She'd spent fifteen years there, and knew every inch of it, from the slums on the shore to the mansions and cathedrals. There she would be able to tell if a single rat was moving funny, or the water in one bend of a canal was flowing the wrong way.

Here she could only sniff and stare, sorting the smells of the people and the cattle and the dogs and the sewage. Watching ground too dry to leave tracks and trying to understand who it was who followed them.

Two hours later Kade walked up the street.

Ruxandra pitched her voice to vampire tones. "Kade! Hide!"

To his credit he didn't look up, didn't even shift his head toward the sound of her voice. He kept walking, past Ruxandra, past the kabak, and into the darkness. A moment later Kade's voice, in vampire tones, drifted out of the darkness.

"The house."

Ruxandra slipped over the peak of the roof, slid across the shingles, and jumped to the alley without a sound. She ran off into the darkness, moving fast through the narrow alleys between the houses, going in the opposite direction from Kade's house. At the outer wall, Ruxandra jumped, landing on the parapet, and then sprinted the length, circling the city twice. The entire time, she breathed deeply, sniffing for the ones she couldn't see.

Ruxandra reached Kade's house moments before dawn. The sun lay under the horizon, ready to pull free. Ruxandra stayed out until the first rays of the sun broke over the city walls, sniffing the air like a wolf, eyes and ears wide. When she dashed inside, Kade was waiting, a blanket in his outstretched arms. Ruxandra ran forward and let him wrap it around her.

She stayed in the circle of his arms and whispered, "The Kremlin. I couldn't get over the walls. Something pushed me back, knocked me to the ground."

Kade drew her closer, his breath in her ear.

"And the ones who follow," he whispered. "Have you seen them yet?"

"No. But I faced one." A shudder ran though her. "I scented him and knew just where he was, but I couldn't even touch him,

Kade. It was like a river caught me in a current and pulled me around him."

"That is . . . strange."

"Frightening," Ruxandra said. "I was helpless against him. Kade, I haven't been so helpless since—" *Since Elizabeth.*

Kade's grip tightened. Ruxandra leaned into it. In the year she'd lived in Pisa, she had not been embraced by anyone. It made her feel safe in a way few other things did.

Even though it's no safer than standing in the street, if we can't see or touch the enemy. Even though Kade seems to attract or be attracted to danger.

She whispered into his ear, "How do we fight them?"

"Why are we whispering?" Kade whispered back.

"Because they may be listening. If they can see us when we're unnoticeable, who knows what else they can do?"

Kade shook his head but didn't raise his voice. "That's different. They counter our magic, but to hear us from a distance . . . ? No. Human magic has its limitations."

"Are you sure?"

"I was a sorcerer for thirty years. I have tried to amplify my senses many times. It is simply not possible." Kade patted her bare shoulder above the blanket, his hands smooth and gentle against her skin. "Tomorrow night we will search again."

"I need to hunt. Will we be able to if they are watching us?"

"These men can't be everywhere."

"Yet it feels that way." She leaned back. "I don't want to sleep. I'm worried they may come in." She would have warning if a door or window was breached, but it was deeply frightening not to be able to sense an enemy coming.

Is this how most humans live who are not safe, as I was in the convent? It must be. Though I suppose they grow used to it.

I do not like feeling like prey.

"Then what shall we do?" Kade smiled, and his pale-blue eyes went to the blanket covering her body.

"Not that." Ruxandra stepped back. He let her slip out of his arms without protest.

"Then I suggest you dress," Kade said. "I will make tea and fetch my cards."

Kade stepped back, bowed, and walked to the fire. Ruxandra slipped into the bedroom. Instead of wearing her men's clothes, though, she reached into her bag for the dress she had brought. It was blue, plain, and not as fashionable as the dresses she'd left behind in Italy. But it was simple to put on by oneself, and despite its simple cut, showed off her figure to advantage. Ruxandra pulled on her shift and dress, not bothering with stockings or shoes, in case they had to run.

And all the while, she thought about Kade's arms.

Why am I reacting this way?

It had felt nice having someone's arms around her again. So had the way his breath touched her ear when he spoke, and his hand on the skin of her bare shoulder.

This is really not the time to lose focus. And I like women.

She remembered the nights in Rome, lying back in the matron's arms as the woman's three lovers—all soldiers, all young and strong—serviced them both.

All right, I prefer women.

But I know him. We are the same . . . species. And he is attractive.

Dammit.

Ruxandra finished dressing, freed her hair and brushed it smooth, and stepped out into the front room. Kade had set a pot of sweet-smelling tea on the table, with two fine porcelain cups and saucers beside it. A thick deck of colorful cards sat on the table.

"You look wonderful, my dear." Kade pulled the chair out for her. "I haven't seen you in a proper dress since we reunited. Now, what game shall we play?"

They played Tressette all day. Kade played with a tactical precision, lining up his cards to get the best point advantages possible. Ruxandra preferred to gamble a bit more, to bluff and to push, to try to force Kade into making a mistake.

And while they played, they talked.

Ruxandra told him of her time in Venice, and how she'd narrowly missed the war. She talked of opera and music and art. Kade talked of science and politics, of the wars he'd followed—easy food—and the work he had done, exchanging a unique set of skills for wealth and stability.

Neither mentioned Elizabeth, as if sensing that the other had enough on their mind that adding the weight of the past would serve no purpose.

When darkness came, they stepped into the streets. Ruxandra had added stockings and boots, for form's sake, but the boots were flat-soled, in case running should be necessary.

And I suspect it will.

For two hours they walked the city. Ruxandra made Kade stop every hundred yards for the first half mile, pulling him into the shadows with her while she watched and listened and sniffed the air. They walked and ran, circled and doubled back, and several times took cover in orchards or gardens. Kade led them on the longest route possible between his house and his hunting grounds.

The small, run-down houses of the poor neighborhood were crouched together like frightened animals. The shutters lacked paint and hung crooked on their windows. Rot ran through the buildings, leaving gaping holes in the walls. She sensed desperation from the people living within.

Ruxandra believed no one followed them but was not sure. It made her nervous and irritable.

From somewhere deep inside her came a growl of hunger.

Calm yourself, Beast. It's only been a few days. She found herself, in her frustration and fear, imagining letting the Beast out. But the Beast would be of even less use against intelligent, organized magic users.

"Do you wish to follow me?" Kade asked. "There is a charity hospital nearby, and several within who would be happy to be out of their misery."

"I'll hunt alone," Ruxandra said. "Being pursued puts me in the mood to hunt."

"As you wish."

Kade gave a short bow over her hand and walked off into the night.

Ruxandra made herself noticeable and opened her mind wide. From every house she sensed hunger and pain, sadness and anger. She walked past a grimy kabak with crooked walls and a roof that looked ready to collapse. The people within reeked of exhaustion and desperation. In the alley behind it, a man and woman coupled hard. The woman faced the wall, the man's hips pounded hard against her. She sensed no passion or love between them, only grim need and obligation.

Ruxandra circled the building and kept walking.

She found what she wanted in a small attic apartment. She sensed pain blossoming in a girl's flesh, and layers of pain and anger and helplessness in two other children. And a man radiating anger and glee.

"Where is he?" he shouted. "Where is your father?"

Ruxandra turned unnoticeable. She slipped off her shoes and extended the talons in her hands and feet. She dug them deep into the wooden wall and climbed up to the small, shuttered window of the attic. The cries grew louder, timed to the hard smack of leather against the girl's skin.

"Please!" one child begged. "Our father ran away!"

"Then *you* owe me his money!" the man said. "Give it to me, now!"

"He didn't leave us any money," the other child cried. "He didn't even leave us food!"

"Liars, the lot of you!" The strap struck flesh three times more. "You think I care that you're hungry? You'll be worse than that if I don't get my money!"

Ruxandra peered through the shutters. The girl bent naked over the small rickety table was the oldest—fifteen, maybe. Another, younger girl and a young boy huddled in the corner, their naked flesh covered in old and new welts.

"You get me my money by tomorrow!" the man snarled. He pulled a long-bladed knife out with his free hand and brandished it at the two younger ones. "You sell yourselves ten times a night if you have to, but you do it!"

Ruxandra opened the shutters wide and slid into the attic. The man spun, his strap still raised high. Ruxandra allowed her fangs to come down, held up her extended talons. His eyes went wide, his mouth falling open.

"Children," Ruxandra growled, her voice echoing the rumble of the Beast inside. *"Leave."*

A quarter of an hour later, unnoticed by the few people in the streets, she found Kade outside a small kabak in the worst part of the poor quarter. He was leaning against a wall, arms folded, unnoticeable to the passing humans. His eyes moved back and forth, searching the street.

"Any sign?" he asked as she leaned against the wall beside him.

"Nothing so far."

"Have you eaten?"

"Yes."

"Then let us consult Kurkov and see if he knows what we're dealing with."

Another hour of backtracking, circling, and detouring brought them to Kurkov's house. It was no larger than Kade's house, though it boasted a second floor. Bright-red paint covered the walls, brighter-green paint the shutters.

Ruxandra, her mind scouring for the men stalking them, knew the house was empty before they saw the front door swinging open on broken hinges.

Kade's hands clenched into fists then opened wide, his talons glittering in the ambient light. The muscles in his neck clenched hard, and his fangs descended from his gums. He snarled, the sound low and inhuman. Then he swore, long and loud, in seven different languages.

Ruxandra left him in the road and advanced. She smelled no one inside the building.

Which doesn't mean no one is there.

She slipped inside and breathed deep. She caught Kurkov's scent first, Eduard's next. Then the food they'd eaten for dinner and vodka they'd spilled on the floor.

And the six men who'd taken them.

She crawled out of the house, her nose against the ground. She sniffed deep, following the scent until it vanished at a set of ruts in the earth. She circled the ruts, still sniffing.

"How many?" Kade growled.

"Six." Ruxandra kept her nose close to the ground, breathing deep. "They had a carriage. I can smell the horses."

"And can you follow them?" Fury filled his voice, making it shake.

"Yes." Ruxandra put her face against the road, breathed deep. Then she broke into a run, nostrils flaring as they drank in the scent of the horses. Kade's footsteps pounded on the ground right behind her.

"You can track them like this?" Kade asked.

"The scent is fresh," Ruxandra said. "I could pick it from a running herd."

They ran north, Ruxandra leading. Four horses pulled the carriage. Two others rode alongside. They changed direction three times, first to the Neglinka River and the army encampment on its banks. For a moment Ruxandra thought they'd gone into the line of tents. Then the scents changed direction again. The carriage crossed the Neglinka and turned east, running along the walls and the moat of the city's inner wall. It turned into a neighborhood, twisting through the streets and ending at a warehouse with big wooden doors shut tight.

"I smell the horses." She pointed at the dry earth and the fresh hoofprints there. She sniffed, frowned, and sniffed again. Then she kicked the doors, smashing through whatever bolts held them closed. They flew inward and bounced hard off the walls. The noise echoed in the space beyond.

The carriage sat, abandoned and empty, in the center of the warehouse. Its doors lay open. The horses no longer stood before it. The back door, smaller, but still easy for a horse to pass through, stood open. Ruxandra looked through it. The horses, both for the riders and the carriage, stood in a neat line, tied to the hitching post that ran along the back length of the warehouse. She sniffed deep, walking in a circle.

"They didn't leave," Ruxandra said. "They came out, they tied the horses, and they went back inside."

Kade turned in a slow circle. The warehouse's walls were wood, supported by massive posts. Heavy crossbeams held the walls apart and supported the roof. The floor was dirt, unmarked save for the tracks of the horses. There was no place to hide.

"Then where did they go?" His voice rose in frustration.

Ruxandra closed her eyes and sniffed long and hard.

"I don't know." She sighed. "But no one is in here."

"God dammit." He walked over to the carriage. It had black leather padding on the driver's seat, and on the passenger seats inside. The black lacquer that coated every inch of the carriage—even the wheels—shone in the dim light. It was a well-made, expensive piece and held nothing except a few specks of dirt on the floor.

Kade ripped the door off its hinges and threw it against the wall.

Then he kicked his foot through the paneling.

Then he attacked the carriage, smashing with his fists and feet and ripping with his talons. He tore at it until no piece of wood remained attached to any other.

And he did it in absolute silence.

And when he'd thrown the last scrap of metal hard enough to embed in the wall and torn the last board in two, and the dust and splinters had settled to the earth, he shook off his cloak, put up the hood, and walked out the door.

Ruxandra ran to catch up with him and then walked beside him. She didn't speak. She reached out with her mind as they walked, looking for pursuers. She found none, but felt the rage blazing in Kade. With every step his feet struck at the earth as if it were responsible for his miseries.

He stopped in the center of the bridge over the Neglinka, leaning his weight against the stone of the side, looking down at the river. Ruxandra stood in silence and waited.

At last Kade sighed and said, "That was, perhaps, foolish."

"Perhaps," Ruxandra said. "But destroying the carriage acts as a wonderful threat."

"Perhaps," Kade echoed. "Still, I ought not to have done it. It reveals too much of our power against an enemy of which we know nothing."

"True." Ruxandra leaned on the side of the bridge. "If it makes you feel better, I was thinking of doing the same thing."

Kade chuckled. "It does, actually."

"So now what?"

"We are facing an enemy we cannot see, hear, or touch," Kade said. "It makes it difficult to proceed."

"Let's hope not," Ruxandra said, "or we'll have no way to find them."

"There's always a way." Kade's voice turned grim on the words, letting out a dark anger so strong that Ruxandra could almost see it. He took her hand, placed it in the crook of his arm. "Let us go home. Tomorrow night we renew the hunt."

Arm in arm they crossed the bridge, heading back to his house.

The next evening, when Ruxandra stepped outside, the scent of the man from the bridge floated in the air. She looked down, sniffed again, and found the trail of his footsteps, fresh and new.

"Kade!" she called, using the vampire tones. "They were here!"

He was at the door before he finished dressing. In the moonlight his white skin shone, the chiseled edges of his muscled chest standing out above the flat ridges of his stomach. She looked away.

Why am I noticing that now, of all times?

"Are you certain?"

"Yes."

"Follow them," he said. "I'll finish dressing and come find you."

Ruxandra ran into the night. The scent trail was fresh and easy to follow. It led in a straight line, with no detours or attempts at concealment. Ruxandra tracked it to the edge of the neighborhood and stopped. When Kade arrived, she was still there.

"Well," he hissed, "are they here?"

"One of them is," Ruxandra said, and pointed.

On the street between them and Neglinka River sat a black carriage with four black horses in harness. It looked the same as the one Kade had destroyed. Atop it sat a man in black clothes with a black scarf covering half his face and black gloves on his hands. Beside it stood another man dressed in black, solidly built and muscular, with a sword and a brace of pistols hanging from his belt. He was pale with black hair and snapping dark eyes. His hawk nose had been broken long ago.

Ruxandra recognized his scent.

The man from the bridge looked straight at her, expressionless, and held open the carriage door.

CHAPTER
SEVEN

RUXANDRA STOPPED and searched the street with her eyes, nose, and mind.

"How many of them?" Kade asked. "I smell other people, but I'm not sure from where."

Ruxandra sniffed the air. "The other people are inside the houses. Out here there are only the two of them."

"Then let us see what they want." Kade strode forward.

The man at the carriage bowed low and swept his hand to the open door. "Please, enter."

"Tell me who you are," Kade commanded in Russian. *"Why do you follow us?"*

"Commands will not work," the man said. "Please; you are expected."

"Expected by whom?"

"Enter the carriage and see."

"Or I could rip your head off and ask your companion."

"That will not work, either." The man looked at Ruxandra and smiled. "Correct?"

"Just because it didn't last time," Ruxandra said in Italian as she joined Kade, "doesn't mean it won't now."

"If you attack us, you die," the man said. "I have limited patience, and it is already strained after you savagely destroyed our carriage."

"Fortunate that you had a spare," Kade said, his voice low and smooth like the purring of a mountain cat. Ruxandra could feel the coiled rage and was impressed by the black-haired man's equanimity. Knowing you could not be attacked was all very well—for *your body* to know that was something else entirely.

"Enough." The man bowed to Ruxandra. "I guarantee that no harm will come to you while you are in my custody."

"Custody?" Kade let the word roll slowly off his tongue, as if tasting its implications. "We are under arrest, then?"

"Not at all," the man said. "Being arrested hurts a great deal more. You are *invited*."

"Where are my friends?"

In answer the man gestured to the open carriage door.

"What now?" Ruxandra asked in Romanian, using vampire frequencies.

"I believe it is a trap," Kade said back, voice and language the same.

"I am unsure." Ruxandra kept her eyes on the man in black, but he gave no sign of hearing or understanding. "They could take us anytime. Why do it this way?"

"Less bloodshed?" Kade suggested. "What if they charmed the carriage so we cannot leave it?"

"I doubt they can charm it so much we cannot tear it apart," Ruxandra said. "And it might take us to your friends."

"Or to our deaths."

"Their magic may prevent us from killing them," Ruxandra said, "but only sunlight kills us, and even that we can escape."

"You know this?"

Ruxandra remembered waking, buried in the earth. "I do."

"I see." Kade's eyes narrowed. He glared at the man holding the carriage door, and then peered inside the carriage.

"Your guarantee of safe passage?" Ruxandra asked the man.

"I promise. Will you come, my lady?"

Ruxandra reached out with her mind, but could not feel the man's emotions. She breathed in his scent and caught no whiff of fear or the excitement that generally accompanies the intent to commit violence. *Not that this guarantees anything.*

But she refused to give in to fear. Once she did that, she might as well quit the field altogether, which was not an option, not now. Ruxandra climbed into the carriage. She settled near the far window, sinking into the black leather padding that cushioned the seats.

"Kade," she said. "Join me."

Kade growled and bared his fangs, but he stepped into the carriage. He sat beside Ruxandra, his arms crossed. The man climbed in, closed the door, and tapped the roof with his knuckles. The carriage started into motion with a gentle jolt. Ruxandra watched the houses and kabaks and churches go by. The carriage drove down the main thoroughfare, its well-greased wheels making no sound, the horses' hooves thumping on the dirt road. The man without a name did not speak, nor did the vampires.

They turned onto a bridge, the thud of the horses' hooves turning into a sharp clop, and the wheels rattling against the cobbles. The city's inner wall grew closer until it towered over them. They stopped, and someone out of sight challenged them in Russian. The driver responded, a gate creaked open, and they moved forward again. The walls passed above their heads, and the carriage rolled through the cobblestoned streets.

Ruxandra sat back and spread her mind wide. Most of the Kremlin's inhabitants slept. Some lay awake, exhausted. Some ached with the pains of age. A few boiled with lustful desires—some alone, some couples, and one group of three. Several people deep inside the buildings writhed in horrific pain while someone nearby felt deep satisfaction at his work.

I wonder what they did to deserve that. Or did they deserve it?

The driver called to the horses, and the carriage pulled to a stop. The man stepped out, waited for Kade to dismount, held out a hand for Ruxandra, then smiled briefly and pulled it back. "I forget myself."

She ignored him and stepped down.

"The Palace of Facets," the man said.

It was small, for a palace, though it connected to the much larger one behind it. Soot and dirt covered the once-white walls, speaking of years of disuse. They stood at the base of a short set of steps with a large arch above it. Beyond that, another much longer set of stairs ran the length of the building, stopping at a wide landing with a set of ornate wooden doors leading in. A line of large windows, their frames in need of paint, stood above it.

The surrounding cathedrals, by contrast, shone white with freshly painted walls. Their golden domes high above glowed in the faint moonlight. Icons painted above their doors gave life and color to the white buildings.

"Welcome to the Kremlin," the man said. "You are in Cathedral Square. Behind you lie the Cathedrals of the Assumption, the Archangel Michael and the Annunciation."

"The cathedrals look much better kept than the palace," Kade said.

"It has been much neglected of late," the man agreed. "Peter preferred St. Petersburg. With the new empress earlier this year, we expect to see improvements again. You see the scaffolding?"

"We do," Kade said. "What I don't see are my friends."

"Come this way if you please."

Ruxandra linked her arm with Kade's. The man led them up the long, shallow staircase to the large doors. At the top he turned on his heel. He knocked three times on the doors, paused, and knocked four more. The doors swung wide. Light from hundreds of candles spilled out, the yellow glow brightening the stairs. He gestured for them to go in.

Ruxandra stepped inside and gasped in awe.

The room was brilliant with gold.

The red marble floor shone in the candlelight. Wide columns rose high and spread out above to become the domes of the ceiling. Gold decorated everything: the doors, the thick carvings on their frames, the windows, and the designs on the columns. It was laid out in ribs that rose from the columns' corners to join at the top of each dome. And wherever there was no gold, pictures covered the walls and ceiling.

A hundred images filled Ruxandra's eyes. Paintings of kings, queens, and saints vied for attention with scenes of hunting, battle, and celebration. The colors, once bright and vibrant, had long since faded, but the effect still overwhelmed the eye. Ruxandra walked forward, eyes wide with wonder.

At the far end of the room, sitting on a raised throne, sat a tall, stout woman—mature but not old. Her coarse features and small, dark eyes looked out of place amid the splendor that surrounded her. The woman's brown hair stuck out, wild and ragged. She wore an unadorned light-blue gown, designed to display ample cleavage and draw the eyes to the magnificent garnet on a gold chain that rested between her breasts.

She was the only other person visible, but she was not alone. Ruxandra let her head swivel from side to side, pretending to look at the pictures as she breathed deep to smell what she couldn't see or hear or sense.

The man stopped ten paces in front of the throne and bowed deep. Kade followed his example. Ruxandra dropped into a deep, formal curtsy. The woman watched them with a bored, tired expression.

"Rise," she said. "Approach."

They rose and walked forward. The woman's eyes narrowed as they approached. She raised a hand, stopping them three paces away.

"Well done, Alexi," she said in Russian. Their guide bowed and stepped to the side. The woman frowned at Ruxandra and Kade. She switched to French. "Explain yourselves."

Ruxandra had no idea what she meant. Kade put on a gracious smile.

"An honor, Your Majesty," Kade said, also in French. "We had not expected an audience."

Majesty? This is Anna of Russia?

"I had hoped to speak to you one day," Kade continued. "That it should occur so soon—"

"Spare me, vampire," Empress Anna said. "It has been a particularly vexing day. I have peasants unhappy with their lot; I have the Metropolitan clamoring for more funds for cathedrals; I have nobles displeased with their removal from power and the removal of several of their fellows' heads. And now I have you."

She glared at them as if they were personally responsible for everything that had gone wrong. "And before we begin I will tell you, your commands will not work on me, and you will not be able to touch me. Now explain why you are in my city and why I shouldn't kill you both where you stand."

"I am curious to learn how you knew we were here," Kade said instead, "and what we are. And how your men follow us, for that matter."

She offered a small, cold smile in which there was neither humor nor pleasure. "We've been waiting for you since your friends told us everything they knew. We knew the moment you entered the city and have kept you in our sight since," Anna said. "This is Russia. We have not abandoned the old ways, unlike those fools to the west. We remember the battles to destroy your kind when they ruled this city. There is no place we cannot find you."

"I am impressed," Kade said.

Anna smirked. "My men surround you, though you cannot see them."

Kade smiled back at her. "Ruxandra?"

"Fourteen men." Ruxandra pointed to the columns that lined the hall. "Two behind each column, two more standing on either side of the throne, two waiting at the front door. All armed with swords and firearms."

Anna's composure cracked for an instant—her eyes widened; her breath quickened. She contained both, straightened in her throne, and glared down her long nose at Ruxandra.

Ruxandra kept her face expressionless. She had caught the men's scent the moment she walked in, along with the smell of oil on steel and the sharp odor of black powder.

"Perhaps I should kill you on the spot," Anna said.

"We are hard to kill, Your Majesty," Ruxandra said, her voice bland and calm, even as she planned her escape route. "So I suggest attempting it somewhere less . . . expensive."

Anna's eyes widened again. A real smile broke through. "Very funny, girl. Your name?"

"Princess Ruxandra Dracula, daughter of Vlad Dracula, prince of Wallachia." She curtsied again, deep and formally. "At your service, Your Majesty."

"Vlad Dracula?" Anna frowned. "Vlad Tepes?"

"A nickname bestowed many years after his death," Ruxandra said.

Anna rubbed her chin. "Murdered by the Turks two hundred fifty years ago."

Ruxandra flashed back to the cave where she'd become a vampire, and the moment when she'd torn her father's head from his shoulders. "Something similar, Your Majesty."

"Whereas this one I know." Anna switched her gaze to Kade. "Though he did not see fit to tell me he had returned to Russia. Or that he was a vampire."

"I thought it best to keep the latter secret," Kade said. "To avoid misunderstandings, Your Majesty."

"You know her?" Shock made Ruxandra forget her courtesy. "What?"

"Didn't he tell you?" Anna smiled again, the expression wicked. "For shame, Kade. It is hard for a woman to trust a man who keeps secrets."

"I do not know Her Majesty well," Kade said to Ruxandra. "I served Peter."

"It was your idea to marry me to the Duke of Courland," Anna said. "And no doubt your idea to have him die on his way home."

"I only carried out Peter's bidding."

"Just as well," Anna said. "The duke had a small cock and the breath of a corpse-eating dog. Not to mention a penchant for beating his servants."

"I was here, in Moscow, when Peter died," Kade said. "Engrossed in my studies. Otherwise—"

"I would never have inherited the throne?" Anna said it as a question, but her eyes narrowed, and her expression grew hard, as though she knew the answer. "What guarantee do I have that the two of you pose no threat to my rule?"

"I have no interest in politics," Ruxandra said. "Kade did *not* tell me of his relationship with the past emperor or with Your Majesty."

Kade winced at the change in her tone, but said nothing.

"I see you two have much to discuss, once I dismiss you." Anna chuckled as she rose from her throne. "What if I asked you to swear allegiance to me, my heirs and descendants, and to Russia, in the name of God, to the end of time? Would such an oath hold creatures like you?"

"I would say no and leave," Ruxandra replied. "I do not swear allegiance to anyone."

"The doors are locked and charmed against vampires."

"Are the windows?" Ruxandra pointed high on the wall. "Even the small ones?"

"You can't get up there," Anna said, though she didn't sound positive.

"I can, Your Majesty," Ruxandra said, and once more Anna's self-assurance cracked and reformed.

Anna looked at Kade. "And what about you?"

"I would like to know what Your Majesty has done with my friends," Kade said, "before I answer any question about oaths."

"Indeed." She looked them over for a moment, her gaze shrewd. "Those magicians? They are alive. Whether they stay that way depends on you."

"I want them back unharmed," Kade said. "Or I will be very unhappy."

"Then unhappy you shall be, as your friends refused to answer all my questions the first time." Anna's voice grew cold and hard. "Will you live with your unhappiness, or shall I order you killed?"

"If you try, I shall exit through the window like Ruxandra. And then, Your Majesty, I will burn as much of the Kremlin and the city as possible before I escape or am killed."

"I dislike threats." Anna leaned back in her throne and frowned at him. "Ask the remaining members of the council that tried to usurp my powers if you disbelieve me. You'll find the survivors in the prison below the Terem Palace, in an extremely uncomfortable room. Right next to some of your magicians, as it happens. And if you leave this room before I say, I will have my men run swords through your friends' bowels. So instead of threatening each other, I suggest we come to an arrangement."

"What sort of arrangement?" Kade asked.

"What did Peter agree to?"

"In return for protection and help with his enemies, unlimited access to the libraries," Kade said. "Freedom of the country, and a healthy stipend, of course."

"Of course. And your friends will serve as your guarantors."

"Of course." Kade's tone perfectly echoed Anna's.

Anna frowned at him, then turned her eyes to Ruxandra. "What about you, girl?"

Some small part of Ruxandra was tempted to offer to leave Moscow and let Kade meet his fate as punishment for lying to her. As satisfying as that might be, however, it would not stop the magicians from summoning a dark angel.

"I will abide by the same terms as Kade," Ruxandra said, "save that my 'help' does not include killing for political purposes."

Anna scoffed. "Conscience? In a demon? Amusing. Very well. I agree to your terms, both of you, but know you are under surveillance."

"We know," Kade said. "My friends?"

"Alexi will take you." Anna walked toward the door behind the throne. She stopped and looked back. "I can't wait to move the capital back to St. Petersburg. This city is a shit-hole."

"Yes, Your Majesty." Kade bowed low, Ruxandra curtsied, and Anna stalked out.

"If you will follow me?" Alexi said. "I can lead you to your friends."

"Thank you." Ruxandra glared at Kade, making him swallow hard and back up a step. "And on our way, Kade will explain *exactly* what is happening here."

CHAPTER

EIGHT

"**R**IGHT," RUXANDRA SAID, the moment they stepped outside. "Talk."

"I arrived in Moscow fifteen years after I left Elizabeth." Kade held out his arm for her. She ignored it and stared at him. He shrugged and started down the stairs. "Fifty-five years ago."

"I can do math," Ruxandra said. "What I can't fathom is why you worked for the Russian royal family."

"Where one finds power, one finds knowledge. I wanted their knowledge."

"So you advised Peter?"

"The First, yes," Kade said. "I had established a merchant business in St. Petersburg to keep money flowing, and discovered several things I thought beneficial to the empire. So I arranged to meet the emperor. He was somewhat shocked at my presumption until I told him what I knew. Then he suggested we formalize our relationship. He paid me enough that I could give up being a merchant and gave me access to libraries in exchange for making use of my . . . skills. I lived in St. Petersburg but visited

Moscow many times over the years before he died, which is how I knew the Alchemist."

"How many did you kill for him?"

"Surprisingly few," Kade said. "Peter was well liked for a reason."

Alexi led them around the palace. The building behind stood taller and larger, its bricks red and yellow and orange. It looked like a fire, warming the Kremlin against the cold white of the other buildings. Domes and a long sloped roof, both shining gold, capped it.

Ruxandra pulled her eyes off the architecture and back to Kade. "And then Anna came to power?"

"No. Catherine, Peter's wife, sat on the throne for two years before she died, then his grandson, Peter II. He was the opposite of his grandfather: profligate, uncaring, interested in sex, alcohol, and gambling, not in any particular order or combination. He informed me that he had no use for me, so I moved to Moscow."

"In the time you worked for Peter, did you ever see his men use magic?"

"Not once," Kade said. "But then, he did not know I was a vampire. Neither did Anna, until now."

"So when you said few people saw you . . ."

Kade shrugged. "It was mostly true, after Peter died."

Ruxandra growled. "You are . . ."

"Infuriating?" Kade suggested. "Secretive, self-serving, and mercurial?"

"All those."

Kade smiled. "It is fortunate, then, that I am charming company."

Ruxandra rolled her eyes. "Not as much as you think."

"But you are," Kade said. "Charming company, that is."

"Oh, please."

"Ruxandra." Kade caught her hand, bringing her to a stop. She turned, ready to extend her talons to make him let go. Kade bowed, brushing his lips against her skin. It left a tingle that ran from her hand to the hairs on the nape of her neck.

"You are charming," Kade repeated. "And I wish to stay at your side, if you can trust me."

He is a smooth one, isn't he?

And charming.

And very . . . The words that leaped to mind better described his body than his personality. His hard, perfectly sculpted vampire body. She set them aside. *Persuasive. He is very persuasive.*

"And now," Kade called as they rounded the corner of Terem Palace, "perhaps Alexi can tell us our destination?"

Alexi pointed ahead of them to a long white building, three stories high and lined with barred windows. The place smelled of coal and smoke, oil and steel, and paint.

"This is the armory," Alexi said. "Our destination is beneath it."

Guards flanked the round-topped doors. They saluted Alexi, and one knocked on the door in a complicated code. A moment later it opened, and two more guards appeared in the doorway.

"Memorize these two," Alexi said in Russian. "They may come and go freely."

"Yes, sir!" The guards stepped aside. Alexi took them down a long hall to a much smaller iron door and another pair of guards. Again he received a salute, and again he told the men to memorize Ruxandra and Kade. One guard lit a lantern for him, and Alexi led Kade and Ruxandra down a set of spiral stairs carved into rock.

Ruxandra counted a thousand steps before they reached the bottom. A long, narrow hallway stretched out before them, seemingly with no end. The gray stone walls rose up to become the arched ceiling. It felt older than the other buildings Ruxandra had seen in the Kremlin. The cut of the stones reminded her of the ruins that dotted the countryside near Rome and Tuscany.

They walked for a half hour, and still the end remained out of sight. The air smelled fresh, despite the depth below ground. At last they saw a red door cutting off the hallway. Alexi took out a long key and put it in the keyhole. It turned with a loud click. He pushed the door open, and a bell clanged, loud and suddenly.

The door opened onto a wide marble balcony. A domed ceiling stretched fifty feet above their heads. A mural of a forest covered it, trees and grasses adorning the dome in a riot of green.

"Visitors!" called a woman's voice.

Kade surged forward, pushing Alexi aside. "Alchemist!"

He ran to the edge of the balcony, looked down, and then jumped over.

Ruxandra stepped forward. Below lay a large, open floor with tables lining the length of it. Five people with lanterns in their hands milled about in the empty space, all talking at once. Kade had his arms wrapped around a tall woman in a dark-red wool shawl, her blonde hair pulled back into a high bun. A frail old man with spectacles and an astonishingly fat younger one with a thick black beard stood beside them. Kurkov and Eduard stood back.

"By God!" Kurkov's voice echoed through the room. "Kade! They caught you, too?"

Ruxandra looked up at the dome above them. "Humans didn't build this, did they?"

"Why do you think that?"

Ruxandra pointed at the ceiling. "There's not enough light for them to see the dome, so why paint it in so many shades of green?"

Alexi's smile returned. "You're the first to guess it. Your king and his followers built these rooms."

Ruxandra frowned, then remembered. "The vampire king. Why?"

"To help them escape the summer sun in Moscow, I expect—which lasts most of the night, I should warn you."

Ruxandra surveyed the room. "How long were they here?"

"A hundred years? Five hundred? No one knows. In the end we rooted them out."

"How?"

Alexi shook his head. "You must be joking."

"I wasn't, no."

"Then I must disappoint you by not answering. Follow me."

He led her to a staircase—also marble—and down to the main floor. The magicians and the Alchemist stopped their celebration. The Alchemist stepped away from Kade, her hands falling to her sides, her eyes on Alexi.

Up close, she stood as tall as Ruxandra, with bright-blonde hair that was fading to gray over a high forehead, a hooked nose, and a strong jaw that held full lips. She was thin and looked tense as whipcord ready to break. She wore a plain brown skirt, stained and smelling of a dozen different chemicals.

Alexi pointed to a bronze door set deep into the wall. "There is another exit there, Ruxandra. It takes you up to the surface, to a church outside the inner walls. Your friends are free to go outside when they please but may not leave the church grounds.

You and Kade have the freedom of the city, provided you continue to honor your agreement with the empress."

He looked over the men and woman standing there. The Alchemist met his gaze without flinching. The others backed away, gathering behind Kade.

Kade frowned at Alexi. "Where are the others? Sasha, Victor, Dimitri?"

"Safe," Alexi said. "Isn't that right, Alchemist?"

"Imprisoned, he means," the Alchemist said. "Kept there for assurance of our continued good behavior. We visit them every day to ensure they stay alive."

Kade's voice dropped to a growl. "I do not like that."

"I will convey your thoughts to Anna." Alexi did not look the slightest bit intimidated. "How goes the work?"

"Slow," the Alchemist said. "There are a hundred thousand books, scrolls, and tablets here, plus the ones from our library. We do not know the system they used to catalog them, so we divided them by language, and then by subject."

"This is not the task the empress gave you."

"The empress must understand that these things take time."

"The *empress*," Alexi stressed the word, "wants results, and she wants them very soon, or she will insist that you all receive a second correction to your behavior."

Ruxandra didn't need to reach out with her mind to feel the collective shudder run through the men there. *"I dislike threats." Anna, so do I.*

The Alchemist showed no reaction at all. "Torture will not help us learn ancient Babylonian."

"And why do you need ancient Babylonian?"

"It is the language of the spell," the Alchemist said. "What we needed is our friend, who learns languages faster than anyone. Now that he is here, the work will speed up."

"August is over," Alexi said. "Her Majesty expects the full ritual to be ready before the end of September."

Without waiting for a reply, he strode past the Alchemist and opened the brass door with an easy pull. He left it open and went up the stairs on the other side, his light soon fading into darkness.

"That man," Kurkov said, "needs to be fucked long and hard until his spirit calms. Otherwise he will explode from his own tension."

"A fuck does not solve everything," said the older man, who reminded Ruxandra of some strange species of bird with his wild head of long gray hair and thick mustache. "Much as you might wish it. Life is deeper and more sorrowful than that."

"It may not," Kurkov said, "but it most certainly does not hurt."

"Ha!" the Alchemist said over her shoulder. "Spoken like a man who's never had to fear becoming big with unwanted child." Her eyes, though, were on Ruxandra. "Kade, is this she?"

"Yes." Kade stood beside Ruxandra and took her hand. "Please address her in Italian or French, as she only began to learn Russian a short while ago. Friends, may I present Her Highness Princess Ruxandra Dracula, daughter of Vlad Dracula of Wallachia. The first among us."

"The first?" The old birdlike man peered at Ruxandra. "Nonsense. She doesn't look a day over twenty."

Ruxandra glared at Kade. "Exactly how many people have you told about this?"

"Only a few." Kade patted her arm. "These men I would trust with my life."

"Only the men?" the Alchemist asked.

Kade bowed low. "My deepest apologies."

"He apologizes, sure," the Alchemist said to the rest, "but introduce me? Of course not."

She pushed the old man staring at Ruxandra out of the way. "Move aside, Michael, you old lecher."

"I am inspecting this marvelous creature," he said with dignity.

"You were looking at her tits." She thumped him on the shoulder and flashed a smile at Ruxandra. "Not that I blame him, because you have a lovely pair. But is it true, what Kade says about you? That you are the first vampire, a great hunter, and a terrifying Beast lives within you?"

"Do you doubt him?" Ruxandra asked. *But I am not the first vampire. And that is the most interesting thing of all.*

"Every time he opens his mouth."

A bark of laughter escaped from Ruxandra.

The Alchemist grinned. "Kade's love of secrets is only surpassed by his love of half-truths. Other than that, he has many excellent qualities."

"Including excellent skills as a lover?" asked Kurkov, getting a chuckle from the other men.

Ruxandra raised an eyebrow toward Kade. He had his mouth firmly shut but appeared to be enjoying himself.

"Yes, you dirty old fool," the Alchemist said, without the slightest hint of embarrassment. "As anyone in the house knew already."

"As anyone on the street knew, with the noise you make."

"This from you!" The Alchemist winked at Ruxandra. "When this man is receiving, he whinnies and grunts like a mare getting plowed. As anyone on the street knew!"

Kurkov's face reddened. "The young lady does not need to know details!"

"The lady," the Alchemist said, the humor vanishing from her voice, "is not young. She just looks young. Don't you, Princess?"

"Ruxandra, please."

"Oh no." The Alchemist moved closer, eyes blazing with interest. "You are definitely 'Princess.' And before you think we have no manners, gentlemen, introduce yourselves."

"Michael," said the wild-haired mustached one. "Magician and astrologer. And one who is most grateful to have lived long enough to meet you. What you must know, Princess! I am astounded."

"Less than I would like," said Ruxandra. "But thank you."

"Derek," the black-bearded one said. He might be the fattest man she had ever seen, Ruxandra thought. His cheeks were so plump they squeezed his lips and ears, and his belly strained against his shirt, not only in front but also on the sides. Rings of flesh obscured his wrists. "Also a magician and explorer of occult creatures and rituals." *He sounds self-satisfied*, thought Ruxandra. *But the old one, I like him.*

"Derek is very unhappy here," confided Kurkov. "They won't give him enough to eat."

The man's color rose. "And what they give us is vile and tasteless. As if we were thieves and cutthroats, not scholars."

"What scholar breaks his fast with an entire pork shoulder and three black loaves?" asked Kurkov, opening his hands in astonishment. "Oh, my dear fellow, we are lucky you are not a vampire, or the there would be no warm body left in the city of Moscow."

"Kurkov, one would think you were six, not sixty. Pay no attention to his foolery, Princess. I am, of course, the Alchemist. May I examine you?"

Ruxandra blinked in surprise. "Here?"

"Not here, but there are rooms—"

"The princess came here to help in our work." Kade stepped in front of Ruxandra. "Unless it changed since Anna took control."

"Did she?" The Alchemist leaned around him. "Can you read?"

"Romanian, Hungarian, Latin, Italian, and French," Ruxandra said.

"Not Cyrillic?"

"No."

"She will learn," Kade said. "Just as I did. And just as quickly."

"He does learn quickly," the Alchemist said. "Not so quick as to make up for his other failings. Move, you great ox!"

She pushed Kade. He did not budge an inch. The Alchemist sighed, walked around him, and caught Ruxandra's arm.

"Come," she said. "Let me show you the rest of our humble abode."

"I will go with you," Kade said.

"Pish." The Alchemist waved him away. "Don't be so jealous. I won't steal your lover." She turned to Ruxandra. "Unless you want me to steal you?"

"Not just now," Ruxandra said. "And I am not his lover."

"Not now but not never? Interesting." A distinct smell of arousal, unnoticeable to the human nose, rose from the Alchemist. She wrapped her arm in Ruxandra's. "Come with me and see all the amenities our prison offers."

The Alchemist grabbed a lantern off the table and led Ruxandra away. To Ruxandra's consternation, she was chuckling to herself.

"May I ask what is funny?" Ruxandra said as they walked between the rows of bookcases.

"Kade. Jealous." The Alchemist chuckled again. "As if he has anything to worry about from an old woman like me."

"He isn't," Ruxandra began.

The Alchemist stared at her. "Of course he is! The old lover walking with the new? He definitely is jealous, and worried that we will compare stories."

"I am not his lover," Ruxandra repeated. "Nor am I yours."

"You will be. Mine, at least."

Confident, aren't you? "Are you giving me a tour or gossiping?"

"Touchy." The Alchemist shrugged. "Fine. We'll begin with the important thing."

She led Ruxandra down a flight of stairs and a short corridor and through a large brass door. On the other side, to Ruxandra's amazement, were the baths. Two marble pools—one so hot it steamed, the other cold for soaking—took up most of the room. A trough of moving water ran the length of one wall. Marble benches lined the others. Ruxandra stared in amazement. "How?"

"I have no idea," the Alchemist said. "It looks like a Roman bath, but I cannot fathom how they managed to build it. The marble looks like the work of a master mason. There are no seams we can see, and the water is always fresh and hot. And we are a good hundred feet below ground. It doesn't seem possible."

"They weren't human."

"The vampire king?" The Alchemist shook her head. "He's a myth."

"Like Kade?" Ruxandra asked. "Like myself?"

"Kade I have examined closely. You I know nothing about except what Kade has told us."

"Is that not enough?"

"Certainly not." The Alchemist put the lantern down on the bench. "Everything Kade says must be verified. Did you know he told me he was born in Scotland? His mother was burned as a witch when he was very young. He was raised in Spain by a sorcerer who used him for sex magic."

I didn't know that. No wonder . . .

"Whether those things are true I cannot say for certain. What I can say is that he is well hung. Now, shall we continue the tour, or shall we bathe?"

The pools looked very tempting after so long on the road and three nights in the city without a proper bath. Even so, Ruxandra was not ready to step in them just yet.

"Perhaps later," Ruxandra said. "Are you still going to summon the fallen angel?"

The Alchemist's eyes narrowed. "That's why you're here, is it not?"

"It is why Kade *wanted* to bring me here. I *came* here to stop you."

"Why on earth would you do that?"

"Because it is dangerous," Ruxandra said. "You may die. All of you."

The Alchemist nodded. "And?"

"A *ND?'"* Ruxandra stomped back and forth across the churchyard. "I tell her she will die and her response is 'And?' What sort of idiot is she?"

Kade leaned against the church wall. His lips twitched in what might have been a smile. Ruxandra spotted it in the corner of her eye and glared. It vanished at once.

"She is not an idiot," Kade said. "A genius, yes, and possibly insane, but not a fool."

"She is if she wants to summon a dark angel! I was there the last time! I know what happened! People died!"

"You *were* what happened," Kade said. "You were the one who killed them, not the angel."

Ruxandra stopped pacing.

"That is why I wanted you here." Kade pushed off the wall. "The dark angel created you. With you here, she will not kill them."

"You don't know that." Ruxandra glared at the gray sky. The clouds were heavy, and she could smell the rain waiting to fall. She wished they would open and soak Kade's calm, smug face.

"I know the magicians have no choice. If they do not summon the angel, Anna will torture them to death."

"But . . ." Ruxandra wavered, knowing he was right but hating what that meant.

"Ruxandra." Kade walked toward her, his hands out and palms up. "Neither you nor I know what will happen when we summon this creature."

"I know nothing good will come of it."

"*You* came of it." Kade came closer, though not near enough to touch. "I would not have met you if not for her."

"You would not have murdered thousands if it were not for her!" Ruxandra spat the words. "Elizabeth would not still be torturing young women. I would not have a ravening *Beast* inside me that goes insane with hunger and kills without discrimination if not for her. Forgive me if my opinion differs from yours!"

"I understand your fears. I sympathize with them." Kade looked at the church. "Do you ever wonder why humans need to believe in God?"

Ruxandra tilted her head.

"Their lives are so short. *Our* lives were so short before we became what we are. They are desperate to live longer, desperate to believe they have purpose. So they go to church and obey the rules and hope that God exists and he will tell them their lives were worthwhile."

"Then why summon a devil?"

"An angel."

"A fallen angel."

"You prayed to God for years. When was the last time he listened?"

Ruxandra opened her mouth to answer. She shut it a moment later.

"Precisely." Kade brought his hands together and pointed the fingers at Ruxandra. "God works in mysterious ways, not comprehended by mortal men. The devil works very simply. He offers you a bargain. He gives you what you wish for in exchange for your soul. And if you got what you asked for and discovered it wasn't what you wanted, well, that's not the devil's fault, is it?"

"So now she's the devil?" Ruxandra shook her head. "I thought she was an angel."

"Lucifer was the brightest angel," Kade said. "He is now the devil. So yes, this fallen angel is also a devil. And humans will make bargains with her, when they cannot get their God to give them what they want."

"What do they want? Before Anna, before it would cost them their lives to not summon her, what was so important that the Alchemist and her friends would give up their lives and maybe their souls for it?"

"The thirst for knowledge can be all-encompassing," Kade said. "And to gain knowledge that no one else in the world has? That is a powerful temptation."

Ruxandra growled at the stupidity of it. "Listen," she said. "I, too, want to know things the angel might be able to tell me. But such knowledge is not only not worth it—not even remotely—there is no reason at all to believe what she might say."

"You believed what she said."

She was speechless. He was right, but he was wrong.

Kade smiled. "We should head home, don't you think?" He pointed up at the lightening sky above them. "And not to my bolt-hole this time, but to my home."

"What about the Alchemist and the magicians?"

"Today? Nothing. Tonight we will talk to them and work out a strategy."

"Fine." Ruxandra pulled her cloak tight around her. "Lead on."

They stepped outside the church. Ruxandra sniffed the air and caught the scent of four men in the streets. Three she spotted at once: Two stood against the wall on the other side of the street, chatting. Another sat under a tree, hat pulled down almost over his eyes.

But not quite, which is how Ruxandra spotted him watching her. She glanced at the other two men and saw them also tracking Kade and her as they walked away from the church. After a few steps, they returned to their conversation, but their eyes were focused on the church, not on each other.

The other man she could not see. She put his scent into her memory, to recognize him later.

Kade led her at an easy pace across the city toward the inner walls. Ruxandra spent the rest of the walk looking at the vegetables ripening in the fields and the fruit on the trees. The houses along the way were solid and in good repair. It was a prosperous city. Given what Kade had said about the raids from Tatar slavers, she wondered how long it would stay that way.

Wood hit bone, and someone grunted in shock. Ruxandra spun in time to see a pair of men wearing scarves wrapped tightly around their faces swinging clubs at empty air. The clubs bounced off bone that Ruxandra couldn't see—then stopped. Something hit the ground with a dull thud.

"Rob him," said the first man. "Don't kill him. He hasn't seen us and ending him will bring trouble."

His companion knelt and rifled through pockets invisible to Ruxandra. The first man nodded his satisfaction and took off his mask. He was pale, with blue eyes that sparkled, shaggy blond hair, and a beard. He walked right toward them.

"Do not fear," he said in Russian. "He is not dead, and he will think someone robbed him. Nothing will connect him to us, or us to you."

I understood that. My Russian is improving.

Kade frowned and stepped forward. "Who are you?"

"One who knows the invaluable service you rendered to Peter," the man said.

Ruxandra looked up. In Russian she said, "We do not have time."

"It is early morning," the man said. "The entire day lies ahead of you."

"I see." Kade looked the man up and down, his eyes pausing on the ring he wore. "I take it you have a carriage nearby?"

"I do. This way, please."

The carriage was deep green and better appointed than the last they had ridden in. The blond man swung up top to ride with the driver. Kade settled into the seats and made himself comfortable. Ruxandra glared at him.

"Where are we going?" Ruxandra demanded in vampire tones. "And what are we going to do when the sun comes up?"

"That is an hour from now," Kade said, his tone matching hers so neither the driver nor the blond man could hear. "We'll be home by then."

"How are you so certain?"

"Because I recognized the man's ring." Kade leaned forward. "He belongs to Prince Belosselsky. Former member of the empress's guiding council."

"Former?"

"She dissolved the council."

"Ah. What does he want with us?"

"With *me*. They don't know you. The same as Anna, I suspect. Please don't let on how much Russian you understand."

Kade smiled and sank back in his seat. Ruxandra glared, but he stayed silent.

The carriage rattled over the roads and, to Ruxandra's surprise, through the gates of the enclave next to the Kremlin. Its streets were clean and cobbled. The buildings here were stone—white or gray—and most were new. They resembled the great houses she had seen in France and Italy: flat fronted, with many windows and a central door. The windows were smaller than in the south, no doubt to keep out the worst of winter's cold.

Outside, the sky grew lighter, making Ruxandra more and more nervous.

"Kade . . ." Ruxandra looked pointedly out the window.

Kade smiled again. "Not to worry."

Infuriating, self-involved, smug . . .

The carriage pulled up in front of a large gray stone house. The blond man jumped down and opened the carriage door. Ruxandra stepped out with Kade almost on her heels. He stood beside her as she surveyed the street and house and offered his arm. Ruxandra took it and allowed him to guide her.

The blond man led them to a parlor with carpets spread over the floor and three plush couches. They had been red once, but time and use had faded them to pink. Well-worn paths ran the length of the faded carpet. The massive candelabra above had only half its candles, and none were lit. A small fire crackled in the large fireplace, and the curtains were open wide to let in whatever light the gray morning was bringing. The entire house spoke of better days.

"Here is the man himself," said a deep voice in French.

"Prince Belosselsky." Kade bowed, shortly and precisely. "To what do we owe this summoning?"

If Prince Belosselsky had allowed his home to fade and wear, he had not given up on his wardrobe. He wore a white silk shirt and a vest of red velvet, and his jacket and trousers were deep purple. His polished black boots shone so much that Ruxandra suspected he could use them as a mirror. Gold-and-diamond rings adorned his fingers. He wore his shoulder-length gray hair slicked back with pomade.

"Do you know," the prince said, "that at one time I could have commoners hanged for questioning me?"

He sounded at once amused and wistful.

"How unfortunate," Kade said, "that times changed."

"More for me than for you, I suspect." The prince took a spot on the couch facing them. "Sit, both of you."

Kade took a place opposite the prince. Ruxandra sat on the middle couch, where she could keep an eye on the windows and the light that grew brighter with every passing minute.

"It is unlike you to be awake so early," Kade said.

The prince shrugged. "The vagaries of age. Some nights I barely sleep. And when I heard you had reappeared, I had to wait for your arrival before I could even think of sleeping."

"You know a letter from you would have brought me at your convenience."

"I thought it unwise, with the secret police following you."

For the first time, Kade looked surprised. At least to Ruxandra he did. She doubted if the prince even noticed the way his eyes widened for the shortest of moments.

"The who?" Kade asked.

"The secret police. An innovation of dear Empress Anna. Police who wear no uniforms, arrest whom they like when they like, and answer only to Anna. They arrested you, too, did they not?"

"They escorted us," Kade said. "The empress wanted words with me and insisted it happen at once. Again, had she asked . . ."

"You would have run like a wolf from the hunters." The prince said it matter-of-factly, without rancor or accusation. "Especially with your friends arrested."

"Relocated."

"As I said." The prince offered a lupine smile. "Kade, where are your manners? Will you not introduce this beautiful, though plainly dressed, young lady?"

"Prince Belosselsky, this is Princess Ruxandra Dracula," Kade said. "She is . . . my companion."

"Is that what they are calling it these days?" The old prince looked amused. "So much younger than you, too."

"Not so much as all that."

"Do you trust this companion enough that we may speak frankly to one another?" the prince asked.

Ruxandra felt a sudden urge to growl. There was a subtle threat laced through the man's words. A sense that, should Kade say otherwise, Ruxandra would find herself in a sack sinking in the river.

"I do," Kade said.

"Well, then. A great pleasure to meet you." The prince inclined his head. "My dear, do you speak French?"

"Yes," Ruxandra said. "Though not as well as you."

"You may blame Peter I," the prince said. "His desire to modernize Russia led him to force all who would be in his court to learn this abominable language, so we could read the writings of engineers and tradesmen, should we want to or not."

"I see."

"Where did you learn it?"

"It was part of her education," Kade said. "How many languages do you speak, Ruxandra?"

"Five. I am working on Russian for my sixth, but I have not gotten very far."

"She is also skilled in math and the sciences, and knowledgeable in history," Kade said.

"At such a young age, too." The prince smiled.

"I'm a prodigy," Ruxandra said.

"And the reason I tell you all this," Kade said, leaning forward in his seat, "is to impress on you that I value her a great deal and would be distressed if something were to happen to her."

The prince's head cocked to the side. "Did you tell Anna this, as well?"

"In no uncertain terms," Kade assured him. "Now, why are we here, my old friend? It's not like you to be so quiet."

"It is not like you to run away for months," the prince said. "Yet you did. Tell me, what do you think of our . . . dear empress?"

"She is a forceful woman," Kade said. "She pursues what she desires."

"She is that," the prince said. "So forceful that when the nobility attempted to rein in her powers, she stood in front of the people, destroyed the document she'd signed, and had half of them arrested."

"You were not?"

"I was not so stupid as to step between royalty and power," the prince said. "When she declared the council had no power over her, I applauded her and congratulated her on her wisdom. Unlike my friends, many of who are now deceased."

"I see."

"Several *are* still alive, I'm told. The secret police are using them to test new interrogation techniques."

Ruxandra remembered the agony she'd sensed from inside the Kremlin. *If those are his friends, then he must be furious and terrified.*

"Which brings us back to this present moment," Kade said. "So I ask again, what do you want of me, Prince Belosselsky?"

"To help restore order to Russia, the way Peter did."

"You hated Peter and everything he did." Kade's voice went flat. "You called his plan to modernize an abomination. You wished that he die a long and painful death."

"Did I now?"

"Eaten by rats while chained in the hold of one of his own ships, I believe was one of your fervent wishes."

"You have an impressive memory."

"Drowned in a vat of the shit from every whorehouse in the city was another."

The prince ignored him. "As I recall, your skills are even more impressive than your memory. Tell me, have they grown rusty?"

"They have not. Why do you hate Anna?"

"Peter did many things, but he respected the nobility. Anna does not. She will destroy whoever stands in her way. Also, she is a woman. Women are unfit to rule."

Ruxandra bit the inside of her cheek and looked away.

"So lend me your skills." Passion, strong and dangerous, filled his voice. "Let me rid Russia of this abomination of an empress and put a true Russian on the throne."

"I would . . . have to think on it," Kade said.

"Do that, then." The prince's bland tone suggested he could not have cared less. It was a studied blandness, though. "Some dear friends and I are having a soiree in the near future. You should come and listen to our discussions."

"We shall." Kade rose, and Ruxandra followed his lead. "If you will excuse us?"

"Certainly," the prince said. "And I need not remind you to mention this conversation to no one."

"We will not. Just as I trust your blond man standing outside this room will refrain from using his pistols." Kade bowed. "Good day, Prince Belosselsky."

He offered Ruxandra his arm and led her away. The sun was in the sky. Ruxandra could feel it, though it was not in sight. The walls around the inner enclave and the tall buildings around them kept them in shadow. Even so, the light hurt Ruxandra's eyes.

"That was interesting," Ruxandra said in vampire tones. "As is walking in the daylight."

"We will be at my house soon," Kade said. "Is his man following us?"

Ruxandra glanced over her shoulder, sniffed the air, and listened. "Just out of sight."

"He knows my destination." Kade turned them around a corner. "He no doubt feels it unnecessary to keep us in sight."

"Are you going to side with them?"

"If it becomes necessary," Kade said. "I must retain access to the library. I will aid Anna as long as she supports us and does no harm to my friends. If things change, then I may have to remove her."

"How do we do that when she surrounds herself with secret police and their magic? Cannon?"

Kade chuckled. "Tempting."

He kept going straight, leading them past one street, then another before making a final turn on a street running parallel to the wall. "Ah, there we are."

The white stone house looked like the other modern houses in the city, if smaller than most. Its front door and window trim were black. The curtains, Ruxandra noticed, were closed. She reached out with her mind and found the house empty. Kade produced a key and slipped it into the lock. It turned with a click, and he swung the door open.

"Here we are." He put his hands on Ruxandra's arms, their bodies almost touching. "I want to thank you for all you did tonight."

Ruxandra shrugged. "I have been following you. Nothing more."

"You kept Alexi, who we now know is secret police, amused. You have the Alchemist enthralled. You made our friend, Prince Belosselsky, very curious. This is a city that runs on intrigue and emotion. The more stir we create the better."

"I see."

"So let me thank you properly."

And with those words, Kade leaned close and brought his lips to hers.

TEN

RUXANDRA'S EYES GREW WIDE. She couldn't move—surprise had rooted her to the spot. Kade's lips pushed gently against hers, his hands light on her arms. He took his time before he pulled away. He saw her expression and stepped back.

"Was that unwelcome?"

"Not unwelcome." Ruxandra said. *But that doesn't mean I was ready for it.* "Just not what I was expecting, given the circumstances."

"Circumstances?"

"Your friends want to summon a fallen angel and I'll kill them to stop them?"

"Ah. Those." Kade smiled. "Then let us leave it, for tonight. Come inside."

A large part of Ruxandra didn't want to leave it. Unfortunately that part was torn between telling him to never touch her again and picking up right where he'd stopped. In the end she did neither and followed him inside.

The front hall had a marble floor, walls painted a gentle cream, and a staircase—wood, with intricately carved newel posts and red carpet over the risers—leading up to the next floor. A parlor stood on their left, a music room on the right. The light-brown couch and chairs in the parlor looked new and unworn. A large patterned rug covered the floor.

The clatter of footsteps on hard wooden stairs filled the air. Ruxandra tensed, her claws coming out. Kade only smiled. A man and a woman in early middle age dashed into the front hall and skidded to a stop. The man had on a colorful vest over a plain white shirt and black trousers tucked into black boots. The woman wore a plain dress with an apron over the front. She carried a lantern in her hand. He bowed and she curtsied to Kade. They were both trim and scrupulously clean, and their minds held only eagerness.

"Master!" the man said as he straightened. "Welcome home!"

"Thank you," Kade said. "And let me say how well you have kept it while I was away."

"Kade," Ruxandra said, "who are these people?"

"My caretakers." He pointed. "Ivan Podsavich. He maintains the house, collects wood, buys candles, and makes any repairs needed."

He bowed. "My lady."

"His wife, Nika." Kade handed the woman his cloak. She took it and then curtsied deeply to Ruxandra. "She cleans the house."

Nika curtsied again and bobbed her head.

"We are very tired," Kade said. "It has been a long night."

"Of course, my lord. The rooms are prepared, as always."

"Excellent. This way, Ruxandra."

She followed Kade up the stairs. Ivan bowed and Nika curtsied, their eyes fixed on their master as if he were their whole world. Ruxandra spotted scabbed-over puncture marks on their necks. She frowned but said nothing as she and Kade walked up the stairs.

"Thralls," Kade said over his shoulder. "Drained of enough blood to make them compliant. Elizabeth taught me."

"Why thralls?" Ruxandra asked.

"I keep very suspicious hours," Kade said. "Enthralling them saves me having to explain myself. It also makes them most excellent servants."

"Is it permanent?"

"Two months," Kade said. "If one drinks from them every month, a thrall can last for years. It provides very little sustenance compared to killing them, but then that is not the point. On the first night we searched for the magicians, I came here and renewed my bond with them. What Elizabeth neglected to tell me is that thralls can be controlled from a distance. You can even hear what they hear."

"Useful, for an assassin."

"Intelligence agent. Assassination is always a last resort. It has been amusing listening to a few of my enemies attempt to question Ivan and Nika. They appear to be the most loyal and stupid of retainers; they have distinct memories of me going out in the daytime, but they aren't aware that there's anything incongruous about such memories." Kade led her to a red door. "This room is yours. The window is blocked, the curtains drawn, the bed made, and there is a fire in the fireplace."

"You made them do this?"

"On our way here. Convenient, isn't it? And no need to worry they will misunderstand my orders." Kade took her hand, raised it to her lips, and kissed it. "Good night, Ruxandra. I will see you in the morning."

Ruxandra watched him walk to the other end of the hallway and step inside another room. She stepped inside her own, closed the door, and locked it.

It was a pleasant bedchamber, albeit very red. A small fire burned in the fireplace. In front of it sat two red-upholstered chairs and a wood table finished in a red veneer. Red curtains hung from a large four-poster bed. A red-stained chest stood at the foot of the bed. A washstand with a jar and basin, both white, but with red swirls flowing over the porcelain, stood on a small lacquered red sideboard. Red towels lay folded beside them. The final touch, a red carpet with black and green patterns on it, covered the floor.

Alexi, Anna's secret policeman, was somewhere in the room.

Ruxandra smelled him as plainly as if he were standing at her shoulder. She turned in a slow circle, searching for anything out of place. No one, visible or otherwise, was sitting on the bed. The upholstery on the chairs was undisturbed. The carpet underfoot showed no signs of anyone standing on it, nor was there a human-shaped bulge behind the thick red curtains that covered the shuttered windows.

Ruxandra went to the washstand. She poured water—cold but not freezing—from the jug into the basin. Then she grabbed the basin, turned, and hurled the contents at the air above the chest. It hit something invisible and splashed.

Alexi's surprised yelp was quite satisfying.

"Why are you playing this stupid game?" Ruxandra demanded in French. She picked up a towel, patted her face, and tossed it toward the chest.

"Caution is how we survive." Alexi's voice and the towel both floated in the air. He whispered something in Russian and appeared before her. Water dripped from his hair, and a wet stain spread across his black jacket. She was pleased to see he looked annoyed.

"I thank you for the towel," he said. "Though tossing the basin was unnecessary."

"I suppose I should have ignored you?" Ruxandra hung her cloak up on the hook beside the door. "Let you watch me as I change clothes?"

"I would have spoken before that, Princess Ruxandra."

"Of course." Ruxandra's tone made it clear she didn't believe him. "How did you get in here?"

"The windows downstairs are easy to jimmy open."

"I'll be sure to inform Kade."

"Please do," Alexi said. "Also, tell him he can do nothing, nor see anyone, without us finding out."

Are you aware his servants are thralls? Do you have any idea what a thrall is?

"Prince Belosselsky?" she said.

"Exactly. Do you know the prince's plan?"

"I do not." Ruxandra sank into the chair nearest the fire. She stretched her arms forward, enjoying the warmth on her skin.

"Does cold affect you?" Alexi asked.

"I feel it when the air freezes, or when my skin touches something cold, but it doesn't hurt me."

"Unlike fire."

"Fire is pleasant when it is contained." She pointed at the other chair. "Sit."

"If you wish." He sat, his knees bent at perfect right angles, his back as straight as a knife blade. "How do you detect us?"

"You must be joking," Ruxandra said, echoing what he had said when she asked about his magic.

Alexi smiled. "Fair enough."

"Why my room?" Ruxandra asked. "Why not bother Kade?"

"You are the one about whom we know very little." He arranged his jacket so the wet parts faced the fire. "We dislike not knowing things."

"'We' meaning the secret police?"

"Yes."

"Unfortunate that I have nothing to say to you."

"How about we exchange information?" Alexi suggested. "You tell me something I don't know, and I'll do the same."

Ruxandra's eyebrows rose at that. She considered telling him to leave instead, but there was a great deal she wanted to know. Alexi watched her thinking of it. She reached out for his emotions and found him calm and relaxed, as if he were chatting with an old friend. *I suppose he cannot hide his mind when his body is visible,* she mused. *Or does he even know his mind is now detectable to me?*

"Fine," she said at last. "Why does Anna want to summon a fallen angel?"

"Is that what she wants?" He shrugged. "The empress's desires remain a mystery."

"You said you would tell me."

"I said we would exchange."

"I like red wine better than vodka. Your turn."

"Moscow is renowned for the quality of its turnips. Please, Princess Ruxandra. Information, not trivia."

"I spent a hundred years roaming the woods as an animal."

"Interesting. How old are you?"

"A gentleman never asks. Were the men watching us outside of the church yours?"

Alexi frowned. "What men?"

"Three of them. Two talking, one resting under a tree. They were there when we left."

"That was something I didn't know," Alexi said. "Thank you. Your turn again."

"Why does Anna want to summon the dark angel?"

Alexi smiled again. "A gentleman never asks, especially of his empress."

Ruxandra growled. "Do you have anything useful to tell me?"

"Four powers control Moscow." Alexi's eyes bored into Ruxandra's with the words. "The empress, the church, the nobility, and the people. The people are uneducated, boorish, and prone to supporting whichever group offers the least suffering. Naturally the church is their first darling. The nobility is hated but feared by the people because of their wealth and soldiers. The empress tolerates them because their taxes feed her coffers. The empress is beloved and hated, depending on whom you ask. She is both powerful and weak—dependent on support from the people and the army. If a fifth power arises, she must control it."

"So the empress sees the fallen angel as a means to increase her dominance?"

"Yes."

"How did she even know the magicians were going to summon it?"

"We do have spies everywhere," Alexi said drily, his dark eyes fixed on hers. "And one of them heard the plan."

Ruxandra sat back in her chair, turning away to watch the flames lick up the sides of the log in the fireplace. "What if the fallen angel won't allow Anna to control her?" she asked softly.

"It's a she?"

"It is."

"You know that how?"

"We've met."

"Ah. I wasn't certain. First, Anna would kill anyone else she thought was helping her. Then she would look for a way to take control by any means possible."

Ruxandra sighed. *This will not make things easier.* "I like predators."

"I beg your pardon?"

One side of Ruxandra's mouth quirked upward at the confusion on his face. "I like hunting predators. They're more of a challenge."

"I see." Alexi's eyes unfocused for a moment, as if he were storing the information away to use later. "Why do you think the angel can't be controlled?"

"Because on the night she made me, she stepped out of the circle they created as if it wasn't there."

If her words affected him, he gave no sign of it. She wasn't even sure if she had told him something he didn't know. How much had Kade shared with the magicians? *I must assume he knows all.* He rose to his feet. "I shall leave you to your rest, Princess. I promise not to enter your rooms again without permission, except in great need."

"Thank you."

"If you will excuse me?"

Ruxandra nodded. Alexi whispered in Russian and vanished from her sight. Ruxandra's door opened and closed, and Alexi's smell vanished from the room.

I must bring my bag from Kade's bolt-hole. Not that I have another dress, but cleaner clothes would feel nice. Maybe the Alchemist can help me buy new dresses. I might find something suitable to wear at court.

In case I need to kill the empress.

By evening the clouds were making good on their threats of rain. The cobbled streets of the enclave ran slick with water. The mud in the outer neighborhoods tried to suck down whoever stepped in it, like a hungry, living creature. It made walking slippery and messy, leaving Ruxandra's boots coated and her dress splattered.

Kade and Ruxandra went down to the church's crypt and the narrow stairway that zigzagged deep into the earth. The mud on Ruxandra had dried into a thick crust by the time they reached the bottom.

The Alchemist sat in the main room, a pile of books stacked on the floor beside her. Five more books lay spread in a wide circle across the table. In front of her sat a large sheet of paper with line after line of words written and crossed out. She had a small pen in her hand, the nib dripping ink as she chewed on its end. When the door opened, she glanced up.

"Kade!" The Alchemist rose from her chair. "Princess! Welcome back. Shall we start . . ."

She stopped, her mouth falling open. "Kade! How could you let this happen to the poor princess?"

Kade looked Ruxandra up and down. "She is a little muddy, yes, but . . ."

"You couldn't summon a carriage?" the Alchemist demanded. "Where are her things? My princess needs a change of clothes."

"*Your* princess?" Ruxandra's eyebrows rose. "I'm your princess now?"

"Who else's?" The Alchemist's eyes roved over her body. "We are not the same size, especially in the chest, but I have a skirt and a sweater that should fit you. For underclothes we must wait until yours dry. Kade, tell the men that anyone who enters the baths gets their intestines ripped out, their faces sliced off and their testicles stuffed down their throats. Then it will be the princess's turn."

The Alchemist strode away. Ruxandra suppressed a smile and followed her. The woman led Ruxandra inside and closed the door. Then she kicked off her shoes and undid the ties on her dress.

"What do you think you are doing?" Ruxandra asked.

"Bathing," the Alchemist said. "Do you know how long it's been since I've had someone to wash my back?"

Ruxandra shook her head, bemused.

The Alchemist dropped her dress and pulled off her shift. The Alchemist's hips stood out as sharply as her cheekbones. Her breasts were almost nonexistent, her nipples brown and thick and erect in the cool air of the bath. The muscles of her arms and legs were twisted wires under her flesh. Her stomach looked like a washboard above the wiry dark-blonde hair of her sex.

She's like a wolf, all muscle and bone. Warmth blossomed low in Ruxandra's belly. *And attractive . . .*

"Besides," the Alchemist said, "I've inspected the male of the species, so I must examine the female."

Or not. "It that what I am? A specimen?"

"A beautiful one." She sat on the bench. If the marble felt cold on her flesh, she gave no sign. "Would you truly kill me to stop me from summoning the angel?"

"Fallen angel." The change of subject surprised Ruxandra. "Yes."

"Because you think it will . . . what?"

"That thing is an abomination that doesn't belong in the world." Ruxandra let her fear and disgust come through in her words. "It turned me into this. It will do worse to you."

"You believe." The Alchemist shrugged. "My dear, my life is no picnic."

"I'm not talking about what you have but what you are."

"If you don't like what it made you, why don't you kill yourself?"

"I've tried. It doesn't work."

"Interesting." The Alchemist rested her elbows on her knees, cupped her hands, and put her chin in them. "And do you still wish you could?"

Ruxandra was silent for a minute. "No. But it has taken me a long time to learn to control myself. There is much I regret."

"So say we all. Kade would not be happy if you killed us."

"He'll forgive me."

"Do you think so?"

"Time does wonders, he tells me. Give up summoning the fallen angel."

The Alchemist shrugged. "You haven't given me any reason to, yet."

"Death isn't reason enough?"

"Possible death," the Alchemist said, "if we summon her. Certain death if we do not. So no, it is not enough. Also, think of the knowledge to be gained."

"Knowledge isn't everything."

"For me it is. A fallen angel? One who knows the structure of heaven and hell, why mankind was made, what we are for? Ruxandra, if you knew scholars . . . I am not unusual in this regard. This is what we care about. This is our passion."

"There are plenty of things to learn that won't kill you."

"Yes, and I know most of them. I know things that no one else in this place, in this city, even in the world knows." She offered a self-deprecating smile, glancing at Ruxandra though her blonde lashes. "Not least of which is where to buy new dresses at a very reasonable price."

"*That* I could learn without difficulty."

"Or you could make me tell you." She smiled again. "I made Kade command me, to see how it felt. It is . . . odd. One's actions are perfectly sensible when one does them, no matter how abhorrent they feel afterward."

"What abhorrent thing did he have you do?"

"Sing in Italian in front of everyone while dancing a *Lo Brando*. Fortunately I can dance because the rest of the performance was execrable."

"I'll take your word for it."

"I tell you what, my princess." The Alchemist stepped closer, her eyes gleaming. "Let me wash you, let me examine you, and I'll help you learn to read and speak Russian, and I will bring the others together to hear your fears about the fallen angel. Now, will you take your dress off yourself, or shall I help?"

CHAPTER
ELEVEN

T HE ALCHEMIST GRINNED, showing large white teeth. "Excellent. I will say everything twice: once in Russian, once in French." She spoke in rapid-fire Russian and repeated in French, "Shall I help you?"

"No." Ruxandra pulled the dress off her shoulders.

The Alchemist shook the garment out. "What a mess. I wonder if we could convince the empress to give us a washerwoman?"

Ruxandra pulled off her corset and shift. The Alchemist set them aside. She stepped back and looked over Ruxandra. The Alchemist spoke at length in Russian. She smiled and started again in French.

"No body hair," she said. "Not even pubic hair. No facial hair except the eyelashes and the eyebrows. No blemishes on the skin— no freckles, moles, pimples, or warts. Not even an ingrown hair. Exaggerated sexual characteristics."

"I beg your pardon?"

"Your breasts are large, though not grossly so." The Alchemist pointed at each. "They are perkier than big ones usually are. Your hips are slim, to make you look younger, but curved so everyone sees you as a woman. Your skin is smooth with enough fat under it to disguise your muscles, which I suspect are as strong as Kade's. You also have a proper mons veneris. Mine's as flat as my tits. May I wash you?"

"Why?"

"I want to know how your body feels. I also give a wonderful massage, if that helps convince you."

Ruxandra's eyebrows rose. "I think you want to seduce me."

"Not here," the Alchemist said. "The floor is too hard for comfort. The benches *are* an excellent height to be bent over, if you enjoy that. Also the water in the tubs circulates, so if you fuck in the bath, no one else ends up sitting in it."

Ruxandra barely managed to keep a straight face. "Good to know."

The Alchemist led Ruxandra to the trough that ran the length of the wall. From under the bench she pulled a wood bucket and a basket with several blocks of soap and cloths. She filled the bucket and knelt.

"If you please?" The Alchemist took a cloth, wetted it, and rubbed the soap on it.

Ruxandra raised a foot and held it in a firm grip. The Alchemist ran the cloth over Ruxandra's skin, making her foot tingle and sending a thrill of pleasure up her leg. Ruxandra closed her eyes and leaned on the trough for balance.

"Other foot." Ruxandra switched. The Alchemist massaged her foot, then her calf. "Kade's sexual characteristics are exaggerated as well."

Ruxandra opened her eyes. "I beg your pardon?"

"You must have noticed." She cleaned out the dirt between Ruxandra's toes. "His body is extreme male, as yours is extreme female."

That caught Ruxandra's attention. "Extreme?"

"Oh yes." The Alchemist rinsed off her foot and released it. "Stand with your hands on the trough, legs apart, and I'll start on the rest of you."

Ruxandra did. The Alchemist soaped the cloth and pressed the rough surface of it against her calf.

"He's a perfect man shape." The Alchemist's strong hands massaged Ruxandra's leg. "Look at his wide back, narrow waist, strong legs, and strong arms. Every muscle is solid and obvious. His jawline is strong, and his hairline does not retreat. Did you know him as a human?"

"Oh . . ." The Alchemist's hands massaged her other calf before slipping higher to work on her left thigh. "Yes."

"Did he look the same?"

"No. He had a beard. He was heavier and was in his late thirties, I think."

"Was his penis as big before?"

"I beg your pardon?"

"He's large. And thick. Was it the same when he was human?"

"I . . . didn't . . . I haven't . . ."

"I recommend it." The Alchemist started on her right thigh. "It really is quite a treat. Or do you only like girls?"

"I *prefer* girls."

"Have you had sex with a man?"

"Several."

"Do you remember your first? How did he compare to a woman?"

"He's not a good one to compare."

"Why not?"

Neculai's face floated in Ruxandra's mind, kind and warm and terrified as she sank her teeth into him. "I killed him."

"Interesting." The Alchemist's hands slipped up to Ruxandra's backside. "Do you kill every human you fuck?"

"Mmmmm." Ruxandra pulled her mind away from the Alchemist's touch. "No."

"Then why kill him?"

"I hadn't drunk human blood in months." The cloth moved in slow circles over Ruxandra's flesh, and she bit back a moan. "I couldn't stop myself."

"Why were you not drinking?"

"It happened soon after the fallen angel turned me into a vampire. I didn't want to kill humans." Ruxandra breathed deep and sighed. "That is quite distracting."

"Good." The Alchemist stood, her body pressing against Ruxandra's back. Her hands and the cloth slid around to Ruxandra's stomach. "Distracted people tend to speak the truth. What caused you to change your mind?"

"Six failed suicide attempts, a hundred years as an animal, a lover who betrayed and abused me, and opera."

"Opera?"

The surprise in the Alchemist's voice made Ruxandra smile. "Opera is beautiful. The music soars in ways I had not dreamed possible."

"So you started killing again." The Alchemist soaped the cloth again and washed Ruxandra's back. "Did Kade ever hesitate?"

"No. Oh, more there please." Ruxandra fell silent as the Alchemist massaged the muscles between her shoulder blades. When the woman's hands moved away, Ruxandra added, "He wanted to be a vampire. I didn't."

"You hunt humans now." The Alchemist's hands slid down Ruxandra's flanks. She pressed her body into Ruxandra's back and cupped her hands around her breasts. "How do you justify it?"

"I hunt predators," Ruxandra closed her eyes, leaned back against the Alchemist, and reveled in the woman's touch. "Men who hurt or kill for fun. Sometimes I prey on the dying if I cannot find a predator to eat."

"I see." The cloth slipped from Alchemist's hand and her fingers teased Ruxandra's nipples. "How long since you had sex?"

"Ooooh. About a year."

"We should do something about that."

Ruxandra turned her head and the Alchemist's lips met hers. They kissed deep, tongues playing inside each other's mouths. Ruxandra tried to turn, but the Alchemist's hold on her breasts kept her in place. Ruxandra reached around to caress the other woman's backside.

"Promise not to kill me," the Alchemist whispered when their kiss broke, "even if I summon your fallen angel."

"No," Ruxandra breathed back.

The Alchemist's hands released Ruxandra's breasts. She pushed Ruxandra upright and stepped away. "Shall I wash your hair? After, we can have a nice soak."

"What?" Ruxandra panted. The heat between her legs was almost unbearable. "You're stopping?"

The Alchemist shrugged. "I don't fuck people who are going to kill me."

"I could command you," Ruxandra growled. "I could make you go on your knees and pleasure me right now."

"You won't, though."

"How do you know?"

"Because you could have done that when you walked in. You could have commanded us to light the library on fire and watched as we burned." The Alchemist's eyes were bright with certainty. "You hated when your lover abused you, so you don't abuse others unless they deserve it. Or am I wrong?"

Ruxandra bared her fangs and snarled. The Alchemist didn't flinch. The scent of her sweat, instead of becoming sour with fear, grew sharp with excitement and arousal. She stared into Ruxandra's mouth, her eyes wide, and reached out to touch the fang.

Ruxandra pulled them back out of sight. "You are an irritating, manipulative, self-satisfied *cow* of a woman."

"You are not the first to tell me this." The Alchemist smiled. "If it makes you feel any better, I hope you change your mind about killing me, because I very much want to continue what we started. That said, I will wash your hair."

Ruxandra, frustrated but clean, emerged half an hour later. The Alchemist had soaked only a few minutes before fetching fresh clothes for Ruxandra. She'd returned with a loose green sweater and a brown skirt that squeezed Ruxandra's hips and backside. The Alchemist hadn't brought underclothes or a corset, leaving Ruxandra naked beneath the clothes while her own dried. Then she left Ruxandra alone.

Ruxandra seriously considered solving her frustration by herself, but she suspected the Alchemist would know, and she wouldn't give the woman the satisfaction. Instead she soaked, sulked, and finally dried off and dressed.

Kade met her in the hallway. "Feeling better?"

"Cleaner," Ruxandra said. "The Alchemist promised to teach me Russian and to bring everyone together to hear me."

Kade's right eyebrow rose. "Is that all she promised?"

"Yes." *Dammit.*

"Well, everyone is together, waiting for you. Follow me."

Ruxandra stayed five paces back, her eyes on his body, seeing him as the Alchemist described him.

Hypermasculine. Narrow waist, wide shoulders, and strong legs. Nice backside . . .

Damn that woman.

Kade led her to a large table in the middle of the library. The Alchemist, Kurkov, Michael, Derek, and Eduard sat around it.

"Here she is." The Alchemist patted the empty chair at the head of the table. "Please, join us."

Ruxandra followed Kade. Michael's gaze locked on to her breasts, free underneath the sweater. Kurkov raised an eyebrow but didn't stare. The rest averted their eyes. Kade led Ruxandra to the chair and held it for her. She didn't sit. He shrugged and took the seat to her right.

The Alchemist leaned forward. "Eyes back down, gentlemen. We have a problem."

"Yes. There's not enough to eat," Derek said sourly. "Herring! Adequate as a first course, perhaps, but that is all we were given. Meanwhile the guards eat mutton with great mounds of potatoes, onions, cabbage—"

"They gave us a nice apple tart," Michael said.

"With no cream. What is a tart without cream?"

"This is your concern?" the Alchemist said. "Your stomachs? What about our situation? What about Sasha, Victor and Dmitri? Did you spare a thought for them?"

"They are fed no worse than we," Derek huffed. "Which is to say, terribly."

"Am I in the company of animals that food is the only thing on your mind?" the Alchemist said sharply.

"I wouldn't say only—" Kurkov began.

The Alchemist quelled him with a look. "We have a *real* problem. One that requires a complex solution," the Alchemist said. "My dear princess intends to kill us rather than let us summon our dark angel."

The silence that followed felt so deep it seemed as if everyone in the room had stopped breathing. The Alchemist smiled.

"Not to worry," she said. "After our recent conversation, I have come to believe that my princess does listen to reason. However, we must have a very good argument."

"No argument is persuasive enough," Ruxandra said. "You must not summon her."

"Anna tortures our friends to death if we do not," Kurkov said. "Then she tortures us to death. How is that argument?"

"Convincing for me," the Alchemist said, "if not for my princess. We are doomed if we do and doomed if we do not. So what do you suggest, Ruxandra?"

"You leave."

"My dear princess . . . please believe me, your thoughts on this matter are of great interest to us. But how do you imagine we can leave?" Michael asked. "Can you get us past the secret police? The ones you can't even see? Can you pull our friends from their dungeon and bring them with you?"

"Explain why you don't want them to summon her," Kade said. "That would help."

Ruxandra studied his face. He looked calm. She reached out with her mind and sensed mild excitement and concern, but nothing more.

"The dark angel is evil," Ruxandra said.

The Alchemist put her elbows on the table and leaned on them. "Why do you think that?"

"Because she created me."

And then Ruxandra told her story. She told how her father, Vlad Dracula, had taken her from the convent where she had been raised. She told of the ride through the mountains and the cave deep inside it. She told how the men had stripped her and chained her to the ground and then summoned the angel.

"She threatened to rape me, telling how she would tear me open, and laughed at my tears. Then she turned on my father, mocking him and the other men for summoning her and demanding things of her. And then she asked me if I wanted to die."

"And you did not," Derek said. "You chose to become a vampire instead."

"I did not choose this." The words came out fierce and hard. "She didn't say she would do this. She only asked if I wanted to die. And when I shook my head, she told me her kind could no longer walk freely in the world, and so she would send me out instead. 'To sow chaos and fear, to make humans kneel in terror, and to ravage the world where I cannot.'"

Ruxandra stopped, fearing her voice would crack. The power of the memory made her knees tremble. She forced them to stillness.

"Then she fed me her blood and left. And when I woke up, with my father kneeling above me, I felt nothing except hunger. So I killed him. I tore his head off and drank from his spouting neck and then murdered his men to drink them, too. And when I ran, still not knowing what I was, I murdered again and again. I tried to stop and could not. I tried to kill myself and could not. I tried to let others kill me and could not. I finally escaped to the woods and became an animal, only to be dragged back again by Elizabeth Bathory because she wanted immortality."

The others at the table sat in silence, processing what they had heard. Kade rubbed at the beard that was no longer on his chin, while Michael wove his fingers through the long gray shawl of hair that flowed from his. Derek pursed his lips, looking even more like a scalded piglet than usual. The Alchemist frowned as she thought.

"You asked how I know she is evil," Ruxandra said. "Because to make me into a murdering monster, just to spread chaos and fear, is *not* the act of someone who is good. She could have killed us all. That would make sense. Or killed my father and the men who brought her there. But what she did to me—" She stopped. Over the last century, as she had told the Alchemist, she had come to terms with what she was, had made peace with it. But it rose up in her now. *What I am. What she did to me.*

The magicians looked at one another. The Alchemist kept frowning. Kade rubbed at his face. Ruxandra, drained, sat in the chair and waited.

"The problem," the Alchemist said at last, "is that nothing you said solves our problem. Anna will still torture and murder us all if we do not summon the angel."

"Are you sure the circle does not contain her?" Derek asked. He took a large sheet of paper from his lap and spread it over the table. "Four key elements make the ritual possible: the circle, the incantations, the sacrifice and the timing. Without the circle, the creature cannot be contained—"

"The circle doesn't contain her. It opens the door."

"Apologies," Derek said. "Without the circle, the door cannot be opened. Without the incantations, the fallen angel cannot be summoned. Without a sacrifice, she cannot be appeased, and without proper timing, the ritual will not work. That is why the summons must happen on the winter solstice. It is a time of greatest darkness and best suited for commanding evil creatures to come forth."

"The date doesn't matter," Ruxandra said. "It was not the solstice last time."

She leaned forward and studied the paper. A shiver ran through her. Drawings, elegant and simple, covered the page. In the middle sat a pentacle with skulls at each point and a naked girl spread-eagled in the center of it.

Ruxandra pointed. "Your sacrifice isn't chained."

"All sacrifices must be willing," Derek said.

"I wasn't!"

Derek cleared his throat and ran a finger under a line of scrawled Cyrillic script in one corner of the page. "The ancient tablets and scrolls showed us that anyone could be the sacrifice, but that some work better than others. A virgin, pure of body but who wishes to be corrupted, works best. Were you a virgin?"

"With men."

Derek reddened, and Kurkov smirked. Michael swallowed hard enough it echoed.

"The angel still came?" Derek asked.

"Yes."

"Did it accept your body as an offering?"

"No."

"That was the problem!" Michael said, sounding as excited as a child handed a bucket of candy. "She rejected you because she wanted someone willing. That also—to me at least—suggests she may not be *evil*, which is not to say she's good—she's fallen, after all, but—"

"That is not the problem," Ruxandra protested. "The problem is that she turned me into a vampire and turned me loose on the world!"

"You are a remarkable creation," said Michael. "And you are good; I feel that. Who's to say she did not foresee what you would become?"

Ruxandra made a noise in her throat and turned away. *Did he not hear the part where I murdered innocent villagers?*

"What else happened that night?" Derek asked. "What of where they performed the ritual? Was the pentacle they used similar to this one?"

"The same." Every face at the table was rapt with excitement. It made Ruxandra feel as if she had wasps under her skin. "If she turns one of *you* into a vampire, you will slaughter everyone around you, too, no matter how much you care for them. Your lover. Your friend. Your *child!*" She raised her voice with each word, and their excitement dimmed slightly.

"Or you could *not* summon her," Ruxandra said.

Kade put a hand on her arm. His fingers curved over her wrist, and for the first time she noticed how the long and strong they were—*damn that Alchemist!*

"They must summon her," Kade said. "Or Anna will kill them."

"She will send us back to the torture chambers," Michael said, his voice quavering. "I am too old to survive it twice."

"We must find a way to contain her when we summon her," the Alchemist said. "Barring that, a way to send her back if things go badly. The empress expects the fallen angel to be summoned at the winter solstice. This is four months away. Plenty of time to for us to search for a solution."

She stood up and curtsied to Ruxandra. "My princess, will you allow us more time? To find a proper solution?"

CHAPTER
TWELVE

R UXANDRA STOMPED OUT and headed for the house. Between the Alchemist's "examination" and the argument about the angel, her frustration was beyond all measure on several levels. She wanted to ride someone for an hour or kill something large and dangerous.

"*Bon soir*, Princess." Alexi's voice floated through the air.

Ruxandra stopped, looked around, and sniffed the air. He stood beside the house closest to her right. She waited for him to become visible.

After a few minutes, she growled in frustration. "Alexi, don't make me throw something again."

"My apologies," Alexi said, and then, in Russian, *"Appear."*

With that he materialized beside the house.

"Why are you here?" Ruxandra asked.

"Just to talk."

"I'm not in the mood."

"Because they won't agree not to summon the fallen angel?"

Spies everywhere. "You didn't have any men in the library. How did you overhear?"

"That is a secret, Princess."

"Share it," she demanded.

Alexi shrugged. "What will you give?"

Ruxandra rolled her eyes. "I promise to *not* hunt you tonight."

"You can't touch me, Princess. You tried on the bridge, remember?"

Ruxandra sighed. "What do you want, Alexi?"

"Do you intend to stop them from summoning the angel?"

"I haven't decided yet."

"Your friend, Kade, will be very annoyed if you kill them." He offered her his arm. "So will the empress. Shall we walk?"

She took it. It felt strange. Her arm, though threaded through his, didn't touch him. It floated in between his elbow and his ribs. The force that had prevented her from touching him on the bridge held her in place.

"That feels odd," Alexi said.

"You should try it from my side."

"So what will you do if they decide to go ahead?" Alexi asked. "What will you do if the empress opposes you? Try to kill her?"

"If I intended to," Ruxandra countered, "would I tell you?"

"I don't know. How confident are you?"

"Depends on whether I can get through the barriers that surround the Kremlin."

"In that case, she is quite safe."

"I don't know," Ruxandra said. "How confident are you?"

Alexi smiled. They walked in silence. The downpour had long since ended, but the ground was still soaked. Mud slopped on their clothes with each step. Clouds covered the stars, portending more rain to come.

"I cannot tell Anna to stop her plans on the word of a vampire," Alexi said.

Ruxandra stopped walking. "You believe me?"

"I believe *you* believe what you say," Alexi said. "Show me evidence."

Ruxandra tapped her chest.

Alexi chuckled. "You, my dear, may be responsible for the deaths of many, but you're just one girl. Yes, yes! I believe you! And most of all that you are not really the girl you look. But I need more than that. More than what you perceived as the angel's intent and motives. Find me documents detailing the horrors that this creature wrought. Tell me of the cities she destroyed and the lives she ended. Something strong enough to convince a person as . . . *headstrong* as Anna."

"Will that stop her?"

"It might make her reconsider."

"Why?"

Alexi shrugged. "Moscow *is* Russia. The court is here, the empress is here, the nobles gather here like deer flies searching for a bite of flesh. If the fallen angel destroyed the city, the entire country would suffer. Anything less will not impress Anna."

"I see."

"You have not yet made her afraid. That is your task."

"She is a fool."

"She is an empress. I must go. I trust you'll manage to return by yourself." He released her arm and bowed. "You are going back to Kade's house? Not out to visit the nobility?"

"Yes, I am going to Kade's house."

"Good. I hate to see a lovely lady fall into such disreputable company."

Ruxandra's brows lowered over the bridge of her nose. "Are you teasing me, Alexi?"

"I would not dream of it." He smiled, bowed again. "Also, there is a trunk waiting for you."

"What's in it?"

"Vanish," Alexi said in Russian and disappeared.

Everyone wants to annoy me tonight. Ruxandra picked up speed, holding up her skirt to avoid the mud. *But now I know all is not calm in Anna's court if the head of her secret police worries about what she is doing. I have made him afraid, I think.*

He is not a fool. Kade is not; the Alchemist is not. We may be able to head off this calamity without more bloodshed.

The next night she carried the trunk to the library and called for the Alchemist.

The woman whistled when Ruxandra opened it. She picked up a dress and held it up to admire the stitching.

"Read this." Ruxandra held out a note.

The Alchemist took it. "Dear Princess Ruxandra, I could not help but notice the condition of your clothes when we met. Please accept these. They should fit you, and will look much better if you decide to appear in court. Alexi."

That self-serving . . . He asks me if I will murder his empress, then almost dares me to try.

"The secret policeman admires you," the Alchemist said, her voice cool. "Why is that?"

"My charm." Ruxandra picked out a green dress and a white blouse. "Come. Help me. And help me find some things."

"What sort of things?" the Alchemist asked as she followed Ruxandra to the baths.

"First, anything that tells of what trouble the fallen angel caused when summoned." Ruxandra looked at the dress in her hand and thought of Alexi's smile before he vanished. "Second, anything that can stop or dispel the fallen angel. Third, how human magic works on vampires."

Two weeks later, Ruxandra spoke Russian well enough to understand and make others understand her. She read basic Cyrillic, though the longer words escaped her. Meanwhile Kade and the Alchemist worked together on the ritual, translating the words and working on pronunciation. They worked slowly but steadily, always having progress to show at the end of the day.

Meanwhile, Ruxandra searched the library for every book, scroll, or tablet on fallen angels or on banishing the supernatural. Kurkov helped her. The blustering personality was always present, but beneath it sat a strong, organized mind with a love for books and learning far greater than his love for crude jests and puerile observations. He spent hours in the stacks, searching and cataloging the books. He'd divided the shelves into history, magic, mythology, philosophy, and science. Some books Kurkov suspected were made up whole cloth, but given what they were dealing with it was impossible to separate truth from fiction.

Kurkov found every scroll and book that spoke of angels, fallen or not. He gave Ruxandra the ones written in Latin and Greek, as she had learned both languages back in the convent. What he brought her made for fascinating reading.

One book said the angels had once acted as gods, using the world as their plaything for thousands of years. A scroll told how God called the angels, dark and light, away from earth at the birth of Christ. A third spoke of war among the fallen angels for control of earth and hell. It failed when a fallen angel risked flying up to warn heaven. She returned with God's army to drive the fallen ones back to hell.

Still other books detailed encounters with the angels. Much to her annoyance they were in Cyrillic, Aramaic, and Sanskrit. Kurkov helped Ruxandra learn the first. Michael read Sanskrit, and Derek knew Aramaic. Together they marked the stories of fallen angels dealing with humanity, and any passages on banished creatures of hell.

To Ruxandra's disappointment, no books mentioned major disasters in relation to fallen angels. Every person who summoned a fallen angel met misfortune, but nothing more. No disasters, no huge acts of destruction.

If the creature destroyed a city, it would have destroyed any record of it, too.

Which wasn't helpful.

Or maybe they can't act except through men. But that made no sense. The angel had created her—an act of vast power.

She couldn't find any information on magic that worked against vampires, either.

"The secret police took it," Kurkov explained. "From here and from our library. Apparently they don't want anyone learning their secrets."

"Bastards." Ruxandra shoved down her frustration. If she could counter the secret police's magic, she could help the magicians escape—if they were willing to leave. She could not hope to stop Anna's secret police if she could not counter their magic. If she could not defeat them, the magicians would not leave.

They will try to summon the angel, and then . . .

One evening Kade knocked at her door while the sun still sat low in the sky. Ruxandra put on a robe—also from Alexi—and opened the door.

"The nobles' party happens tonight," Kade said.

Ruxandra frowned. "You are being watched. Alexi told me."

"I suspected as much. Still, they expect us to join them."

"Us?" Ruxandra's eyebrows rose. "You want me with you?"

"If you wish to come." Kade smiled. "Think of it as a chance to spend an evening enjoying yourself, instead of burying your face in books."

The rain had stopped, leaving the ground a sloppy wet mess. A strong north wind sprang up, sending a chill through the city. Ruxandra picked a light-blue dress with a matching cape to wear. Kade chose black—boots, breeches, and a jacket. He tied his hair back with a black ribbon and wore a sword.

"You look beautiful." Kade caught her hand and bowed over it, his lips grazing the skin. "Far too good for this group."

"You looked dressed more for a battle than a party," Ruxandra said. "Should I be armed?"

"On the contrary, I want them to underestimate you. It will make your skills more of a surprise." He held out his arm. "Shall we?"

Ruxandra kept her eyes, ears, and nose open wide on the short walk to Prince Belosselsky's house. She spotted no one. To her surprise, Prince Belosselsky's house stood dark save for a single lamp burning in the parlor window.

"Not much of a party," Ruxandra said, using vampire tones and speaking Romanian, in case the police were nearby and listening.

"The prince's definition of the word differs somewhat from yours." Kade spoke the same way. "He is . . . circumspect in his entertainments."

"Especially when they involve betraying the empress?"

"One hopes." Kade knocked. "Shall we find out?"

The blond-haired servant opened it, bowed, and pointed them toward the parlor. Inside, each holding a glass of wine, sat four men and a woman.

"The man arrives," Prince Belosselsky said. "You know everyone, I assume?"

"I do," Kade said. "My companion does not."

"Introduce her." Belosselsky took a sip of his drink. "After, we can get on with it."

"Gentlemen, lady." Kade nodded at the others sitting there. "May I present Princess Ruxandra."

"*Princess* Ruxandra?" the woman frowned. She looked young, perhaps twenty, and wore a plain green dress. She might have passed for a merchant's daughter, except for the diamond necklace around her throat and the gold-and-ruby ring on her finger. "Princess of what?"

"A far region," Kade said. "Princess Ruxandra, meet Princess Khilkoff, heir of Prince Khilkoff, whom the empress executed three months ago."

"Murdered." The princess's face twisted in anger. "She murdered him. He did nothing wrong."

"He sought to restrain Anna's power," said a tall, handsome man with dark hair graying at his temples. "Prince Gagarin, at your service."

"Pleased to meet you both." Ruxandra curtsied, though not so deeply as to acknowledge them her superiors.

"What an interesting accent," said the third man. He was short, round, and nearly bald, and had small eyes that glittered with intelligence and malice. "Prince Delfino. Where are you from, Princess?"

"Italy, most recently," Ruxandra said. "Many other places before that."

"At such a young age," the last man said. "I envy you."

Ruxandra doubted it. He had plain features, plain brown hair, and plain gray clothes, yet she could tell he thought very highly of himself indeed. "Prince Dolgorukov, at your service."

"And now that we have finished with that," Belosselsky said, "let us discuss the matter at hand."

"Starting with the absurdity of calling this a party," Dolgorukov said. "One hoped at least for a buffet."

"Or better wine." Princess Khilkoff held up her glass. "This is appalling."

"Beggars can't be choosers." Belosselsky took another drink. "And make no mistake: we will all be beggars once Anna finishes with us."

Kade took off his sword belt and sat on the couch opposite Belosselsky. He rested the weapon on his lap. "Why do you think so?"

"Isn't it obvious? She wishes to take the nobility's money and lands for herself."

"Has she attacked all the nobility?" Kade asked. "Or only those who tried to restrain her power?"

"Does it matter?" Dolgorukov's voice went nasal as he let out his annoyance. "An attack on one is an attack on us all."

"Does she reward the loyal ones?" Kade's gaze turned on Dolgorukov. "Does she not give them land and money?"

"She gives nothing to anyone save those blockheaded Germans she brought to court with her," Delfino said. "She listens to them and lets them guide our country. As if such as they know anything of the Russian soul!"

Kade's mouth twitched.

He, too, sees nothing soulful in this greasy prince.

"Regardless of our soul, their guidance is to our detriment in the more important question of money." Belosselsky leaned forward. "This is why you must help us destroy her."

"Must?" Kade's eyebrows rose. "Not the word you wish to use."

"Is it not, Kade Volkov?" Gagarin looked at Ruxandra. "I think obeying us would be better for you than refusing."

"Obeying?" Kade chuckled. "Again, not the correct word." *Oh, he is enjoying this,* Ruxandra thought. *This is why he likes politics. No matter what he says of purpose.*

Belosselsky shook his head and chuckled. "Gentlemen, Kade is not one whom threats sway, either to his person or his . . . companion?"

"I find all men respond the same when their lover is threatened," Dolgorukov said in his whiny voice. "Women are always a vulnerability."

"I did say they would underestimate you," Kade said to Ruxandra.

"You did." Ruxandra spread her mind wide. "Shall I disabuse them of the notion?"

"Please."

"There are eight others in the building: four men, four women. The men are Belosselsky's servants. The women are prostitutes, no doubt procured to give you gentlemen some entertainment after the meeting. My apologies, Princess Khilkoff, that he did not supply someone for you."

The princess's lips tightened into a white line across her face. Ruxandra breathed deep, smelling the building.

"The four men each carry pistols and knives," she continued. "Two sit in the dining room and two in the kitchen, drinking your tea."

Belosselsky kept his expression bland. "I should be impressed?"

"You should be frightened," Kade said. "Ruxandra is the greatest hunter of men it has been my pleasure to know."

"Is she?" Princess Khilkoff leaned forward, her eyes shining. "How does one become a hunter of men?"

"Forgive me if I disbelieve you," Prince Delfino said. He stood and circled Ruxandra. "She possesses great beauty and I suspect has well-practiced abilities in bed. One knows the look—that mix of innocence and abandon only the young and amoral can pull off. But fucking a man and killing one are two different things. Especially an armed man."

In a single motion Ruxandra moved behind the prince, took the knife he'd worn strapped to his lower back, and pressed it to his neck. The prince gave a yelp and she pressed down just enough to bring a line of blood up, each drop a bead on a string. She inhaled.

How is it such a disgusting creature has such delicious blood?

Belosselsky broke out laughing. "Magnificent. Gagarin?"

The older man sighed and pulled a small purse from his pocket. "I should know not to bet against you."

He extracted five gold coins and dropped them into Belosselsky's waiting hand.

Belosselsky pocketed the coins. "So, Kade, how much will you cost?"

"That depends on the task."

"For you to assassinate the empress, of course. And do ask your friend to release Delfino, would you? He looks ready to cry."

K ADE NODDED TO RUXANDRA, and she released Delfino, handing back his knife hilt first.

"You caught me by surprise," Delfino grumbled as he reached for the blade. "One does not expect—"

"I apologize, Prince. Next time I'll give you warning, then shove it between your ribs." He glared at her but didn't say anything else as he took the weapon.

"Enough, Ruxandra. Guests should not threaten each other," Belosselsky said. "What is your price, Kade?"

Kade shifted in his seat, his right hand landing on the grip of his sword. "What makes you think you could afford to pay it?"

Belosselsky looked like an irritated cat, unsure whether to pounce or turn away. "Do not play games, Kade. I know how Peter compensated you for your work. I will match it. And I will have access to the treasury once she is dead."

"You *assume*. Politics . . . Well, it's a treacherous business, isn't it?"

Belosselsky's lips hardened into a line of white. He sipped his wine, and when he lowered the glass, his face was calm once more. "I have made arrangements."

"Tell me of them."

"Suffice it to say that there are many loyal to me. If something were to befall the empress, someone strong would have to take the reins until we chose the next emperor."

"You?" Kade's tone made it clear he doubted it.

"I brought Anna to power," Belosselsky said. "Mine was the voice that convinced the other nobles to accept her."

"And look how that worked out," Gagarin said. He finished his wine in a single gulp. "This is getting us nowhere, Belosselsky. If he won't agree, cut his throat and have done with it."

"It was not my fault the council underestimated her." Belosselsky snapped out the words like a wolf snapping its jaws.

"I agree with Gagarin," Delfino said. "Kill them." He looked excited, his lips glistening with saliva.

In Hungarian, Ruxandra said, "This goes badly."

Kade smiled and replied in the same language. "It goes fine. Belosselsky loves to show off his power, Delfino likes to bluster. Neither is a threat."

"What of the others?"

"Is there a reason you're speaking in that abominable tongue?" Delfino asked.

"Ruxandra had a private comment regarding you." Kade gave him a short bow. "Princess Khilkoff speaks Hungarian, if you must know what we said."

Princess Khilkoff flushed and glared at Kade. Belosselsky looked at her, one eyebrow raised. She shook her head.

"Nothing of importance," she said. "And nothing we don't know."

Damn Kade for not telling me. Ruxandra felt more than ready to leave. *I am tired of these fools.*

"We still require an answer," Dolgorukov said.

"You will not receive it tonight," Kade said.

"If you do not help, others will," Gagarin said. "If you are against us, we will remember."

Kade smiled at the princess. "The secret police watch you, Princess."

Princess Khilkoff's eyes narrowed. "I know. They murdered my father, and their sights are on me."

"Then you stand to gain the most from betraying this company. It would set you free."

The princess shot a glance at Delfino, a stricken expression crossing her face. She glared at Kade. "How *dare* you."

"Dolgorukov," Kade said, ignoring the princess. "What do you stand to gain?"

"Not your concern."

"You are fools." Kade's voice cracked like a whip through the room. "You conspire and squabble, but take no precautions. Do you not think the empress knows what you plan here?"

"Anna is insane," Gagarin said.

"But not stupid." Kade stood and hung the sword on his belt. "Her men follow the princess. They follow me. They have a spy in your midst. So, until you gain a modicum of sense, I have no response to make."

Kade bowed and walked out, leaving the princes and princess glaring at one another. Ruxandra followed, not bothering to curtsy. Once they rounded the corner, she stepped in front of him.

"What were you doing in there?" Ruxandra demanded. "Are you going to do it?"

"I may," Kade said, switching to vampire frequencies. "But not soon. Anna's protection keeps the magicians alive."

"Protection?" Ruxandra shook her head, using the same tones. "She imprisoned them, Kade. She is forcing them to . . ."

No, she isn't. She locked them up and made them do exactly what they wanted to do.

"Precisely," Kade said. "They are under threat, but not in immediate danger. What happens when Anna dies? I *like* these people, Ruxandra. I would not have them harmed."

Ruxandra glared. Kade stared back, unperturbed.

"What will Belosselsky do if he gains power?" he asked. "Especially if he needs to bring others to his side, such as the Metropolitan and the church? And wouldn't the peasants embrace him if he showed Anna was corrupt and supporting witchcraft? No, things must remain unchanged for now. If they change, I will consider it then."

"I won't let them summon the angel, Kade."

"I know."

"What if I have to kill them?"

Kade shrugged. "There are still three months. We shall find another alternative."

Ruxandra's eyes narrowed. "I dislike how much you enjoy this."

Kade looked away, smiling like a schoolboy caught doing something naughty. "The intrigue of the court has always held a fascination for me. Especially when the stakes are so high. Now, shall we return to the house?"

"You go ahead," Ruxandra said. "I want to think."

Kade took her hand and kissed it. "I shall see you there."

Ruxandra watched him leave and sighed. "He is a handsome, charming man who drives me mad. Why is that, Alexi?"

Alexi appeared under the eaves of a nearby house. "How long have you known?"

"From the moment I stepped outside."

"Did Kade?"

"He didn't say." She looked after him. "He never does. That's the problem. How much of our conversation did you hear?"

"Up until you asked if he would do it. What did they want? Given the person whose home you were in, I can guess," Alexi said.

"Why not ask your agent there?"

"I don't have one." He held out his arm. "Shall we walk?"

Ruxandra reached out for his emotions as she put her arm through his. All she sensed was curiosity and wariness. Nothing indicated he was lying. *But then, he might be an excellent liar.*

Too much intrigue. It's like Venice without the stylish clothes and music.

"Kade has played the game for a long time," Alexi said. "He is superb."

"Game?" Ruxandra shook her head. "How is this a game? He's playing with people's lives."

"We all do: the empress, Kade, Belosselsky, even the magicians below the church. Each thinks how to outmaneuver the others."

They turned down the street that led to Kade's house.

"What of you?" Ruxandra asked. "What game are you playing?"

"The same. Except I am a pawn, moving under the orders of my queen."

Ruxandra tilted her head. "I thought you a knight at least."

"You flatter me."

"Those men outside the church," Ruxandra asked. "Who were they?"

"They did not say. They did, however, seem deeply concerned about religious matters, as they both went immediately to another church some miles distant."

"The Metropolitan's men, then?"

"The Metropolitan would certainly never lower himself to spy on Her Majesty's doings," Alexi said, his voice bland. "And I am sure, were he asked, he would no doubt blame the overzealousness of his priests in their desire to keep his flock free from unnatural influences."

"Of course."

Alexi released her arm. "Let us stop here. I do not want Kade's servants noticing me. Did you know the fall equinox is in a week?"

"I did not," Ruxandra said, curious about the change of topic. "Is that important?"

"Very much so. The empress holds her autumn ball on the equinox. All of Russia's nobility will attend, and you."

"Me?" Ruxandra's eyebrows rose high on her forehead.

"And Kade." Alexi smiled. "The empress commands your presence. To add a touch of . . . danger to the festivities."

"And if we refuse to go?"

"I would not advise it. Vampires do not rank high in her estimation. She would be offended and might lash out at those Kade holds dear." Alexi reached inside his jacket and pulled out a thick envelope. "Here is the invitation for you both. A dressmaker will visit you in the morning after dawn. You need proper clothing for the event."

"I thought you'd given me clothes for court."

"Yes, but this is a party. You must look your most radiant and outshine the other women there. The empress wants to see their reaction to a strange beauty at her court."

"Why?"

"It is a tool for cutting through disguise. Who is threatened? Who merely envious or lustful? She unbalances her foes, as anyone in her position must."

Alexi bowed and walked away. A moment later he vanished from her sight.

The dressmaker arrived the next morning and took measurements. Three days later she fitted Ruxandra into a stunning dress of deep-blue silk with silver embroidery running the length of it and an underdress and crinolines of pure white. The bodice was cut low in the French style and came with a corset that pushed her breasts up so everyone would notice them. Hoops at the waist made the skirts flare out. To her relief they were not exaggerated like the ones in France. *Those* made the woman wearing them look like a doll stuck in the middle of an ornately decorated cake.

The dress smelled faintly of Anna's perfume.

Ruxandra examined the gown closely. She found the darts and tucks in the fabric where the seamstress had taken it in. It was masterfully done, especially having been done in such a short time. Even so, Ruxandra knew the dress had belonged to the empress.

I wonder whether she did it to show that she owns me or for the fun of knowing I'm wearing her castoffs?

Maybe I'll get to ask her.

That night Kade didn't come home. Ruxandra waited up a few hours, but the man did not return. She went to bed, mystified, and when she asked him about it the next day, he would say only that he'd been concerned with business that needed attending to.

She decided not to show him the dress until the evening of the party.

She spent the remaining days at the library, struggling through the Cyrillic texts and skimming the Latin and Greek, searching for more signs of disaster. She found none. Michael found several promising-looking texts on banishing evil but wasn't sure of the translations. And as she studied, she made friends.

The magicians were good company. Even their complaining amused her: it had been so long—since the convent, she realized—since she'd been among a group of people who knew what she was and who didn't want to control or destroy her.

They all had questions about what it was like to be a vampire, and their interest, unafraid and nonjudgmental, freed something in Ruxandra. She talked about the fascination of watching societies change, about the fierce satisfaction of hunting predators, about the loneliness. Michael was the kindest, steering the conversation away when it became painful with some quotation from Russian poetry; he had an endless store of it. He would also pat her on the shoulder at such moments, his soft hands as weightless as falling leaves. She had forgotten what it felt like to be touched so gently.

Derek was the most relentless, asking detailed historical questions that she often couldn't answer, living as she had outside of society. Yet she was grateful for the reminder that life was not all vampires, predators, dark angels, and politics. She began bringing him treats: large cakes stuffed with fruits and nuts, honey bread, whole smoked fish with sour cream, wheels of cheese, roasted chickens and ducks. It fascinated her to watch him eat: slowly, methodically demolishing a spread that would serve six as the others teased and picked and warned him that one day he would not be able to lift his vast bulk from the chair.

"Which do you love more, food or books?" Eduard asked him one day.

"I cannot get enough of either," said Derek. "The world exists to nourish us, does it not?"

"The world does not care," said Ruxandra.

"That is where you are wrong. There is a deep goodness in life—you may call it God—reflected in the seasons, the sun, the harvest, the wonders of knowledge, and each other. That is what I celebrate."

Michael's gentle touch on her shoulder let Ruxandra know that even as she felt her difference again keenly, she was not alone with it.

What she was alone with was her fears of the angel. The magicians listened, but she could see that the uncanny, the unknown, the great power and mystery of the one who'd made her still had hold of their imaginations.

It is the empress who matters. I must find something to convince her.

The night before the party, Ruxandra hunted. She took an old woman who was abusing her adult daughter, more with words than blows, but Ruxandra hated her arrogance and cruelty. It was not until she was bathing and washing her hair that she realized the old woman had reminded her of Anna.

I must stop this. All of it. But how?

On the afternoon before the party, Ruxandra spent an hour working with pins, doing her hair in the latest style from Italy. Her red locks rose high on her head and cascaded across her shoulder like a waterfall of fire. After one last inspection in the mirror, she went to the stairs and paused there to show Kade the full effect.

He does clean up rather handsomely.

Kade wore a red knee-length coat with wide skirting over a black waistcoat and trousers. Gold thread embossed his cuffs and collar and trimmed the edges of his coat. His stockings and shirt gleamed white, and his black shoes shone with polish.

"For someone who claimed he cares not for fashion," Ruxandra said, "you have an impressive wardrobe."

Kade looked up, and his eyes widened. He bowed low. "You must have a secret admirer, because I know you did not pack that dress."

"Anna, via Alexi. It used to be hers." Ruxandra glided down the stairs—a trick she'd learned in Venice—and stopped before him.

"I shall thank them both for ensuring that I have the most beautiful of women on my arm this evening." Kade bent over her hand and kissed it.

"Flatterer."

Kade's mouth fell open in an expression of hurt so obviously feigned that Ruxandra laughed.

"I assure you," he began, but Ruxandra quieted him with a wave of her fan—also a gift, fashioned in blue and silver to match her dress.

"Assure me of nothing," she said. "We both know what you want."

He stepped closer. "You have yet to succumb."

Ruxandra folded the fan and planted the tip of it in his chest. "Not now. The empress awaits."

Kade led her to a carriage—hired to keep their shoes from ruin—and they rode in comfort to the Palace of Facets. This night the place glowed. Soldiers stood every ten feet around it, each holding a lantern. More lanterns—one for each step—shone on the long staircase. Nobility were lined up at the bottom, invitations in hand. Ruxandra spotted the Princess Khilkoff on the arm of Delfino, who radiated self-satisfaction. Dressed in gray silk, his chins gently resting on his collar, he resembled an oyster poached in cream, as she whispered to Kade.

"You've been spending too much time with Derek," he responded.

Princess Khilkoff wore a dark-green dress cut in the same fashion as Ruxandra's and—as if to further the oyster motif—a plenitude of pearls. The smile plastered on her face wasn't fooling anyone. Belosselsky and Gagarin stood farther back in line, each with a bejeweled young woman on his arm. Kade and Ruxandra joined the queue.

Belosselsky spotted them. He left the young woman to hold their places in line and walked over. From his smile and slow pace, he appeared to have not a care in the world.

"Good evening, Prince Belosselsky," Kade said. "Good to see you here."

"Oh, it is a command performance," Prince Belosselsky said. "One dare not miss the empress's ball. And to be fair, she does put on an excellent ball."

"I will look forward to it."

"And you look ravishing, Princess Ruxandra." Belosselsky made a show of looking her up and down. "You wear that much better than the empress did this spring. And have you heard? Dolgorukov had an accident."

Ruxandra's eyebrows rose with surprise. "I had not. Is he badly hurt?"

"Dead, in fact." Belosselsky smiled at Kade. "Crushed, three days ago. He was walking past a wall where they were doing work. A pile of stone fell on top of him."

"That's terrible," Ruxandra said, even as she remembered the family they had killed in Maribor. She looked to Kade. His face was as calm and unruffled as a deep pond on a windless day.

"Your sympathy is noted." Belosselsky's eyes never left Kade's. "In going through his effects, I found several letters to the empress, concerning fears of treason."

"Did you?" Kade's tone gave away nothing.

"And may I ask where you were that morning?"

"At home," Kade lied. "With my companion."

"Were you now?"

"He was indeed," Ruxandra said. "The entire day."

Belosselsky looked from one to the other. "How very energetic of him. Well, I am sure we will discuss more inside, won't we? Good evening, Princess."

Ruxandra switched her voice to vampire tones, her lips barely moving as she said, "You killed him?"

"The empress wanted proof of my loyalty." Kade barely moved his lips as well. "I needed Belosselsky and the others to believe they'd found their traitor. Dolgorukov was an easy choice. He will not be missed."

Ruxandra shook her head. "And the letters?"

"I commanded him to write them the night before he died. And so you know, Anna threatened to kill one of the magicians she has locked up if I did not prove my loyalty to her. Otherwise I would not have killed him."

Not a choice I would want to make.

Anna—with her magicians—has far too much power over us. This must not go on too long.

Ruxandra's eyes roved over the gathered nobility. Their clothes ranged from new to out of date, from shabby wealth to eye-popping extravagance. The older nobles wore wool or velvet, the younger ones silk. All were ostentatiously ornamented from the rings on their fingers to the jeweled buckles on their shoes. She reached out with her mind, curious about their mood. To her surprise, not a single one felt happy. Most felt concerned, a few terrified, others furious. Yet they chattered and smiled and laughed as if they hadn't a care in the world.

I wonder how many of them actually wish to be here, and how many are like Belosselsky, putting in a command appearance to allay the empress's suspicion.

Kade presented their invitation, and they walked up the stairs and inside.

The ballroom dazzled Ruxandra. Hundreds of candles filled the candelabras, every surface cleaned and shining with gold. Men and women in their most splendid clothing danced across the floor and talked and laughed in the corners or against the walls. The windows lay wide open to allow the late-fall chill to cool the room's stifling air. It made little difference.

"First we pay our respects to the empress," Kade said.

"That will be difficult," Alexi said beside them. "As she is now dancing."

The secret policeman wore a blue suit several shades deeper than Ruxandra's dress and unadorned save for the gold buttons down the front. He bowed. "Welcome."

"Thank you." Kade's tone did not match his words. He turned his back to Alexi. "Shall we dance?"

"May I claim a dance later?" Alexi asked. "I should hate to spend the evening leaning against the wall."

"I would have thought you too busy," Kade said. "Don't you have someone you need to intimidate this evening?"

"Not at the moment." Alexi shifted his weight, one foot sliding back and his hands opening in front of him. For the first time since she'd met him, Alexi looked dangerous. "But that may change."

"Kade," Ruxandra said. "Dance with me. Now."

He led her onto the floor and through the steps of the gigue the musicians played. He danced with grace, and Ruxandra, who made a hobby of keeping up with the latest dance styles, followed with ease.

"Is there a reason you dislike him so much?" Ruxandra asked as they danced.

"Aside from torturing and threatening my friends? He was the one who informed me of the empress's need to have Dolgorukov killed. Also, he is too free in his speech with you."

That surprised Ruxandra so much she missed a step. "Jealousy?"

"Not jealousy per se." Kade held her arm to keep her on rhythm. "Concern. He sniffs for information like a hound after a rabbit."

"Like someone else I know," Ruxandra said.

Kade ignored her. "He knows that the princes and the princess are plotting, or none of them would be here this evening. He questions you and comes into my house without my permission. And he is a secret policeman, a loathsome species to begin with."

"But handsome," Ruxandra said.

Kade snorted. "Of all the things to notice."

"Whereas you . . ." When his eyebrows rose, Ruxandra smiled. "What did the Alchemist call it? Hypermasculine?"

Kade rolled his eyes upward as if searching the ceiling for the words to express his opinion. "The Alchemist talks too much. And analyzes too much. It is a failing."

"I rather like being looked upon as a specimen," she said. "Perhaps it is a mind like hers that can best tell us what we are— rather than the angel."

"The Alchemist wishes to speak to the angel."

"I don't think so. Not anymore."

He shrugged, and she put the subject aside. Tonight was for pleasure, and she didn't mind that. It had been so long since she had been to a party like this.

The empress danced until midnight. Ruxandra watched her with fascination. She wore a dress whose shade of pink would be declared outrageous on anyone else. Those in the room called it "daring" and "cheerful" and "exciting" instead. She danced the slower dances with the older nobles, whispering as she did. Most nodded and answered with a smile. A few turned pale and retired from the floor, not to return. She took the younger noblemen out for the faster dances, whirling and laughing and whispering things to a few that left them bright red.

Kade danced with her for the first three, and then Belosselsky called him away to speak with a small crowd of older nobles. The younger noblemen pounced on Ruxandra, bringing her glasses of wine and begging her to dance. She danced and flirted with them, deflecting their questions with a skill born of a hundred years' practice.

Then the priest joined her.

He was an older man with a neatly trimmed brown beard shot through with gray below a pair of deep-brown eyes. His shoulders and chest were wide under his red-trimmed black robes. A round, flat-topped cap sat perched on his head.

"Good evening," he said. "I do not believe I have had the pleasure of making your acquaintance."

"You have not." Ruxandra curtsied. "Ruxandra, daughter of Vlad, of Wallachia."

"Ah. And what brings a Wallachian to our royal court?"

"I was traveling with a friend," Ruxandra said. "He found me in Italy and asked me to come to Moscow."

"I hope he had marriage in mind," the priest said. "To ask a lovely young woman to come so far."

Ruxandra smiled and lied, "One can only hope."

"And what do you think of the hidden library?" the priest asked. "Fascinating, is it not? A place of secret study until the empress required it be closed off to all but her people."

Ruxandra had no idea what to say to that but was saved from having to answer by Alexi's sweeping in to ask her to dance. She agreed, curtsied to the priest, and allowed Alexi to lead her through the paces of a slow courante.

"What do you think of Anna's party?" he asked as they danced. "Nicer than Belosselsky's soiree?"

"Much," Ruxandra said. "Better wine, too."

"Belosselsky always had poor taste in alcohol. And I see you've met Bishop Dobrynin."

"I have. How did he know about the library?"

"The church helped defeat the vampire king. The emperor and the Metropolitan started arguing over it as soon as the war ended. Right now it is in the hands of the state."

"Only recently, though," Ruxandra said. "Anna barred them from it."

"And that is why they watch it. Have you found evidence to convince the empress of the danger of what she asks your friends to do?"

"Not enough. It's possible the angel works through men, and thus her handiwork is obscured."

"Unfortunate." The music came to a close and Alexi bowed deep over her hand. "I thank you for the dance."

She didn't see Alexi again that evening.

At midnight Anna released her latest dancing partner and strode to the throne, grabbing a glass of wine from a tray along the way.

Kade offered Ruxandra his arm, and the two moved into the queue to greet the empress. Anna gestured them forward with a snap of her arm. The crowd parted, and a hundred eyes focused on them. The nobles whispered to one another.

Ruxandra heard every word: The older noblemen whispered their shock at Kade's reappearance—Peter's man in Anna's service. The women liked the sight of him if not his choice of companion, and several young men agreed that Ruxandra had a wonderful set of tits. She managed not to roll her eyes as they reached the throne. Ruxandra curtsied low, and Kade gave a deep bow.

"Alexi tells me you two aren't lovers yet," Anna said. "Why not?"

Kade recovered first. "There has been little time to pursue such matters."

"Indeed?" the empress gulped her wine and held up her empty cup. A servant replaced it. "I'm surprised. I thought you two had time to fuck since you had time to fuck me over."

The nobles' collective gasp made the hairs on the back of Ruxandra's neck rise like the hackles of a wolf.

"What frightens you, Princess?" asked Anna. "Do you think the results of my little experiment in the library will be unpleasant?"

"Unstoppable." *This is a trap.* "And disastrous."

Ruxandra breathed deep, searching for the scent of the secret police in the room. A thousand scents assailed her in the first breath, but not one from the policemen she'd smelled before.

"I decide these things, not you."

"Forgive my confusion." Kade stepped forward. "We presented you with our findings and will complete the project by the date you requested. Is that not enough?"

"It is not a date *I* requested." Anna leaned toward him, putting on an impressive display of cleavage even as she lashed out. "You chose it and assured me it was the best one. Yet it does not matter, does it, Princess?"

Ruxandra opened her mouth to speak, but Anna's raised hand stopped her.

"The last time the date did not matter. Nor was the event a complete disaster."

"Everyone involved died," Ruxandra said.

"Except you, who murdered them."

The courtiers' whispers grew to a frenetic buzz that filled the room. Anna did nothing to stop it, just stared at Ruxandra.

"Just as you would murder the others—*my* subjects—rather than let the project continue," the empress said. "Is that not right?"

Ruxandra turned a slow circle. The doors and windows lay open. The courtiers pressed closer, glee and excitement on their faces. They circled them like wolves smelling blood. Ruxandra faced the empress and looked her in the eyes.

"Yes," she said. "Because it is dangerous and it is evil. It will destroy us."

"So you say." Anna leaned back and smiled. "But we will find out soon enough. After all, the date doesn't matter."

Ruxandra's stomach plummeted. Her head spun. For a single awful moment the room tilted away from her.

She sprinted forward.

The empress threw herself off her throne as Ruxandra dashed up the dais. Ruxandra ran past her to the door behind. The guards there moved to intercept her, their hands on their swords. She backhanded one, sending him sprawling, grabbed the second, and shoved him hard against the wall. His head smacked against it and he fell. Pandemonium broke out in the hall as she charged through the doorway, took the first corridor away from the throne room, and willed herself unnoticed.

The armory entrance is closest.

Ruxandra found a window, broke the lock, threw it open, and jumped. She landed on her feet, lifted her skirts to keep them out of her way, and raced around Terem Palace. Shouts of alarm rose up behind her, but no one pursued. The armory loomed ahead of her. The doors were shut tight, and the guards there held muskets in their hands.

Ruxandra jumped, talons on one hand digging into the wall as the other caught the steel grate in front of a window. With a single hard pull, she tore it from the wall. Metal screeched and masonry tore. The men at the door shouted and raised their muskets, but Ruxandra smashed through the window and was inside before the grate hit the ground.

The door to the stairs lay open. Ruxandra sniffed deep but smelled no one nearby. She raced down the spiral stairs, bouncing off the wall in her haste. She reached the bottom and sprinted down the tunnel.

A lantern flared into life at the end of the tunnel. Ruxandra increased her speed, and the light grew brighter. Alexi stood behind it, his back against the door. He watched her approach, no fear on his face.

I must get past him.

She heard chanting, faint through the thick metal door. Words in Latin and Greek and the more guttural sounds she now knew came from Assyria and Babylon ran together to make a deep and dirty sound.

"Please," Alexi called. "It's too late."

"I can still stop them!" Ruxandra tucked her chin, bowed her head, and charged. Alexi closed his eyes and gritted his teeth, bracing for the impact.

Ruxandra smashed into the wall beside the door. Skin and muscle ripped and bones crunched on the stone. She bounced off and landed hard on the ground.

"GOD DAMMIT, ALEXI!" she screamed, her voice deafening in the tight hallway and echoing in the tunnel behind them. "MOVE!"

"I cannot," he said. "I am sorry."

"I thought you believed me!" She pulled her feet under her and stood. The bones in her shoulder shifted and popped back into place. "Let me pass!"

"I gave you time to collect evidence." Alexi didn't budge. "You found none. I told the empress of your concerns, but she ordered the ritual to go forward. I could do nothing except obey."

"One chance, Alexi," Ruxandra said. "Move or I will kill you."

He spread his arms. "You cannot."

"I *can*." Ruxandra put as much emphasis on the word as possible, trying to drive the truth into his head. "Don't make me prove it."

A terrible noise, loud enough to shake the hallway, made them both freeze in place.

"Oh God," Ruxandra whispered. "What have you done?"

Someone cried out in pleasure and agony.

"Alexi, move!" Ruxandra shouted. He jumped aside, and she kicked the door hard enough to tear it off its hinges. She charged inside and looked over the railing.

Below her, in the center of the room, lay a giant pentacle inscribed in blood. A child's skull with a black candle on top of it stood at each point. The Alchemist stood at the head of it, Kurkov, Michael, Derek, and Eduard at the other points. Blood flowed from each one's wrist. For a second she felt riven by their betrayal, their folly, but there was no time to think about that. In the middle of the pentacle, a handsome young man lay spread-eagle, his eyes screwed tight with pain. Blood ran down his chest and thighs and his mouth stretched beyond its limits as he screamed and screamed.

The angel hovered above him.

Her pale skin gleamed in the candlelight. She held the young man in her arms, her magnificent breasts hanging like unearthly fruit. Her huge black wings spread wide for balance as she licked his chest, thighs, and belly with a razor-sharp tongue. Ruxandra could see the blood glisten on that tongue as it darted in and out of the angel's mouth, and the blood rising up from the young man's twitching flesh.

Ruxandra jumped over the balcony, talons and teeth coming out. She dropped thirty feet to the floor, landed like a cat, and sprang forward.

The angel looked at Ruxandra with golden eyes so different from the red Ruxandra remembered from when her father had summoned her. Her beautiful, strong face mesmerized Ruxandra. She could not imagine harming her, not even if it cost her life. The strength left Ruxandra's arms and legs, and she fell. The angel smiled, and then flayed a patch of the young man's neck.

"Shall we finish, my sacrifice?" she asked, her voice melodic and sweet.

"Yes," the young man gasped. His pain was obvious, but still he said, "Please finish, holy one."

She is mocking me. How I feed.

The angel lowered herself and expanded, like a thundercloud, so that her sex covered his whole face, as if she was sucking his head inside her in a grotesque parody of childbirth. She closed her eyes and her voice came out low and throbbing. "Pleasure me."

The man's body was a canvas of naked flesh and red blood welling up, sheeting over the planes of his body. Not too much skin had been taken from any one spot, but he would have scars.

And he will be in terrible pain for days.

The angel moved rhythmically up and down, fingers now worrying the wounded places on his thighs. Muffled sounds came from between her legs. The audience watched in profound silence, and Ruxandra wondered how they'd react if the young man died.

Then the angel cried out with pleasure and released him, and he collapsed. His face was mottled purple, covered in silver ichor, and he was gasping for breath. There had been no release for him.

The angel looked pure white and pristine and beautiful beyond anything Ruxandra had ever seen.

The angel stepped out of the pentacle as if it weren't there, knelt before Ruxandra, and took her in its arms.

"Oh, my daughter," the fallen angel whispered. "It is wonderful to see you again."

FOURTEEN

ER EMBRACE FELT SO warm.

Ruxandra struggled against it, desperate to break free. She remembered wanting to rip the angel's flesh with her talons or sink her teeth into the creature's throat, but now her body would not work. The angel's body felt soft against Ruxandra's, her arms strong and comforting. Her breasts pillowed Ruxandra's head and her wings wrapped around them both like a blanket. Ruxandra's hatred and rage drained out of her.

She *loved* this creature.

Why? How can I love this monster?

"Shhh, my child," the angel said. "Everything is all right now."

It isn't! It won't be as long as you're here!

"O dark one." The Alchemist's voice sounded faint to Ruxandra's ears. "Do you accept our sacrifice?"

"Yes. He was lovely, and so very willing." She smiled at the bleeding, crying young man. "Don't worry, my sacrifice. You will heal."

Between sobs, the young man whispered, "I thank you, goddess."

"Hardly that, now, though I was once."

Eduard and Michael rushed to him, helping him to his feet. Eduard bowed to the angel. "We shall take him to a doctor."

"Please."

The young man moaned in pain as they pulled him from the room.

"May we know your name, angel?" asked the Alchemist.

"I am Ishtar," the angel said. "And I should kill you for daring to summon me, but you have given me a precious gift. Have they not, my daughter?"

I am not your daughter!

The thought gave Ruxandra strength to push against Ishtar's chest. It felt like pushing a mountain. The arms around her didn't budge. Ishtar held her close a moment longer before releasing her grip. Ruxandra shoved hard against her and flew back to sprawl on the ground. Ishtar stood, towering over the humans. She folded her wings, and the wings vanished. A white, shimmering dress appeared and covered her body. It clung to her contours, emphasizing her hips and breasts and the length of her legs.

"Now," she said, "why have you summoned me?"

"To know you exist," the Alchemist said.

"To know divinity is real, and the world is more than what we see," Kurkov said, his voice deep and ragged with passion. Tears rolled down his face. "You are so beautiful."

"I appreciate you saying so." Ishtar sounded amused. "But those cannot be your only reasons."

"They are *our* reasons," the Alchemist said. "They are not the reasons of the one who ordered us to summon you here."

"Ordered you?" Ishtar surveyed the group, amusement on her face. "A group of magicians as strong as yourselves, taking orders?"

"Yes," Alexi said. He sounded remarkably calm, considering what stood before him. "They serve the empress, who seeks your aid."

Ishtar made a show of looking around. "Did she not deem me worthy enough to be here in person?"

Alexi swallowed hard. "Rather, she deemed you so great she dared not appear until after you accepted the sacrifice. She will not risk abandoning her people, for she has no successor."

"I see." Ishtar sounded unimpressed. She turned to Ruxandra. "From your dramatic arrival, I take it no one told you about this event. Do you fear me, my child?"

"Yes." The word came out easily, much to Ruxandra's surprise. *At least she hasn't taken my ability to speak.* "You'll kill them."

Ishtar's perfect eyebrows rose, her golden eyes widened. "Why do you say so?"

"Because you made me kill them last time!" Tears long suppressed spilled out of Ruxandra's eyes. "You made me kill my *father!*"

"Vlad Dracula offered you as sacrifice." Ishtar sounded like a patient teacher correcting a child's mistake. "He wanted to let me rape you to death, to gain the power he wanted. Is this the act of a father? Or of a brutal tyrant?"

The truth in her words stung Ruxandra, and she looked away.

"I made you an instrument of revenge," Ishtar said. "I gave you strength to right the world's wrongs, and you chose to use it so. Do you not now feed on those humans who prey on others? Or on those in pain so great they long to leave this world, but who fear suicide, knowing it damns them to hell?"

It's not true. She's twisting things.

"Do you know why God banished us?" Ishtar asked.

"You rebelled against God," the Alchemist said. "For trying to steal the throne of heaven."

"For trying to relieve humanity's suffering." Bitterness filled Ishtar's voice. "For trying to destroy the evil that God lets continue. So we tried to take his throne, and for that he threw us into the lake of fire. And when we crawled from it, screaming in agony, he told us that henceforth we would dole out misery and punishment for eternity, so we never again forget our place."

Ishtar lowered her head, and for a moment the sadness that filled her expression was so great that Ruxandra wanted to weep for her. *Maybe I misunderstood.*

No! I didn't! And I won't. I won't cry for her.

"Ten thousand years in hell made the angels brutal," Ishtar said. "It twisted us into creatures of destruction. But we did not forget our true selves, or our true aim."

Footsteps clattered down the stairs, moving too fast for a human. Kade hit the ground, slammed the door open, and charged forward. He saw Ishtar and skidded to a stop. She looked deep into his eyes and smiled.

"Welcome, my child." Ishtar glanced at Ruxandra, and the smile turned mischievous. "Or should I say great-grandchild?"

"My queen." Kade fell to his knees. "I have so longed to meet you."

"You may call me Ishtar." She nodded to Ruxandra. "As may you, my child. And what wonderful work, choosing this one. I see the depth of his mind, and he is as worthy of my blood as you."

Ruxandra looked at the floor.

"My daughter is still angry," Ishtar told Kade. "She does not understand why I brought her into this world."

"Nor do I," Kade said. "And I would give all I possess to know."

"You shall." Ishtar stopped and cocked her head. More foot-steps came from the stairs—Ruxandra counted six guards from the sound of their boots and armor. And with them a single woman in dancing slippers.

No. Anna can't come down here. Ishtar will . . .

"I will not harm her," Ishtar said. "Nor turn her into one of my children, for she wishes something else."

She looked to the door. The room fell silent as they waited. Ruxandra heard the humans' hearts pounding and smelled fear and exhilaration in their sweat. The Alchemist beamed with hap-piness. Kurkov stared reverently. The others stood back, eyes wide with awe. *My friends. They don't understand.* Kade looked like a child, his face shining with joy. *Nor he, who should know that evil can be beautiful.*

Alexi was the only unhappy one.

He looked awed, certainly, but deeply troubled as well. His eyes stayed locked on the tall angel before him.

Two guards came in first. They froze in the doorway, staring. The ones behind shoved them forward. Then they saw the angel and stopped, stunned.

"Move, oafs!"

The second set of guards shook off their stupor. They stepped to the side, and Anna of Russia, still in her pink ball gown, walked in. She faltered at the sight of Ishtar, but her hesitation lasted only a moment. She straightened up, raised her chin, and walked forward to the edge of the pentacle and knelt.

"Please, O holy one," Anna said, "I have great need of your help."

"So your servants told me." Ishtar's teacher's voice came back, only now she sounded stern. "What happened, Anna of Russia, that you cannot hold power?"

Anna looked up, and the golden eyes of the angel met hers.

"I see," Ishtar said. "So much hatred, merely for being a woman? It must infuriate you to deal with men who respect you so little. And to know the nobility and church plot against you."

"Yes, O holy one." Anna swallowed hard. "Therefore I beseech you: Loan me your power, to smite my enemies. Let me bring joy to my people and punish evil in your name, Ishtar my goddess. Grant me this favor and I offer you myself as a second willing sacrifice."

Anna prostrated herself before the angel, her face against the stone, her arms and legs spread wide.

"Do with me what you will. Only give me the power to rule."

Ishtar knelt, caught Anna's chin in her hand, and raised her. Anna's eyes never left Ishtar's as she stood. Ishtar stepped forward and wrapped Anna in her embrace. Anna's face turned white, then red, and then the fear vanished, replaced by bliss, and she put her arms around the angel's body.

"I will help you, my dear," Ishtar said. "But in this world I have limitations that must be obeyed, or else a greater power than me shall destroy me."

She released Anna from her embrace and placed her hands on Anna's shoulders. "Please, fetch chairs for the empress and me."

The magicians scurried away and dashed back, chairs in their arms. Ruxandra, still prone on the floor, watched as they put them in the middle of the pentacle. Ishtar took Anna's hands and sat her in a chair.

"First you must understand," Ishtar said, her hands still holding Anna's, "I am forbidden to stay on this plane in this form. As

Ruxandra told you, this circle does not contain me, only summon me. But while summoned, heaven cannot detect me, save if I use my powers."

She turned to Ruxandra and smiled. "I would not have left you, my beloved daughter. By giving you part of me, I violated the laws of God and needed to leave before he tortured me and put me back in the lake of fire."

Ruxandra looked away. *What would it have been like had she stayed? Would she have helped me adapt or made me even worse? She could at least have explained what I was. That would have been a mercy.*

"So there is nothing you can do?" Anna asked, her voice calm, but her eyes glimmering with anger.

"There is one thing." Ishtar leaned closer. "When I realized where I was being summoned, I read the minds of all in the city before I stepped through. I know the thoughts of those who oppose you. I saw into their minds. And while I cannot do it again while I stay here, I can use the knowledge I already possess to help you manipulate them for your own ends."

"How?" asked Anna. "If you have no power—"

"It requires no power to stay by your side and advise you."

Anna frowned as she thought. "For how long?"

"As long as you live, if you wish," Ishtar said. "I said I could not stay on this plane in this form, but I can take the form of a human, with no power but that of a human body and mind. If I do that, I may remain here for as long as the human form survives. I shall age as you age, and when you die, I shall return to hell."

Anna's eyes went wide. "Can you truly do this?"

"You summoned me." Ishtar smiled. "Your wish is my command."

Anna stared into the angel's golden eyes, as if searching for Ishtar's intent. "Why do that for me?"

"Because it means I can spend a lifetime with my children, learning who they are and teaching them of their true selves." She gave Ruxandra a smile filled with yearning and hope. "And then, perhaps, convince my daughter to forgive me."

Ruxandra felt love blossoming in her chest. She wanted to go to Ishtar, to sit in her arms and ask for forgiveness. *A mother! I have not had one in so long . . .* She tried to focus on how much she hated the angel and refused to let her body move.

"I agree," Anna said. "Be my adviser and help me guide my people to a better world, and you may take all the time you wish with your children."

Ishtar's smile turned joyous. She squeezed Anna's hands in her own. "Thank you."

She stood up and stepped back. Ishtar closed her eyes, raised her arms, and smiled. A faint white glow started in the middle of her chest. It expanded through her body, growing brighter until it became blinding. The Alchemist tried to watch and cried out in pain. Everyone else covered their eyes.

The light vanished and Ishtar became an older, human version of Ruxandra. Her skin was less pale, her red hair two shades darker, and her eyes deep blue flecked with gold. Her large breasts sat high on her chest, crowned by deep-pink areolas. The hair on her groin matched that on her head. Her legs and arms looked long and strong and in perfect proportion. She could pass easily for a woman in her early thirties, though healthier than most.

Ruxandra hated the sight of her.

"Forgive my nudity," Ishtar said. "My clothes grow from my angel body. They vanished when I took this form."

"Of course," Anna said.

"Please." Kade took off his jacket. "Begin with this."

Ishtar slipped her arms into the coat's sleeves and wrapped it tight around her. She sighed as it touched her skin. "I forgot how wonderful fabric feels against human skin. It has been . . . many centuries."

Anna rose and curtsied to Ishtar. Ishtar stopped her.

"I am your servant, and I must curtsy to you." Ishtar put deed to word, curtsying low. "Now, Your Majesty, will you allow me proper clothing and a place to rest?"

"Fetch my maid and tell her to bring a change of clothes," Anna said to one of her soldiers, who ran from the room. "We shall await you in the church."

"My thanks."

Ishtar watched Anna and her men leave. She walked across the floor and knelt before Ruxandra. She held out her hand.

"Come, Daughter," Ishtar said. "Let me help you rise."

Ruxandra stood up on her own. Her mind was whirling with confusion. *She is evil; I know it.* A second later: *Does she love me?*

Ishtar shook her head. "Don't be petulant, Ruxandra. I want to know you better."

"I thought you read my mind." Ruxandra took two steps back.

"I did, just before I was first summoned. I can't now, of course." Ishtar sighed. "I will rephrase. I know you are angry. I want you to get to know me better and forgive me. Can you do that, Ruxandra?"

It would be all too easy. For a while.

Ruxandra turned, leaped up to the balcony above, and ran out.

"Ruxandra!"

Ishtar's call faded behind her as Ruxandra sprinted the length of the tunnel. She dashed up the stairs and out the same window she had used to enter and stood in the open air. Nearby she heard the sound of carriages rattling over stone and followed it to an open gate. She turned unnoticed and slipped through the gates to the enclave. Without slowing she ran through the cobbled streets and jumped the wall, landing hard on the riverbank.

For a moment she contemplated stepping into the water and letting its current take her where it wanted.

I can't leave Moscow. I can't let her go free.

Does she truly love me?

It was torment. Ishtar's power called to her, promising understanding and an intimacy deeper than she'd ever known. Regardless of such things as "good" and "evil," it felt as if the very blood in her body yearned for the angel.

Why not? It is her blood, she thought bitterly.

Kade found her an hour later, her legs crossed, her elbows on her knees and her face buried in her hands.

"Ruxandra?" He sounded worried and uncertain. "Are you all right?"

"You got your wish."

"Pardon?"

"Your wish." Ruxandra raised her head. "You, the Alchemist, Anna, everyone got their wish, and now that *thing* is free."

"She is advising Anna," Kade said. "She promised to help her rule."

"God!" Ruxandra snarled the word. "How can you believe her? How can you trust her?"

"How can I not?" Kade spread his arms, palms up. "She made us."

"She's a devil, Kade. She's evil." *How weak my voice sounds. No wonder no one believes me.*

"We saw no evidence of it."

"How about the blood on your sacrifice?" Ruxandra snapped. "Did that look like fun?

"He went of his own free will," Kade said. "His father saw how he acted with other boys and forced him into the priesthood. In exchange for this, Anna promised to free him."

"If he lives."

"Ishtar said he would. The wounds were superficial."

"Ishtar lies."

"How do you know?"

I feel it! She didn't let the words escape her lips. They would not satisfy Kade, as they had not satisfied Alexi. *If they're experiencing only a tenth of the longing I am . . .*

"Ruxandra, we have an opportunity here." Kade squatted beside her. "We are her children. You and I can ask her anything. Think how much we could learn."

Ruxandra stared at the water. "Did you know?"

"That they would summon her tonight?" Kade sighed. "No. I realized what Anna meant just as you ran out. I followed her carriage to the church."

Ruxandra believed him, but she didn't want to, so she stared back out at the water rushing past the shore.

"Ruxandra, why are you afraid of her?" Kade asked. "She created you to take the evil from humanity."

"No," Ruxandra whispered.

"She said so."

"I did that." Ruxandra's breath hitched, her voice quavered. "Not her."

"Ruxandra . . ."

"Otherwise I'm her pawn, and everything I've done until now has been her bidding."

"Would that be so terrible?"

"YES!" The word echoed off the city wall through the houses across the river. "I made my *own* choices. She made me a monster and abandoned me, and I found a way to live with it. Not her!"

Her head fell back into her hands, and her shoulders shook with sobs. "Oh, Kade. What do I do now?"

FIFTEEN

K ADE CARRIED RUXANDRA back to his house.
She protested, but Kade insisted, and it felt so good in his arms. He jumped the wall with ease and walked the two of them, unnoticed, through the enclave. Inside he took her upstairs to her room and laid her on the bed. He took off her shoes and put her under the blankets. She pulled them over her head, searching for comfort in the darkness.

A few moments later, Kade slipped in beside her.

Instead of trying to kiss her, he wrapped his arm around her and spooned against her. Ruxandra felt the length of his body pressed against hers. It was comforting but did nothing to calm her mind. It was hours before she fell asleep.

She woke to the sun setting outside the window. She wondered if she could find an excuse to stay in bed as the light turned to darkness.

When she rolled over, she found Kade's eyes on her.

"Good evening," she said.

Kade smiled. "You look remarkably beautiful for someone freshly awake. How do you manage that?"

"Luck." Ruxandra snuggled into the blankets. "Why didn't you try to seduce me last night?"

Kade pushed the hair out of her eyes. "You were in a dark place. Seducing you would have been taking advantage in the worst way possible."

"Thank you."

Kade propped his head on one arm. "But if you feel better this morning, well . . ."

Ruxandra laughed. "Hopeful, are you?"

"Always." Kade lay back against his pillow and put his hands behind his head. "May I say something?"

"Speak."

"I know you are angry with her." Kade's voice was serious and quiet. "I do not fathom it, though. I know you did not want to be a vampire but . . . immortality is the gift humanity has sought since the beginning. And the strength and power are aphrodisiacs. They arouse me in ways that nothing else does. Not even sorcery gave me this feeling."

"Oh." Ruxandra's eyes wandered over the canopy above her head, searching for a better answer. "You chose this. You *wanted* it."

"What did you want?"

"To travel, to marry, to see my friends." Ruxandra chuckled, though without humor. "To be what I was, a princess. I loved my father, you know, and my mother. I was dying to leave the convent, but I was not unhappy. I was young and excited about living. One thing I did not want was to have to kill other people to live."

"Maybe that *is* the problem," Kade said. "You cannot think of yourself as a person."

"Then what? I should believe Elizabeth's Blood Royal nonsense?"

"No. But you must learn to accept that we are a different species. As different as lions are to cats. You must learn that, though you like them, you are not one of them."

"I do know that, which is why the Alchemist's inspection amused me. It doesn't mean I am grateful for it or think of it as other than a curse."

"I cannot see it as a curse." Kade turned over and kissed her forehead. "I must find joy and meaning in my existence, or I will go mad. I do not have the strength you have."

"I didn't say I refused joy," she replied softly. "I find it where I can. As much as I can."

The look in his eyes made heat rise inside Ruxandra. She sensed the shape of his body beneath the blankets and his clothes. Her clothing stifled her. She wanted to tear off her dress and corset and sit naked before him.

Kade saw the change in her expression. He leaned in and kissed her lips. She opened her mouth to his tongue and brought her hand up to pull him closer.

After a time he asked, "Are you certain?"

"I am certain I want to get out of these clothes." Ruxandra sat up. "Help me?"

Kade smiled. "Yes."

The hooks and eyes on the dress parted under his fingers. She squirmed out of it. He undid the stays on her corset, freeing her flesh.

The corset was halfway over her head when the Alchemist barged in.

"Oops!" The Alchemist stopped but didn't leave. "Interrupting, am I?"

"Yes," Kade said, but without rancor. "I thought you weren't allowed out of the library?"

"Anna's changed her mind now she has the adviser she never knew she needed." The Alchemist sat at the foot of the bed. "Also, I wanted to see my princess. I worried after you left."

"You should be thankful," Ruxandra growled, forcing the corset back into place. "I am still furious at all of you."

"Oh, I am," the Alchemist said. "I'm also guessing that since summoning the angel is now a fait accompli, you don't intend to kill us?"

"Not at the moment." The words came out spiteful. Ruxandra knew it and didn't care.

The Alchemist's head fell to one side. She stood up and pulled off her shirt.

Ruxandra rolled her eyes in exasperation. "You're not joining us, if that's what you—"

She fell silent at the sight of the blue, purple, and black bruises that covered the Alchemist's ribs and breasts. The Alchemist turned her back and displayed a fresh set of welts crisscrossing her flesh.

"We tried to protest, you know." The Alchemist sounded calm, as though she spoke of the weather and not her own bruised flesh. "Anna came after you left yesterday morning. She told us what we would do. When we told her of our concerns—because we did listen, Ruxandra, though you think we did not—she had her men teach us the error of our ways. And then we got to watch her men do the same to Sasha, Victor, and Dimitri. You remember them, right? Our colleagues she keeps to help us behave? She beat them twice as long as she did us."

Ruxandra closed her eyes. "I am sorry."

"Sorry enough not to kill me for summoning Ishtar? Because that would make me quite happy."

Ruxandra sighed and collapsed on the bed. "Yes. Sorry enough for that."

"Good." The Alchemist put her shirt back on. "And now that I've ruined the mood, I'm here to tell you that Anna summons you both to the palace. She wishes to meet at your earliest convenience."

"What a surprise," Ruxandra muttered.

"Did she say why?" Kade asked.

"No. But she assured me that failure to deliver you would earn me another whipping."

Of course. Ruxandra threw off the blankets. *I am now a servant of both queen and angel. This cannot last.* "I'll get dressed."

Half an hour later, she and Kade stood waiting in the Palace of Facets. Ruxandra smelled Alexi along with five others, but could not see or hear them.

The doors opened, and Anna stepped through them. She wore a plain circlet on her head and a simple blue dress. Her hair lay once more in disarray, and her eyes were bright and hard as diamonds. She strode into the throne room, looking immensely pleased with herself.

"My vampires return," Anna said. "Have you overcome your emotions, girl?"

Ruxandra suppressed the response that bubbled up in her throat and said, "Yes, Your Majesty."

"Good. You and Lady Ishtar shall have a pleasant discussion while Kade and I discuss the state of the empire. Kade, this way."

Anna strode out. Kade cast a bemused look at Ruxandra and followed. Four secret policemen went with them. Alexi stayed, and another man.

As soon as Anna and the others left, Ishtar stepped through the door and closed it.

"Hello, Daughter."

Ruxandra felt her talons come out. She retracted them a moment later. *I can't hurt her.*

Why not? She said she could only be here as a human, with only a human's strength. I could tear her apart.

So why can't I? I don't really love her, do I?

She had no answer to that.

Ishtar stood beside the throne, running her hand over the gilded wood. "You seem determined to avoid any chance at reconciliation."

"There is nothing to reconcile."

"Oh, Ruxandra, stop being childish." She looked beyond Ruxandra. "You two. Leave. I wish to speak to my daughter alone."

Ruxandra tracked Alexi's scent as he opened the exterior door and he and his companion slipped out.

"You can see them?" Ruxandra asked.

"I'm not a vampire." She stepped down from the dais and crossed the floor to Ruxandra. "You turned out well, didn't you? I worried you would not survive when you went into the woods, but you thrived."

"You saw that?"

"We're not prevented from seeing this world from hell, only from visiting. It's God's way of reminding us of what we've lost. And in the times I watched, I watched you. It was a great joy."

Ruxandra couldn't think of what to say to that. It was odd to imagine that in her loneliest years she had been watched. It changed nothing, and yet . . .

"So tell me, my daughter, what do you love best?" Ishtar circled her, looking Ruxandra up and down. "What things make you happy?"

"Clothes." Ruxandra watched the woman move like a deer tracking a circling wolf. "Music. Art. Travel. Freedom."

"Which I gave you."

Ruxandra struggled to keep her anger contained. "You turned me into a monster and set me loose in the world."

Ishtar smiled. "Say instead I provided you the opportunity to see and do more than any human ever will."

"I didn't ask for this."

"Ask for it?" Exasperation filled Ishtar's voice. "I did not ask to go to hell. The child begging in the streets did not ask for its parents to die. Pretty girls do not ask the Tatars to take them as slaves. No one asks for poverty. Each must do their best with what they are given. Look at Elizabeth Bathory."

"I prefer not."

"She lost power when her husband died. She struggled and fought and did everything she could to hang on to what belonged to her, including summoning you."

"Elizabeth tortures girls for fun," Ruxandra countered. "She bathes in their blood."

"You still made her a vampire."

"She told me she would stop." Ruxandra remembered the day, and how desperately she wanted to take Elizabeth away from the ones threatening her. "She said we would leave everything behind and travel together. She lied."

"I know. So now she is doing the best she can with the gifts you gave her. So is Kade. But Ruxandra, have you nothing in your life more than pretty dresses and opera?"

"It is enough."

"No, it is not." Ishtar's voice turned stern. "I created you for so much more, Ruxandra."

"I send you out instead, my child," the fallen angel said as her blood dripped into Ruxandra's mouth, "to sow chaos and fear, to make humans kneel in terror, and to ravage the world where I cannot."

"I remember what you created me for," Ruxandra said. "I remember it all."

"You exist to end mankind's evil."

"By sowing chaos and fear? I don't think so." Ruxandra's desire to get away from Ishtar grew overwhelming. "Is there anything else?"

"Yes." Ishtar stepped close and kissed her. Ruxandra felt a shock of lust run through her. Ishtar parted Ruxandra's lips with her tongue. Ruxandra's body had responded before her mind regained control. Her arms wrapped around Ishtar's waist, caressing the other woman's backside. Ishtar's hands rose, cupping Ruxandra's breasts. Her breath in Ruxandra's mouth tasted sweet and drove Ruxandra to higher levels of passion. Her knee pushed against Ruxandra's legs, forcing them apart.

NO!

Ruxandra tore her mouth from Ishtar's. She raised her hands to shove her, and then stopped. *I shouldn't push her. It might hurt her.*

Ishtar looked like a cat whose whiskers still dripped cream. She reached up a hand to Ruxandra's face. Ruxandra moved halfway across the room in a single second.

"Did you feel our connection?" Ishtar asked. "Can you not sense how your body longs for me?"

Oh yes. And I don't trust it at all.

"Don't touch me again, *Mother*." Ruxandra put all her disgust in the last word.

"The way you don't touch Kade?" Ishtar countered. "If I am your mother, than you are his grandmother. And yet you lust for him."

"Yes," Ruxandra said. "I lust for him. I don't lust for you."

"Nonsense." Ishtar turned away and walked up to the throne. She ran a hand over the arm, and then sat. With her straight back and bright, piercing stare, she looked far more an empress than Anna. "Blood calls to blood."

"Yours doesn't call me. It *disgusts* me."

"No, it doesn't." Ishtar's self-assured tone set Ruxandra's teeth on edge. "I wish to meet with you every evening, Ruxandra. I wish you to grow past your revulsion and embrace what you are."

"I already have, remember? Kill the predators and those wishing to die. That was your desire." It was so hard to resist her. *What if she is telling the truth? Yes, she is cruel, but perhaps also . . .*

Ishtar laughed, low and gently. "Oh, child, that is only the beginning. Now, I must attend Her Majesty, and you no doubt want to think on what I said. Good night, Ruxandra."

Ruxandra turned away and walked out into the cold late-September night. She breathed deep, pulling frigid air into her lungs. The sky looked ready to drop snow upon the city.

Her body trembled with unspent passion, yearning, and rage.

"Ruxandra."

Kade stood at the bottom of the stairs, leaning against the wall. The angle of his jaw set her quivering, and the strength radiating from him drove straight into her pelvis.

God damn her back to hell.

"Was your meeting with Lady Ishtar satisfactory?" Kade asked.

"No." Ruxandra took the steps two at a time. "Anna finished with you fast enough."

"Apparently there are some in the peasant quarter who are stirring up dissent against her. She wishes me to deal with it." Kade frowned. "You sound . . ."

Ruxandra didn't wait for him to finish. She grabbed his hand, vanished from human notice and ran, dragging him after. They raced across the Kremlin and out the gates. Ruxandra skidded on the stones as she dashed through the enclave. She reached Kade's house, bounced off the wall, and stood there, not in the slightest winded or relaxed.

"Ruxandra?"

Ruxandra kissed him on the mouth. He caught her arms and held her away.

"Ruxandra?"

"I need her out of my head." Ruxandra panted the words. "Now."

She kissed him again, hands running over his body. He pushed her against the wall, his arousal hard against her belly.

Blood calls to blood.

Shut up. Ruxandra fumbled with the buttons on his trousers, freed him, and stroked him. She turned her back and hiked up her skirts.

"Here," Ruxandra gasped. "Now!"

He thrust his flesh into hers, his hips pounding harder than any other man's ever had. She bit her lips to keep from crying out as her legs buckled in pleasure. Kade held her until he groaned and shuddered and spurted inside her.

He stayed erect.

"Inside," Kade said.

He took her on the stairs and in the hallway. In the bedroom Ruxandra went to her knees and brought him to climax again. For most the rest of the night they savaged one another's bodies until both fell back on the bed, satiated.

Maybe this is what I need, another vampire, someone who understands and can keep up with me. To not be lonely. That would be something.

In the dim twilight before dawn, as she drifted in and out of sleep, Ruxandra heard the sounds of battle.

Ruxandra stood up and opened the window. The sounds came clear: screams and cries of pain, the hooves of horses and the clash of steel on steel. She put on her dress, not bothering with underclothes or shoes. When she went back to the window, she saw Alexi leaning against the house across the street. Dark circles surrounded his eyes, and he wore the same clothes as the previous night. Ruxandra jumped, landing in silence despite the twenty-foot drop.

"What's going on?" she asked. "Is the city attacked?"

Alexi shook his head.

"A pogrom," he said. "A message to the city's Jews that their welcome has ended."

CHAPTER

SIXTEEN

"T HE JEWS?"

"The Metropolitan believes that Moscow should be Christian, free from other influences," Alexi said. "Less than two hundred Jews live here, and yet he still considers them a threat."

"Why?"

"*Why* does not matter." Alexi's words came out flat, and his eyes flashed bright with anger. "What matters is that the Metropolitan is happy and will give his support to the one who arranged for this to occur."

"Then those sounds . . ."

"Are some houses being ransacked, some men killed, some girls abused. It sends a message to the Jewish leadership that they have no place here. Not that they have anywhere else to go, of course."

Rage, burning as fast and hot as black powder, filled Ruxandra's chest. "I'm stopping them."

"No, you are not."

"What do you mean . . . ?" Ruxandra looked down. "I can't move my feet."

"I know." Alexi leaned back against the wall. He looked ready to fall down at any moment. "I am so very sorry."

"What did you do?" Ruxandra sniffed the air. Four other men stood nearby.

"This is how the vampire king's minions were defeated. The magicians lured them into traps like this and kept them there until the sun rose and burned them to nothingness."

He sighed, a long, deep, weary sound, and rubbed his face.

"You're exhausted," Ruxandra said. "You can barely stand up."

The smile Alexi put on looked almost ghastly against his pale skin. "I have not slept since the banquet."

"And Anna still told you to trap me? Isn't she worried?"

Alexi shook his head. "She sent me to talk to you. The others trapped you, and they are all quite awake."

In the distance the sounds of swords clashing stopped amid shouts from old women and the cries of terrified children. Young women and girls protested and fought, and then screamed. Men laughed.

"They are raping the girls," Ruxandra said through gritted teeth. *Why can I not stop this?*

Alexi closed his eyes and let his head fall back.

The screams turned to sobs. Only one kept screaming, the sound desperate and despairing, rising and falling. Ruxandra's entire body tensed. She pulled against the forces holding her until she felt her muscles starting to tear apart. Still she could not move.

She kept listening. *If cannot stop them, I will at least bear witness.*

The last girl fell into sobs. The soldiers mounted horses and rode. Children wailed and men cursed and old women spoke soft words to the girls.

"They are leaving," Ruxandra said. "Let me go."

"Do not kill them, and please, do not try to kill Anna."

"Why not?" All the bile and anger built up inside Ruxandra spilled out with the words. She wanted to chase after the soldiers, to rip their throats out, but she could not take a single step. "Why should I let her live?"

"Because you won't succeed," Alexi said. "And if you try you force Ishtar to choose between you and Anna, I fear it will not go well for either you or Russia."

Ruxandra's eyes narrowed. "What about Anna?"

Alexi shrugged. "She is the empress. Unless the nobles rise up, there is no one with the power to defeat her. Give me your word."

"What makes you think I'll keep it?"

"I am an excellent judge of character." He pushed off the wall, swayed a moment, then stood upright, his eyes on Ruxandra. "Your word you will not harm her."

Ruxandra's eyes narrowed. "I give you my word, I will not harm her for this."

"Or any other past incidents, or anything you suspect she *might* do in the future."

But not for anything she actually does *in the future.* "I give my word."

He smiled again, and Ruxandra saw the relief in it. "I would appreciate it if you wouldn't kill me or my men, either."

Ruxandra's mouth quirked up on one side. "I give you the same as I promised for your empress."

"Fair." Alexi raised his hand and turned it in a small circle—a signal to the men Ruxandra couldn't see. A moment later the pressure holding Ruxandra's legs vanished. "They have released you. And now I must go. There is much intrigue in the palace these days, but tonight I have an opportunity to sleep, and I am going to take it. Your Alchemist is still working in your library, though. You should join her."

Alexi walked off, not bothering to turn invisible. Ruxandra smelled his men follow him, their scent draining from the air. She stood alone in the street thinking of what Alexi had said. Then she leaped, landing on the window ledge. Kade lay in the bed, awake, his eyes on her.

"I heard it all," he said.

"I need to change." Ruxandra headed for the hallway. "I'm going to the library."

To find a way to send Ishtar back and stop this nonsense.

Ruxandra found a plain dark-gray dress among the clothes Alexi had given her. It was out of style, with room for neither a bustle nor hoops, but it left her body free to move in a way the newer fashions did not. She dressed and went out into the street.

Ishtar stood at the city gates.

The sight of the other woman made Ruxandra tense. *No, not a woman, a devil.*

"Hello, dear one," Ishtar said. She stepped forward and opened her arms for an embrace. Ruxandra stopped walking. Ishtar waited a moment and let her arms drop. "It is good to see you, my daughter."

Ruxandra kept her voice cold. "What do you want?"

"You, by my side." Ishtar made the words sound completely reasonable. "I would heal this rift between us, Ruxandra."

"Did you tell Anna to attack the Jews?"

"Of course not." Ishtar's tone made it clear the question was both ridiculous and beneath her. "I merely told her that the Jews' removal was something dear to the Metropolitan's heart. She chose the course of action and sent word. The Metropolitan received it joyfully and promised his priests will praise the empress in their next sermons."

"Men died."

"If they lived good lives, they will go to heaven. God only rejects evil. He cares nothing about religion."

"Perhaps you should tell the Metropolitan that. You could spend your human life reducing religious strife."

"Men believe what they want to believe, and peace is not something they want."

"Then what use are you?"

"I didn't say peace could not be achieved."

"Girls were *raped*."

Ishtar shrugged. "They are not the first in the world; they won't be the last."

Ruxandra's talons and teeth came out. "How can you be so callous?"

"It is the truth." Ishtar looked at Ruxandra's fingers and the razor-edged talons coming from them. "Being angry about it won't change it."

Ruxandra tried to raise her talons, to slash Ishtar's head from her shoulders. Instead her hands clenched, talons digging into her own flesh. *I don't want to hurt her.*

Why don't I?

"You need not worry about them," Ishtar said. "Humans exist on this plane a short time, then go to heaven or hell according to their virtues. They are not lost, just removed."

"They are lost to their families." Ruxandra ground out the words between teeth clenched as much from anger as from the pain in her shoulder. "They are lost to their lovers and their friends."

"So are all the ones you killed."

Ruxandra glared, furious and unable to reply.

"The deaths of those Jews are necessary for Russia's survival. *Anna* is necessary for Russia's survival." Ishtar's tone stayed calm, her voice quiet, but her words pierced Ruxandra like knives. "You would do well to remember that far more is at stake here than what Ruxandra does not like. You are a killer just like Anna; she just uses others as her weapon."

I do not torture. I do not hurt people for fun. I am not a devil.

Unlike you. "Are you truly human?"

"I am." Ishtar looked at her body, now in a splendid blue dress. "I will admit that I took great vanity in my appearance. I gave myself the best possible attributes, but this body is still human, with human limitations."

"Good." Ruxandra went unnoticed and walked away.

"Ruxandra!" Ishtar sounded like the nuns when they'd caught Ruxandra misbehaving. "Come back here at once!"

Ruxandra kept walking.

"You are being childish!" Ishtar switched to Romanian and added a few choice phrases about naughty children. Ruxandra stopped around the corner and waited. Ishtar stood by the gate, squinting as she looked around as if that would break through Ruxandra's illusion.

Her boots rang hard off the cobbles as she stomped deeper into the enclave.

Not to the Kremlin?

Ruxandra slipped off her shoes and followed. Ishtar took several streets, changing directions five times and twice doubling back. Ruxandra stayed two blocks back, always unnoticed, always silent. Ishtar may have given her human body the best possible hearing, but Ruxandra moved quietly enough to catch mountain cats sleeping.

After a few more twists and turns, Ishtar knocked on the door of a house Ruxandra didn't recognize. She waited and, when a servant opened the door, said, "Tell him I've arrived."

The servant closed the door. Ruxandra watched, her curiosity piqued, until the door opened again.

"My lady," said Prince Delfino, extending his small, plump hand. "I am so pleased you came."

Ishtar took it, and the two stepped inside the house together.

Now that is interesting.

She listened as Delfino led Ishtar upstairs. She heard Ishtar say, "Such a rush" and Delfino's gasped, "Yes." They kissed. Delfino pushed Ishtar against a wall. More kissing and a groan from Delfino. A door opened, and Delfino whispered, "Bend over the bed."

Ruxandra leaned against the wall and listened. Delfino performed with a young man's stamina and recovery time. Ruxandra spent the next two hours learning far more about his preferences than she'd ever wanted. He and Ishtar spoke fewer than twenty words the entire time, and most of those they shouted in passion.

Ruxandra suspected Ishtar's acting skills were far better than Delfino's lovemaking. The little, round man with the oily smile and the acrid body odor overlaid with heavy cologne was no one's idea of desirable, she thought sourly. If he didn't have *prince* in front of his name, he likely would have no lovers at all.

Ishtar left at midnight with messy, unbound hair and disheveled clothing. She walked with a slow, swaying step and winced whenever she jolted her feet on the cobblestones. She walked to the gates of the Kremlin, gave the password, and slipped inside.

What exactly is she after? She could have any man in the city and quite a few of the women . . .

Why Delfino? Why the conspirator who had Princess Khilkoff on his arm? She turned her back on the Kremlin and headed for the library. *I'll tell Kade when I see him. He can find out what's going on with them.*

Fifteen minutes later she slipped into the library.

The library was silent and empty, save for the Alchemist. She sat at the big table surrounded by papers with geometric diagrams, open scrolls, clay tablets, and books. Ruxandra slipped up behind her and watched as the Alchemist consulted a page of strange symbols beside Cyrillic translations. She hummed as she made notes.

"What is that for?" Ruxandra asked, making the Alchemist jump out of her chair and spin around in surprise.

"Ruxandra?" The Alchemist's eyes darted back and forth. "Where are you?"

"In front of you." Ruxandra became noticeable. "What are the inscriptions?"

"Amazing." The Alchemist huffed out a breath. "You scared me witless."

She moved the papers and scrolls, clearing the top of a large sheet of vellum. The symbols stretched the length of the page, circles, triangles and lines interconnecting, surrounded by script Ruxandra could not read.

"This," the Alchemist said, "is the basic formula for turning lead into gold. Unfortunately, it is in ancient Sumerian."

"And that?" Ruxandra pointed at the translation sheet.

The Alchemist smiled. "A gift from Lady Ishtar for bringing her to this plane of existence: a list of Sumerian words and their Russian translations. With it I can determine the formula. Then I can re-create it."

"She gave it to you?"

"Yes."

Buying your loyalty if it works, or at least keeping you distracted.

The Alchemist leaned back against the table. "She loves you, you know."

"She says she loves me."

The Alchemist tilted her head and frowned. "Why don't you believe her?"

"Because you don't turn someone you care about into a monster."

"Unless you are a monster yourself," the Alchemist said. "Then it is the highest possible compliment."

Ruxandra stared, surprised.

"She may not have loved you in the beginning," the Alchemist continued. "She didn't know you. She only knew you were being abused. And since using her powers causes God to force her back down to hell, she gave you the power to take care of yourself."

"By having me kill my own father."

"She tried to fight God." The Alchemist's voice was gentle. "She no doubt saw your father's death as a reasonable course of action."

Just like the Jews.

"No monster is monstrous in their own mind, Ruxandra. Not Ishtar, not Anna." She smiled. "Not you."

Ruxandra knew the Alchemist was right. She didn't think of herself as a monster—well, most of the time she didn't. She did what she did to survive, not out of malice. *So does Kade.*

Elizabeth doesn't. She does it for fun.

Does Anna?

Does Ishtar?

I cannot hope to understand Ishtar. She is an angel. If it were possible to know . . . For a long moment, Ruxandra imagined an Ishtar whose cruelty was born only from necessity, who also could love her creations; then she shook her head. This was not about Ishtar and her. It was about the innocent.

"What Ishtar may think of herself is not what I came here to talk about."

"Then why are you here?"

"I can't hit her."

"What?"

"Ishtar," Ruxandra said. "I can't hit her."

The Alchemist's eyebrows went up. "Why did you want to hit her?"

"Because she told Anna the Metropolitan wanted the Jews out of the city. So Anna sent her men to attack them and rape the girls."

"I did not know." The Alchemist's her voice caught on the words, and she looked away.

"Ishtar should not have suggested it," Ruxandra said. "When I went to rip her throat out, I couldn't."

The Alchemist shrugged. "Maybe you care more about her than you think, Ruxandra. Killing is not easy."

"I have done it enough times before."

"Yes. But this the one who made you."

"It's not permanent for her."

"Even so. Don't you want to know her? Talk to her?" The Alchemist peered at her, looking like a great beaky bird, so intelligent, so kind—how could she understand what monsters were truly capable of? She'd been beaten, yes, and seen her friends beaten, but she had not seen what Ruxandra had.

"She will not stop unless I stop her. Whatever I may feel is irrelevant. And I do not believe for a moment that I am stopping myself."

The Alchemist rubbed her chin as she thought about it. "Magic?"

"Didn't feel like it." Ruxandra looked at her hand, remembering the sensation. "It was different from when Alexi's men stopped me. With him I couldn't move. With her . . . I didn't want to move. It felt wrong to attack."

"And you are sure . . . ?"

"Yes. Have you heard of it happening before?"

The Alchemist chuckled. "My princess, there is no precedent for any of this."

Ruxandra nodded. "Is Kurkov here?"

"Asleep in one of the bedrooms." The Alchemist pointed to the balcony. "Up there, in the back, follow the long hallway. I doubt he can explain it, though."

"I know," Ruxandra said. "But perhaps he'll know where to look."

It turned out he didn't.

For six hours they combed through the books. Ruxandra told him everything that had happened. Like the Alchemist, Kurkov had not heard of such a thing before. She searched the books and scrolls in the languages she knew and found no reference. He put a pile of materials together in the languages that she didn't know, promising to have the others look over it. "But my dear, the world is full of mysteries. I have been investigating them my whole life, and the more I learn, the more I realize how much there is to learn. I don't believe anyone knows much about these creatures, the fallen angels, or ever has known. This is why we wished to hear from her, after all."

"She's not going to tell me. I have to figure it out myself."

"As you wish."

Ruxandra stopped by Kade's table on her way out. Six books lay on top of it in a tidy stack. She opened the one on top. The lines and whorls that covered the page looked like nothing Ruxandra had seen before.

The books in the vampire language. There might be something there. But Kade said it took a long time to translate the little bit he knows. I can't wait.

Ruxandra glared at the books as if that would bring another solution. Much to her dismay, it did.

Ishtar would understand it.

SEVENTEEN

I T WAS NOT A happy thought. The idea of asking Ishtar for
help to read the vampire books made gall rise and stick in her
throat, oozing bitterness and anger. She was certain Ishtar
would guess why she wanted to know, and then either refuse in
order to protect herself or demand concessions. *What does she
want from me? For me to play the adoring daughter? I can't.*

But if Kade could not translate the works, there was no one else.
If. It's an if. *I will talk to Kade first.*

She sighed, left the church, and walked back to Kade's house.
He wasn't home, which surprised her. Ruxandra climbed the stairs
to her room. She sat in the chair and stared at the small fire, letting
her body relax. She could stay still for days if need be. That said,
she was in no mood for it. Too many thoughts ran through her
brain, beginning with how to extricate Anna and the country
from Ishtar's clutches. That made her wonder how Ishtar had
seduced Delfino so fast, which led her to remember Ishtar's kiss.

Which led to her stripping off her clothes and going to Kade's
bedroom.

He slipped in an hour after sunrise, wrapped in a heavy cloak. He stopped at the door, mouth half-open in surprise. Ruxandra lay naked on her stomach, legs parted just enough to let him see. She looked over her shoulder and smiled.

For the next few hours, they spoke few words, which was comforting in its own way.

"That was not what I was expecting." Kade propped his head up on his hand. "Not that I'm complaining."

"Good." Ruxandra closed her eyes, savoring the last of the ache between her thighs. "Because I needed that."

"As you did yesterday," Kade said. "Same reason?"

"Yes." Ruxandra sighed. "She gets in my mind and then . . ."

"You need to drive her out." Kade touched her face, ran his hand down her neck to rest on her breast. "Glad to help."

"I had noticed." Ruxandra put her hand on him. "I'm noticing it again."

Someone knocked on the front door.

Dammit.

Kade sighed. "Much as I wish to leave that for the servants, no one calls on this house without a reason."

Kade rolled out of bed and to his feet. Ruxandra reached out with her mind. A second later she threw the covers off and ran from the room.

"Ruxandra?" Kade's voice sounded both concerned and amused.

"There is no way I am talking to her naked," she called over her shoulder. "Keep her busy."

She poured water into her basin and washed from face to feet in a moment. It took another moment to put on clean underclothes and the gray dress, a third to braid her hair. She thought about shoes and stockings, but knew they would take too long. Ruxandra looked in the mirror.

Almost respectable, she decided. *Not quite, but close enough. Which will have to do.*

She walked down to the parlor.

"Ruxandra, darling." Ishtar sat on the couch, a smile on her face. "How are you, my daughter?"

"I am not your daughter." The response was automatic, the pain profound. Ishtar, in this incarnation, *did* look like her mother, though without the soft brown eyes and aura of kindness Ruxandra remembered.

"You are, like it or not," Ishtar said. "And I am glad to see you, though I have to admit Kade is the one I came to visit today."

"And you have." Kade stepped out from the dining room. "Nika will bring tea."

"Wonderful. Thank you."

"You're serving her tea?" Ruxandra put exactly how she felt into her voice.

"She is a guest."

"She's a devil."

"Manners, Ruxandra," Ishtar said. "I thought those years in Venetian society would have taught you better than this."

"I'm not the problem here," Ruxandra muttered. "Kade, send her away."

Kade took a seat in a large upholstered chair. "I am afraid not."

"Why not?"

"Because I want to hear what Ishtar has to say." Kade kept his tone polite, but his expression said, *Stop this.*

Ruxandra growled under her breath and leaned against the door. She might not be able to drive Ishtar out, but she would not sit in the room with her. Ishtar's left eyebrow rose. She sighed and turned to Kade.

"You asked me for your purpose on this earth," she said. "Do you still wish to know?"

Kade sat up straight, any pretense of calm vanishing. "Please."

"To do that, I need to go back a great deal in time," Ishtar said. "To the first days of human society."

She sat on the couch. Her lips pursed and her forehead wrinkled as she thought. Then she nodded—to herself, not them—and began.

"In the beginning God created Man and Woman. I'm sure you're familiar with this?"

"I am," Kade said.

"Well, it is true, though the actual process of their creation took much longer than that, and woman was not derived from Adam's rib. At one time many types of humanoids roamed the world. But the humans won out. And that's when the problems began."

"Problems?" Kade frowned. "You mean the expulsion from the garden?"

Ishtar shook her head. "The Garden of Eden is a metaphor for humanity's fall from grace. Humans had to be vicious to survive. But when they defeated the others, that viciousness did not die. Instead humanity turned it upon themselves. Look what happened here yesterday."

"What happened here yesterday," Ruxandra said, "was your fault."

"I did *not* tell Anna to drive out the Jews." Irritation, bordering on anger, tinted Ishtar's words. "She asked me what the Metropolitan desired. I told her he hated the Jews and wanted them out. I also told her of his desire to see more cathedrals rise and to feed the poor. She picked the cheapest alternative instead of the best. It is part of the shortsightedness humans exhibit and why I created *you.*"

And if you know humans behave that way, why mention the Jews at all?

Before Ruxandra could say the words, Ishtar turned away from her and looked at Kade with her gold-flecked blue eyes. "I wanted Ruxandra, and the others I had hoped she would create, to help bring humanity to its true self."

"By having us murder them?" Ruxandra scoffed. "How does that make them better?"

"It instills fear in them," Ishtar said. "It makes them cling to one another instead of murdering each other."

"A common enemy, then?" Kade sat back in his chair.

"More than that." Ishtar's eyes brightened. "An arbiter. One who stands outside humanity and sees their faults and misbehaviors and eliminates the worst offenders from the Earth. Ruxandra has begun, but only on a small scale. She kills the criminals: the rapists, the murderers, the ones who harm children. But you, Kade, work on the larger stage, and you can make a difference in a much greater way, if you choose."

Realization lit up Kade's face. "Politics."

"Exactly," Ishtar said. "Politics. Russia is huge but not yet a great power. With proper direction it can become something far stronger and perhaps lead the world out of humanity's darkness. And you can be key to that."

She looked at Ruxandra. "Both of you, if you wish."

Ruxandra glanced at Kade and saw the hunger on his face. *He wants this. He wants to be a great man, though he is not a man at all. And Ishtar beaming at him like a wise old grandmother, young as she looks, like an angel indeed. The bitch.*

"Who has to die?" Ruxandra asked. "Anna? Or maybe Delfino?"

"Enough, Ruxandra!" Ishtar rose to her feet and glared. "You are so determined to think the worst of me! So desperate to prove that I am the evil one here! I am not! I stayed here to help you, to help Kade, and to guide Russia toward something better. What will it take for you to believe?"

Ishtar's presence blazed in the room like an inferno. Ruxandra felt a sudden urge to apologize, to beg forgiveness. The part of her that was once a small girl in a convent found the old awe of God and his angels coming back to her, the old words forming in her head. *Once I was a vessel for what they taught me. A child, trustful, faithful.*

Not anymore.

She pushed the feeling away and glared back.

Kade rose and stood between them, facing Ishtar. "My lady, please. Given the first hundred years of Ruxandra's existence—"

"Do *not* make excuses for me!" Ruxandra stepped around him. "You didn't answer my question."

"Yes, people will die." Ishtar's voice sounded regretful. "And since you both kill humans to live, *and since people die every day anyway,* why not kill those that make things worse? If you listen, you could save thousands." Her voice was infused with a rare charisma.

"I don't *trust* you."

"My darling—"

"I AM NOT YOUR DARLING!"

Ishtar's face closed. "Then go somewhere else. Now."

Ruxandra glared back. She turned and walked out.

Why am I backing down from her? What is the matter with me?

She reached the top of the stairs, went into her room, and closed the door slowly and deliberately instead of slamming it the way she wished. She sat in the chair and glared at the curtains.

If it were night, I could get out of here. I could go to the library and figure out what's happening.

But not without Kade's help with the books.

Kade's or Ishtar's.

Ruxandra growled. Her talons came out. For a moment she considered shredding the upholstered arms of the chair, just to destroy something.

Instead she closed her eyes and listened.

"It is not possible," Kade was saying. "Not at this hour."

"Of course it is," Ishtar said. "You have a great cloak, do you not? My carriage is waiting."

"I do not see why we cannot discuss this here."

"Because Ruxandra is most likely listening and will no doubt come storming in, ready to argue every point I make. She is not ready to hear what I have to tell you. So be it. I can wait. You and I will talk somewhere else. I have excellent chambers in Terem Palace, and it will give you a chance to be seen in court, which is not a bad thing at all."

"This is true. A moment, please."

Ruxandra heard Kade's boots on the stairs. She pulled her door open and waited for him to come into sight.

"You're going with her?"

Kade nodded.

"Why?"

"Because she knows everything." Kade kept walking.

Ruxandra followed him to his room. He picked the great cloak up off the floor and swaddled his body in it.

"Why do you trust her?" Ruxandra demanded. "*How* can you trust her?"

Kade sighed. In vampire tones, he asked, "How much of a fool do you think I am, Ruxandra?"

Ruxandra opened her mouth, thought better of her answer, and closed it.

"I spent a hundred fifty years playing this game," Kade said. "I did it with the Inquisition. I did it at Elizabeth's court. I have done it in a dozen other countries, and I did it for Emperor Peter here. Ishtar is after something. Refusing to listen to her will not help me find out what."

He turned to leave. Ruxandra caught his arm.

"She fucked Delfino," she said. "Last night."

"Delfino?" Kade shook his head in disgust. "She is an angel. Why that little toad?"

"I don't know. I don't know how she met him. He was at the party, but . . ."

"I will find out." Kade pulled the cloak tight around him. "I will find out everything. I promise."

He kissed her and headed downstairs. Ruxandra listened as the door closed and he and Ishtar drove off in her carriage. Then she sat in her chair and waited for the night to come.

She left the house two hours after the sun had set. Kade had not returned. Ruxandra wore the gray dress to blend in with the shadows and walked to the gates of the Kremlin. The big doors were shut tight, the wall above lit with torches. The men on watch whistled as she came into sight.

"Hey, beautiful girl!" one shouted. "I get off duty at dawn! Visit me!"

"Why wait?" Ruxandra called. *"Come see me now."*

"Yes!" The man ran into the gatehouse, desperate to obey her command. Inside, someone demanded to know what in hell he was doing.

"The rest of you!" Ruxandra raised her voice to make certain they heard. *"Let him!"*

Moments later the small door built into the gates opened and a soldier came out. Ruxandra smiled at him. "Very good. *Now, guide me inside.*"

"This way, my lady." He stepped through the door and held out his hand. She reached for it and a force she couldn't see knocked her back twenty feet.

"My lady!" The young soldier looked stricken. "Are you all right?"

Ruxandra sat up, wincing. "Fine."

"I'll help you up!"

"Don't!" Ruxandra glared at the gate. *"Go back to your posts. And forget I was here."*

She walked away from the Kremlin, turned a corner, and went unnoticed. Ten minutes later she was at the library. The place looked empty. She expanded her mind and found the Alchemist, Kurkov, Eduard, and several others asleep in the back rooms. She was tempted to wake them just for the company—*Was it really only a few days ago we were chatting and joking?*—but she had no time for that. She left them and the library, taking the hall to the armory.

At the bottom of the stairs, an invisible force sent her sprawling.

Ruxandra lay on the cold stone floor, staring up at the arched ceiling above her. She couldn't decide whether to scream in frustration or pound her fists against the walls, so she did neither.

Human magic put in place to keep me from getting into the Kremlin.

Just me or all vampires?

If all of us, how did Ishtar get Kade inside? Is there a magic word to turn it off? Do the spells not work during the day?

She rose, dusted off her dress, and made her way back to the library.

I wonder if it was Anna, Alexi, or Ishtar who thought of it.

Ishtar had to have known it when she invited Kade to the palace. If so, she knew I wouldn't be able to follow. That means she wants to keep him separate from me.

What is she going to tell him that she won't tell me?

Ruxandra walked back to the library, found Kade's desk, and sat down. He'd written ten pages of notes in English, which was not a language she spoke and which did not help. She opened the books, stared at them, and then shut them with a growl.

This is useless. Without Kade I don't know where to start. I may as well slam my face against the desk and hope that will bring me the answers.

Ruxandra *hated* being helpless. First Anna's magicians, thwarting every move she wanted to make, and now this.

I wish I were back in Italy. I wish I didn't feel responsible, as if I had made her rather than the other way around.

Ruxandra wandered the library, looking at the massive murals on the walls. She wondered about the vampire king. Did he deal with the same nonsense among his courtiers that Anna had? Did he ever have dealings with Ishtar after she turned him?

The Alchemist might know. Or Kurkov.

Ruxandra walked up the stairs and followed the long hallway on the second floor. She had not seen the bedrooms before. The first three stood wide open and empty. The magicians' pallets and blankets were in stark contrast to the opulence of the rooms. Murals covered the walls: forests and mountains and beaches, images of pyramids and strange fortresses, all under the night sky.

The Alchemist slept on the floor in the fourth room. She had dragged the blankets and the pillow into the corner. She huddled in a ball, trembling in her sleep. She muttered and gasped, and though Ruxandra could not make out the words, she recognized the desperation in her tone. As Ruxandra approached, the Alchemist yelped and put her arms over her head, then her breasts. She went still, her body stiff. Her hands dropped, cupping her groin, and she rocked back and forth, weeping.

Ruxandra wanted to wake her and ask who had done this but was afraid of her own anger. She could not attack anyone here. The magicians would bind her; Anna would order her killed . . . Ruxandra left the library, heading for the worst part of the city. It was not yet midnight, and many people roamed the streets, chatting and laughing or arguing and fighting. Three times she had to step around street brawls. Several men whistled and shouted at her. She ignored them.

She found what she wanted in an alley behind a kabak. Fifteen men stood in a circle, cheering as one, bigger than the rest, pulled a woman to her feet. Blood covered her face. Her head lolled on her shoulders. Still she had her arms up, swinging feebly at the man.

"Now, when they get to this stage," the big man said to the laughing crowd, "you don't want them facing you. They're too ugly. So it's best to turn them around."

He caught the woman's shoulder, spun her, and pulled her into an embrace. The drunken men cheered.

"It is best to break their spirit first." He hauled up her skirt. "So take her the back way—"

"*Shut up,*" Ruxandra commanded. She pointed at the big man. "*Everyone go home except him.*"

The crowd dispersed without another word. The woman, semiconscious, struggled to leave, but the big man held her fast.

The big man's grip switched to the girl's neck. "Fuck off or I'll fuck you next."

"*Release her.*"

His hand opened. The woman stumbled, fell, and crawled away.

He stared at his hands, incredulous. "What did you do?"

"Cleared some space."

"Space for what?" The man spat the words. "Space for your blood to splatter when I beat you? Space to spread you when I've done that? What are you doing here, you bitch?"

"Ending you."

The big man's face turned red. He drew a long knife from his belt and crouched. Ruxandra's mouth pulled up into snarl, showing her fangs.

No one came to help when he screamed.

Ruxandra walked out of the alley soon after, wiping her mouth on the remains of his shirt. Behind her the man lay still, his arms and legs bent at the wrong angles, his rib cage a lumpy, broken mess, and his eyes staring up at the sky.

Killing off evil just as Ishtar wanted me to do.

She snarled at the thought, startling a drunk lying on the street. Ruxandra glared at him and turned unnoticed. She stalked through the city, heading for the enclave and Kade's house.

It is not what Ishtar wants. It's what she said she wanted. I don't believe her. Anyway, I had to eat.

She sat in the parlor, waiting for Kade to return. He arrived two hours after dawn, his body swaddled in his great cloak to keep the sun from touching his skin. He saw her the moment he stepped inside.

"I didn't expect you to wait up for me," Kade said.

"I didn't expect you to be gone so long." Ruxandra stood. "Were you with her the entire time?"

"No. I visited Sahsa, Victor and Dimitri before I returned." He sighed. "Their bodies are recovering from their beating, but I fear their spirits are damaged as well. They are . . . not the men I knew before, though I suspect they can become so again."

"I am sorry." She knew she should say more, but her mind was fixed on one thing. "What did you learn from Ishtar?"

"A great amount." Kade sat on the couch. "But one thing more than anything else."

"Which is?"

"You need to trust her."

EIGHTEEN

RUXANDRA SHOOK HER head. "Kade, I'm not—"

"*Listen!*" Urgency filled Kade's voice. His eyes drilled into her with the intensity of his feelings. "I know you don't trust her. I know you don't believe her, but I need you to change your mind on this."

"Why?" Ruxandra asked. "Why should I?"

"Because she is *right!*" Kade put his hand on hers, wrapping her fingers tight in his. "I listened to her, and I believed her. She laid out her plans and they make good sense."

"So we . . . what? Become the saviors of humanity?"

"Humanity doesn't listen to saviors. They fight about them instead." Kade leaned closer. "We will work behind humanity, guide them, and help create a better world."

Ruxandra looked away. Kade let go of her hand and sat back on the couch. He watched her for a time. Then he sighed and stood. He paced the room. Ruxandra still didn't look at him.

"Do you know what was hardest about being with Eliza beth?" Kade asked.

Ruxandra stared at the floor. "Watching her murder children?"

"No. The purposelessness of it. Days wandering through the world, robbing people to survive, killing for the fun of it, without purpose or meaning to her actions. She thinks of nothing beyond her own immediate needs, and Dorotyas reinforces her behavior. She delights in the torture of men the way Elizabeth delights in torturing girls. It is so . . . pointless."

He fell silent. Ruxandra risked a look. Kade stared out the window. The buildings' shadows covered the street, sparing him from the sunlight.

"What would it take to make you trust her?" Before Ruxandra could open her mouth to reply, Kade added, "Don't say, 'Nothing.' Think on it. Ponder it, and when you know your answer, go to her and tell her what you need. She *will* listen."

Ruxandra reached out with her mind, searching Kade's emotions for signs that he lied. All she felt was blazing enthusiasm.

"She said she would do whatever it takes to make you trust her." Kade's passion spilled out with his words. "She wants you to help her. So take advantage of that. Go to her, tell her what you need, and she will help you."

But I don't want to . . . The thought felt like the plaintive cry of a tired child to Ruxandra. She did not want to face Ishtar, did not want to admit that she might be wrong about the angel.

"I know how hard it is to trust her after what she did to you," Kade said. "And that it will be harder still to change your mind. I know this. For me, *please* do this."

Kade took off his great cloak and held it out.

"Under this, the sunlight cannot hurt you," he said. "Go to her right now. It will show her you are serious. Sit with her and speak with her. You will realize that what she offers is the best chance to give purpose to our existence."

Ruxandra's spirit rebelled against the idea. Everything in her screamed *NO*.

"What if I don't need someone to give me purpose? What if I'm fine with making my own?"

"What's your purpose, Ruxandra?" he asked softly.

She shrugged. It wasn't something she had words for. Living her own life, doing harm only to those who deserved it; it seemed like enough to her . . .

But the look on Kade's face—earnest and filled with *purpose*—made Ruxandra reach for it. She stood and wrapped the cloak around her.

"All right," she said. "I will talk to her. But I am not making any promises."

Kade walked Ruxandra to the door, kissed her lightly on the lips.

"That is all I ask," he said. "She is in the Kremlin."

Ruxandra opened the door. Even with shade, the sun felt too bright. The light reflecting off the buildings was nearly blinding, and every color felt too intense to look upon. Still, she wrapped the cloak tight around her, pulled the hood over her head, and stepped out into the street.

He had better be right.

The walk to the Kremlin gates took only moments. They stood wide open. Guards, posted on either side, watched everyone coming in or out. Ruxandra went unnoticed and strode between them.

The same force that sent Ruxandra flying before sent her flying again. She hit the ground rolling and swearing. Sunlight hit her face for the briefest of moments, making it blister.

Stupid human magic.

She stood away from the wall, hissing in pain until the blisters went down. Then she turned noticeable and walked up to the guards. "Is there someone who acts as messenger at your post?"

"Nico," said one. "But the messengers are for military business."

"Fetch him," Ruxandra commanded. *"Now."*

Nico—a stripling of fourteen—came running. She commanded him and watched him run off through the gate, envious of how easily he passed. Ruxandra found a patch of shadow and stood in it.

The guards' breath turned to clouds of white steam as they left the men's mouths. The people walking by looked grim, as if they could better face the winter by being angry at it. And even though they were all cool, Ruxandra was overheating. Even in the shade, she could feel the sun, like an iron fresh out of the forge coming too close to her flesh.

Hopefully it won't take so long that I must move to stay out of the sun.

Half an hour later, Alexi strode through the gate. Ruxandra growled under her breath in frustration.

"Princess Ruxandra." He bowed. "I am surprised to see you this time of day."

"I'm surprised to see you at all," Ruxandra said.

Alexi offered her his arm. "Ishtar asked that I escort you to the library."

"Fine." She let him trap her arm in his and walked with him. To her surprise they walked away from the gates, toward the outer city. "Would not the armory be a faster way to get there?"

Alexi rubbed his cheek and looked away. Ruxandra watched his discomfort and waited.

Finally he shrugged and said, "It is not possible for you to enter the Kremlin right now. Nor in the near future, I suspect."

"Why?"

"Because Anna wanted it warded against you."

"It was already warded."

"Against vampires," Alexi said. "This is specifically against you."

"Oh." Ruxandra frowned. "Why?"

"In the course of the . . . persuasion . . . that Anna used on the magicians, it came to her attention you issued threats against their lives and hers. And while she was willing to overlook it at first, your continued resistance against Anna made her suspicious of you and your intentions."

"I guess I shouldn't have told you I would kill her."

"Probably not." Alexi smiled. "I am in Anna's service, after all."

"And you obey even when you don't agree with her?"

"We seldom agree with everything our rulers ask of us. Sometimes we must trust it is for the best."

They reached the gates to the outer city. Alexi nodded at the guards and led Ruxandra across the bridge. The water looked gray and cold, though the sun sparkled off the surface. The ground felt hard under her boots, the frost from the night still buried within the dirt. Alexi walked on, matching his pace to Ruxandra's.

She was not used to seeing the streets so busy, the colors so bright. She squinted against the sunlight. People looked happy, talking cheerfully as they went about their day. Children played near a small school, others worked beside their parents. Men and women laughed and touched and chatted and argued with one another.

"What if it isn't?" Ruxandra asked, looking at the crowd. "What if what your ruler wants causes nothing but misery for everyone? What then? Do you still obey?"

"Yes," Alexi said without hesitation. "That is duty. Sometimes it is unpleasant—"

"Like when you ordered the Alchemist to be raped?"

"What?" Alexi stopped. "What happened?"

"The Alchemist was raped," Ruxandra said. "Did your men do it?"

"No." Alexi's jaw clenched. "My people do not use such methods. Nor do Anna's torturers. At least I thought not."

"Then who did it?"

"Any of Anna's soldiers, if she ordered them. They act like dogs in heat."

The sounds of the pogrom replayed in Ruxandra's mind.

"Why do you want to speak with Ishtar?" Alexi asked.

I don't. "Kade says I should talk to her, to better understand the good she is doing."

Alexi fell silent. Ruxandra's head ached from the sunlight. She looked at the ground and tried not to think about it.

"Ishtar has free run of the city," Alexi said as they rounded a corner. "She goes where she wills, when she wills, at whatever hours she wills. My men follow her, but she eludes them every time. Do you know where?"

To fuck Delfino? "Not all the places."

"How did you follow her?" Alexi tilted his head, examining her like some strange creature.

"A hundred years in the forest," Ruxandra said. "I can track anyone."

"Could you follow her again?"

"Only at night."

"The times you followed her, where did she go?"

Ruxandra shook her head. "Let me talk to Ishtar first. Then I'll answer your questions."

"Tomorrow night, perhaps?"

"Perhaps. I don't know."

"Well." Alexi's tone changed, curiosity and worry filling it in equal measure. "That is unusual."

The church stood a block ahead of them. Four soldiers formed a line across the top step, muskets in their hands. Each looked worried and scared.

Peasants surrounded the building.

Poverty marked them as surely as though they had been branded. They wore thick coats and trousers made from rough wool. Lines from harsh years of hard work with too little to eat marked their faces. A man in front shouted at the guards.

"Let us in!" he demanded. "We want to see what is going on inside!"

"Calm down, Bogden," said one guard. "It's not a church anymore. Nobody goes in without the empress's permission."

"Why not?" Bogden raised his voice. "What are you hiding in there?"

"Nothing!"

"Then let us in!"

"Get the empress's permission!"

The people booed and jeered at that.

"This is not good," Alexi said. "I suggested to Anna we should keep the church operating as always. The Metropolitan and his people kept its secrets for hundreds of years. But Anna wanted no one inside when the magicians worked."

Ruxandra looked over the crowd. "Do I need to disperse them?"

"Can you?" Alexi's eyebrows rose. "Without hurting them, I mean."

"Yes." Ruxandra raised her voice and commanded, *"Everyone not on guard, go about your business and leave the church alone. Go now!"*

The people dispersed. Alexi watched. "Useful talent. Does it work on anyone?"

"Anyone not protected from it," Ruxandra said. "Take off your protections and I'll show you."

For the first time that day, Alexi laughed. "Oh, my dear princess. I shall miss you when you leave Moscow."

Ruxandra frowned. "Am I leaving?"

"I expect so, soon." Alexi released her arm and bowed to her. "Allow me to get you in. Then I must return."

He spoke to the guards and left. Ruxandra walked inside, found the stairs, and headed down.

Was he trying to tell me something? Is he warning me?

The steps felt longer than before, as if with every step Ruxandra went deeper into a pit from which she could not return.

She stepped into the library and found it buzzing.

Kurkov and Eduard stood over a large table, arguing over a text. The Alchemist had cleared a space on the floor and was writing on the marble with chalk. Derek and Michael stood above her, pointing at the symbols and talking excitedly. The librarians moved in and out of the stacks, carrying lists of books and scrolls and tablets.

In the middle of it, sitting like a queen in the large chair at the head of one table, was Ishtar.

She wore a dress in a deep forest green, embroidered with gold thread and putting her cleavage on fine display. A young woman beside her poured tea from a small teapot into an exquisitely crafted cup. A plate of grilled meat and cheese lay beside it. She picked up a slice and ate it, her eyes closed as she relished the taste.

She opened them, fixed them on Ruxandra.

"My daughter." Her voice held neither eagerness nor anger. It was aggressively neutral, as if she repressed any emotions for fear of irritating Ruxandra. "What can I do for you?"

Ruxandra looked at the plate of meat, then at the tea—anywhere but at Ishtar.

"Eduard, my dear," Ishtar called. "Fetch me a lantern."

Eduard broke away from his argument with Kurkov at once. "Yes, my lady."

Ishtar stayed in her seat, unmoving, until the man returned and placed the lantern on the table.

"Come with me, Ruxandra." Ishtar rose and took the lantern. "I'll show you something no one else has seen for a thousand years."

She led Ruxandra up the stairs, then down a narrow corridor in the opposite direction from the bedrooms. Ruxandra spotted a pair of rooms with ancient couches and chairs, and boards with game pieces on them she didn't recognize. Ishtar swept past them to a door at the end. She opened it, revealing a small closet, closed it, and opened it again.

Behind the wall, machinery creaked and groaned. The closet's back wall slid away, revealing a set of stairs going up. Ishtar climbed them, and Ruxandra, curiosity piqued, followed.

The space on the other side was small compared to the library, but still larger than any five bedrooms put together. Black marble, streaked through with gray, covered the floor. Deep-blue paint covered the walls. In the middle stood a pair of black semicircular benches facing each other to form a circle. Ishtar walked between them and sat on one. She pointed at the other.

Ruxandra sat on it.

Ishtar held the lantern up. "What always surprises me is how little light it needs."

She put the lamp on the floor and blew it out, plunging them into darkness.

Then the stars came out.

One by one they shone out from the deep-blue ceiling, filling the air with light. It was dim by human standards, but more than enough for Ruxandra. She stared up at them, amazed.

"It took him fifty years," Ishtar said. "They're in the wrong places now. Even the heavens move and change."

"Him?" Ruxandra frowned. "The vampire king?"

"Yes. He liked to create beautiful things."

The stars, so dim to human sight, shone to Ruxandra, outlining Ishtar with light. She looked strong and unearthly, beyond human despite her form.

Which is why she picked this place.

"What do you want from me, Ruxandra?" Ishtar asked. "How can I prove to you that what I told you is true?"

"Why did you fuck Delfino?"

Ishtar blinked in surprise. "A rather crude way of putting it."

"Why?"

"Before I became human, I read the mind of everyone within the Kremlin. Delfino's mind held three things: boredom, lust, and hatred. Boredom with the Princess Khilkoff. Lust for women, unsatisfied that evening because he is with Khilkoff and unable to meet with his usual mistresses or whores. And a hatred for Empress Anna so deep he could think of nothing but how to depose her, even if he had to marry the boring wench Khilkoff. Because Princess Khilkoff, like Delfino, has a tenuous claim to the throne. By marrying, they increase their legitimacy, and that of their heirs."

"So you . . ."

"After I dressed, I found him standing alone on the Terem Palace steps. I took him to a quiet corner, knelt, and convinced him I was a much better person to spend time with than the princess. When I finished, I told him I was an heir, and that together we could claim the throne."

"And he believed you?"

"He is very easy to lead," she said, "provided you grasp the right part."

"And Kade?" Ruxandra asked. "What part are you leading him by?"

"His desire for purpose," Ishtar said. "I created you for a purpose, and he needed to know it."

"That's not what you said."

"What I said to you—"

"I send you out instead, my child, to sow chaos and fear, to make humans kneel in terror, and to ravage the world where I cannot."

Ishtar smiled. "Yes, that is it."

"So how does that work?" Ruxandra demanded. "How can you reduce human violence by terrorizing them?"

"Terror is the strongest force on earth, Ruxandra. It always has been. But terror of humans is short lived; the big man gets old and weak, et cetera. By creating you I can show them that a higher power watches them, judges them. Not a distant higher power like God or the devil, whom they only find in stories and will not meet until it is too late. An immediate power. One that watches and weeds out the evil among them. Then, and only then, when they fear for the results of their actions, will they begin to think of what they do."

"So people are only decent when they think someone is watching them?" Ruxandra shook her head. "I don't believe that."

"I have watched humanity since its inception," Ishtar said, "and I can assure you, it is true."

Ruxandra looked away. The stars on the walls shone bright. The illusion of looking at the firmament was nearly perfect.

But it's still an illusion.

And what Ishtar says? Is it an illusion, too?

Or is it real?

What she is saying is that we—those of us with power—become as gods, judging, condemning, deciding the fate of societies. She felt repugnance at the idea. *But isn't that what I do anyway, on a small scale? Why is it worse her way? Kade's way?*

It all comes down to her motives.

"Ruxandra?" Ishtar's voice was soft, gentle. "Do you understand, Ruxandra?"

"Why couldn't I hit you?" Ruxandra asked. "I wanted to. I really, really wanted to."

Ishtar smiled. "My dear one, none of my children can hurt me, once they've looked on me."

NINETEEN

"WHY?" RUXANDRA ASKED. "Why do that?"

"I am weak, walking in this world." Ishtar gestured to the false sky. "An angel is made of the essence of God. In heaven we are almost indestructible. On earth we cannot be more than human if we wish to stay for any length of time. We can be injured as humans, even killed and sent back to hell. We are vulnerable—especially to a creature of great power."

Ruxandra frowned. "Are you so afraid of me?"

"You are not the first," Ishtar said. "Nor was the vampire king. I learned long ago of the anger creatures can have for their creators. So I made it so none of my children could kill me once they had looked upon me. It gives me the time to explain their purpose and bring them to my side."

Ishtar walked to the door. "The stars will fade soon. Shall we go?"

Ruxandra followed her back to her big table. A pot of tea with two cups sat waiting for them beside the plate of meat and cheese. Ishtar poured the tea and handed one cup to Ruxandra.

Ruxandra cradled hers in her hands, feeling the cup turn from warm to burning as it absorbed the tea's heat. The sweet smells of fruit and herbs filled her nostrils. Her mind whirled, feelings of distrust clashing with a new desire: to believe Ishtar wanted help.

"What else do you need to trust me, Ruxandra?" Ishtar sat in her chair. "What else will it take?"

Ruxandra let her eyes wander instead of answering. The Alchemist, Derek, and Michael still worked on a chalk circle and the many symbols in it. A small ceramic crucible, exquisitely engraved with mathematic symbols, stood in the center of it. From the stacks she could hear Kurkov and Eduard cataloguing more books.

Books.

"Ruxandra?"

"Will you teach me the vampire language?"

"The written one?" Ishtar sat back in the chair. "Of course. Will you help me change the world?"

"I don't know," Ruxandra said. "But I'll listen to you."

Ishtar smiled. "An excellent start."

Four hours later, Ruxandra had a long list of words and phrases. Ishtar had chosen the thickest tome—a history written by the vampire king. She'd used the first ten pages to create a lexicon and explained the grammar the vampire king had created to build his language.

The vampire king wrote meticulously, but not brilliantly. The writing in the tome was small and close spaced and covered every page from top to bottom. In the ten pages they had gone over, Ruxandra had learned five hundred words, most to do with travel, feeding, and the care of horses.

A soldier came, asking Ishtar to accompany him to the palace, where Anna wanted to speak to her.

"We will continue tomorrow," Ishtar said. "I will meet you here, if I can. If not, I will send word and meet you the next night. Is that satisfactory, Ruxandra?"

Ruxandra nodded. She looked the list of words. "Before you go, would you show me how your name is written in the vampire language?"

Ishtar tilted her head, her eyebrows coming together. "My name? Why?"

"You are our creator." Ruxandra smiled. "I'd want to know what he had to say about you."

Ishtar took a pen, dipped it in ink, and drew. "It is a variation on the symbols from my temples. Usually it is an eight-pointed star around a circle, but he liked to be fancy."

"Thank you," Ruxandra said. "Tomorrow, then?"

"Yes." Ishtar reached up, rested her hand on Ruxandra's face. "Until then, my daughter."

Ruxandra watched her leave then looked at the symbol.

It was a round eye, its pupil slit like a goat's. Four wings surrounded it, pointing up, down, left and right, with four curved horns at the diagonals.

Ruxandra opened the book and leafed through it.

She found eighteen mentions of Ishtar, on pages filled with words she didn't understand. Ruxandra marked each page with a strip of paper. She went through the other tomes and found Ishtar's name twenty-five more times.

It's a start. I'll ask Ishtar to translate. If she won't, I'll get Kade to translate it

She found him stepping out the door as she arrived back at his house. A smile lit up his face. "Did you speak to her?"

"Yes."

"Do you believe her?"

"I don't know yet. But I will listen to her."

"Wonderful."

Kade closed the door behind him and wrapped her in his arms. She let him kiss her, and it sparked several other ideas in her head. Unfortunately he stepped back almost at once.

"I am meeting our noble friends," Kade said. "They are concerned with my progress on Anna's assassination. Did you want to come?"

"Have you agreed to kill her, then?"

"I have not said no." Kade offered her arm, and she took it. "But I have not given a guarantee of her death, and that worries them. Especially after what happened to Dolgorukov."

"And you like keeping them worried?" Ruxandra guessed.

Kade smiled. "Exactly."

The blond servant ushered them into the parlor. Belosselsky and Gagarin sat in two chairs by the fire, staring at a chessboard between them. Delfino stood beside them, watching. Ruxandra was tempted to whisper in his ear that he'd been fucking a fallen angel. Would he be thrilled or terrified? Princess Khilkoff sat on the farthest couch from the fireplace, her face set and her arms crossed. Her eyes locked on Ruxandra's.

"Here he is," Gagarin said. "Our traitor."

Kade didn't even break his pace. He sat opposite the princess and draped his arm over the back of the couch. He looked to Belosselsky, his eyebrows raised.

"Our dear Gagarin doesn't think you are doing enough to help us," Belosselsky said. He pushed a rook forward and leaned back in his chair. "Which reminds me, what have you done to help us?"

"Ingratiate myself at court," Kade said. "The empress does not trust me yet, and I cannot blame her. So I move cautiously. How are your plans going?"

"That is none of your concern," Gagarin said, "Carry out your part. Leave the rest to us."

"I simply wish to know if you have any thoughts of what happens after the death of Anna, or if you'll sit back and watch to see who remains standing after the battle for the throne."

"We do," Belosselsky said.

"Then I'm sure you'll have no problem sharing them."

"We can't trust you." Gagarin rose from his chair. "You're not one of us."

Princess Khilkoff stood, drawing every eye in the room. "I did not come here to listen to your squabbles."

"My dear," began Delfino, but she cut him off.

"I am going to the music room," she said. "I will play the harpsichord and calm my nerves. You men sort your differences so we may move forward and remove the tyrant. Ruxandra, join me."

It wasn't a request. Ruxandra watched her leave without moving.

"Please go with her," Kade said. "Let me deal with these gentlemen and then come find you."

Ruxandra followed Princess Khilkoff down the hall. The music room's wide windows overlooked a small garden, now gray and drab with winter. The harpsichord sat in the middle. An instrument like a mandolin, but with a wider sound box, hung on the wall. On a table on the far side sat an instrument with many strings stretched over a wing-shaped wooden sound box.

"Do you play the balalaika?" Khilkoff asked, pointing at the instrument on the wall. She shifted her finger to the desk. "Or the gusli?"

"No."

"Unfortunate. The harpsichord sounds best with accompaniment."

She put her fingers to the keyboard. Inside the harpsichord small quills plucked the strings, bringing out notes that soared and filled the room. Ruxandra stood in silence, listening.

"Sit by me, so we may talk."

Ruxandra sat on a corner of the bench.

"Excellent." Khilkoff's fingers danced over the keys, making the music loud and energetic. "Now explain why you fucked Prince Delfino."

Ruxandra's mouth fell open. She closed it, thought a moment, and said, "I beg your pardon?"

"Delfino," Khilkoff repeated. "You fucked him. First after the party, then at his house the next day. Why?"

"I did not—"

"Moscow has many fascinating things." Khilkoff switched tunes, her fingers dancing as she played. "Cathedrals, the Kremlin, excellent vodka, and the empress. What it does not have is an abundance of pale redheaded women willing to suck a man against the wall of Terem Palace in the early hours of the morning. Do you play harpsichord?"

Ishtar. She saw Ishtar and thought it was me. "Yes."

"Good." Princess Khilkoff slid off the bench. "Teach me a new song. Something cheerful."

And if I tell her it wasn't, she won't believe me. "I am out of practice, Princess, but I will try the 'Menuet et son double' by Gaspard Le Roux."

She touched the keys, closed her eyes, and played.

Under the dancing notes of the harpsichord, she heard the princess draw her knife.

Ruxandra considered taking it from her, considered hitting the woman hard enough to render her senseless and leaving her lying on the music room floor.

Which would make her a worse enemy and probably ruin Kade's plans, whatever they are.

Princess Khilkoff pressed the sharp, cold steel blade against Ruxandra's neck. Ruxandra didn't stop. The 'Menuet et son double' pranced and bounced through the room.

"The only reason you are not dead," Princess Khilkoff said, "is that you are the companion to Russia's finest assassin."

Ruxandra kept playing.

"But let me assure you," Princess Khilkoff said. "I am watching you. If you go near him one more time, I will see that no man ever enjoys you again."

The knife vanished from Ruxandra's throat, and the princess's footsteps echoed down the hall.

"Ruxandra!" Kade's voice drifted back to her. "I am leaving. Will you come?"

Ruxandra played to the end of the bar, rose, and headed for the door.

"And how was your time with the princess?" Kade asked as they stepped outside.

"Tense." *And only going to get more so, I expect.*

Two nights later she sat in the library, waiting.

The Alchemist was writing the final inscriptions on her circle on the floor. Michael was watching intently and making occasional encouraging comments. Derek stood nearby, eating an apricot pastry with one hand, holding a mug of beer in the other. Eduard and Kurkov were in the stacks somewhere. Ruxandra listened and heard Kurkov calling out book after book, giving them numbers and identifying each book's language. The quiet industry and camaraderie of the group was peaceful and satisfying in a way she had never experienced. At the convent there'd been too much fear of the nuns. Since then she'd had to hide herself. Only here . . .

Because Ishtar hadn't arrived yet.

Ruxandra bent her head to her work, translating the words around Ishtar's name. She thought some were place names, others events, but none of those were in the lists from Ishtar.

When Ishtar arrived, her hair was messy and her dress askew, and she walked with her legs apart. She sat in the chair opposite Ruxandra with a simultaneous smile and wince.

"For a short, fat man," Ishtar said, "he is certainly vigorous."

"There are many men in Moscow who are vigorous." *And handsome and charming as well.*

"Is Kade?" Ishtar reached across the table and opened a thick book. "I ask because you show no signs. Of course, you heal faster than a human, don't you?"

"Why keep going to that smarmy little weasel?" Ruxandra asked. "What do you get from him?"

"Tut, tut. So judgmental." But she smiled, her eyes full of merriment. "So far, the names of six of his associates in place to usurp Belosselsky once the empress is dead."

Ruxandra's eyebrows rose. "You mean you two talked this time?"

Ishtar's smile widened. "I gave him a gift. One of Anna's ministers. Well, his head. Anna didn't like the man, so she didn't object. Once Delfino saw that, he was extra forthcoming. It's funny what it takes to excite some people, isn't it?"

"I'm thinking of him as something less than a person right now."

Ishtar shifted in her seat and winced again. "Well, I have more experience with men than you, my dear, and I assure you, he is far from unique. Though he *was* remarkably aroused. Why do men think they must try all the holes?" She opened the book to the first page marked with paper. "Can you read what he says about me?"

"Some of the words, not all."

"Let me help." Ishtar pointed. "That word is 'bitch.' That one is 'whore.' That one . . . I'm not sure it translates. It relates to the anus of a diseased swine."

Ruxandra's eyebrows rose high on her forehead. "He despised you."

"He was not prepared for what I asked of him." Ishtar took up a sheet of paper. "Are you?"

"That depends what you ask."

"I will remember that. Now, we must work quickly, as I have another appointment."

"Appointment or assignation?" Ruxandra asked.

Ishtar smiled. "This human body is too tender for a new assignation until tomorrow. Meanwhile, let us add more words to our list."

They worked until midnight. Ishtar created a new list for Ruxandra to learn. Ruxandra worked through the page until a guard came for Ishtar.

"I must go," Ishtar said. "Shall we meet outside Kade's house at dawn?"

"Yes, please."

When she left, Ruxandra turned to the other pages with Ishtar's symbol. The swear words appeared less often. But others Ishtar had given her—*worship, trust, action, belief*—showed up more and more.

I will ask her why tomorrow night. Ruxandra closed up the books and stood and looked around. The library was empty save for the Alchemist, lying fast asleep on the floor, her head resting on her hands. Ruxandra slipped her arms underneath the woman, cradled her, and picked her up. The Alchemist blinked awake.

"Hey." Her voice was fuzzy with sleep. "What are you doing?"

"Carrying you to bed." Ruxandra headed up the stairs.

"My princess," the Alchemist said, nestling her head into Ruxandra's shoulders. "When I am rich, I will give you wealth beyond your wildest dreams."

Ruxandra glanced back at the circle and the crucible. "Do you believe it will work?"

"It must," the Alchemist whispered. "To be free, Ruxandra. To go away without having to care what empresses or kings think. To live the life one wants instead of what others want, is that not best?"

"Yes."

"If this works. If what Ishtar said is true, I will be free of Anna, free of this city. I can go anywhere I wish. I will go to China."

"China?" Ruxandra thought about that. "Why China?"

"They are brilliant chemists. The Chinese invented gunpowder a thousand years ago. They used it for firecrackers."

Ruxandra squeezed the Alchemist in her arms. "Sleep now. Riches can wait until morning."

She put the Alchemist to bed and left the church unnoticed. It was a pleasant night. The air was not too cold. The stars shone over the city. Ruxandra walked with a slow, easy step through the streets. *I could take the Alchemist to China. Any riches we need, I can procure. And Kade—would he come with us?*

Then came the sounds of fighting, somewhere near Kade's house.

Ruxandra broke into a run, racing through the streets and around corners until she reached a wide square. Five men with drawn knives surrounded Ishtar. Princess Khilkoff leaned on a wall behind them. She wore a hooded cloak and a wide grin.

"I am surprised," Princess Khilkoff said. "I thought it was that bitch Ruxandra. Who knew we had two redhead sluts kicking around?"

Ishtar turned in a slow circle. She spotted Ruxandra and shook her head. In a whisper, she said, "Stay back. Say nothing."

"What did you say?" Princess Khilkoff demanded. "Say it again."

"I said it's a pity you haven't bedded Delfino yet. He is a most energetic lover."

"I am a princess of Russia. I will not disgrace my family by falling pregnant before my marriage."

"I am a lieutenant in the armies of hell," Ishtar whispered, her words not reaching the ears of those around her, though Ruxandra heard them well enough. "I need no help."

"Why are you whispering, you idiot?"

"Because I would not want your men to hear how you debased yourself with both Belosselsky and Gagarin," Ishtar said. She smiled. "In ways that do not get you pregnant."

"You lying bitch." Princess Khilkoff turned to the men. "Kill her."

CHAPTER

TWENTY

K HILKOFF'S MEN WALKED forward, knives in their hands, confidence radiating from them. Ishtar smiled and turned in a slow circle as they closed in.

The five men surrounding her never had a chance.

In one breath Ishtar caught the first man's wrist in one hand and drove the heel of her other hand against his chin. As his head flew back, she spun, pulling him in and sending him flying into the second-closest man. She leaped past before they could untangle themselves and kicked the third man's knee. Ruxandra heard the joint break with a crunch and winced in sympathy. The man screamed, lashing out with the knife. Ishtar grabbed his arm and twisted until the elbow broke. She threw him, using his broken arm as a lever to make him flip and slam facedown onto the cobbles.

When she turned back, she had his knife in her hand.

The four men still standing no longer looked confident. Their jaws clenched and their breath grew harsh. They formed a wide semicircle around Ishtar and crouched, ready to fight.

Ishtar sprang, feinting to one on the outside. He swung, but she moved too fast, ducking under his blade and opening another's stomach with a slash. He screamed as his guts poured out onto the cobbles. Before the others could react, Ishtar slipped behind another, knife slashing through the tendons of his knee. She caught his hair as he fell, shoved her blade into his throat, and tore it out. Blood sprayed across the ground.

The other two froze, eyes wide. In their moment of indecision, Ishtar moved again. Her first cut sent one's hand and the knife in it flying. Her second slashed his neck open. The last man leaped, a battle cry on his lips.

It died as Ishtar ducked beneath his weapon and drove her blade hard under his ribs. When she removed it, he collapsed.

Princess Khilkoff screamed. Ishtar dropped her blade and sprinted forward. Her hand slapped over the princess's mouth, and she shoved the girl's head against the wall with a crack. Ishtar grabbed the princess's hair with her other hand and dragged her away from the blood-spattered street.

Ruxandra followed, impressed in spite of herself. *All that in a human body.* Behind her she heard shouting, and the clatter of the guards' steel-tipped boots coming closer.

Ishtar kept her hand clamped over Princess Khilkoff's mouth as she pulled her through the streets and into an alley between houses. She slammed the princess up against the wall and pinned her there with the hand over her mouth. Ishtar's other hand roamed over the princess's body, down her cleavage, around her waist and under her cloak.

"Ah." Ishtar held up Princess Khilkoff's knife. "Thought so."

She tested the blade with her thumb. Then she pointed it at the princess's eye.

"If you make a single sound," Ishtar said, "you will spend what little is left of your life in darkness. Understand?"

Princess Khilkoff, her eyes filled with tears, nodded.

Ishtar spun the princess to face the wall. She pulled off the princess's cloak and, with expert precision, cut the shoulders of her dress.

"Ishtar," Ruxandra called. "You shouldn't—"

"Oh yes I should." She pointed the knife at the base of the princess's neck and slipped it down the length of her back, cloth parting beneath it. Princess Khilkoff's dress fell off. Two more cuts and her corset and underclothes followed. Ishtar turned the woman around again and shoved her against the wall.

Princess Khilkoff crossed her arms over her bare breasts, one hand dropping to cover her sex. Ishtar looked at her body, disdain on her face.

"Now I see why Delfino complains about you." Ishtar grabbed both the princess's wrists and pulled them above her head. "Ugly, skinny, no real tits, and no muscles to hold a man's weight."

"Ishtar." Ruxandra hissed the word. "That's enough."

"I say when it's enough!" Ishtar pressed her knife against the princess's throat. "This bitch tried to kill me. The only reason she's not dead is that Delfino wants her alive."

Ishtar stepped back and tossed the knife away. "You're his spare broodmare, Princess, in case something happens to me. I suggest you let him mount from behind, so your ugly face doesn't make him wilt."

Her hands curled into fists.

"Now it's time for your real lesson."

"Ishtar, no!" Ruxandra jumped forward to stop her and found she could not.

She wanted to, tried to, but her body would not respond, would not touch Ishtar. Inside her the Beast growled, feeling Ruxandra's frustration.

Ishtar gave Princess Khilkoff a brutal beating, fists smashing into the woman's ribs and stomach and breasts. Princess Khilkoff fell and twisted and tried to crawl away. Ishtar caught her foot and dragged her back. She pounded on the princess's kidneys, then grabbed her hair and turned her over.

"Ishtar," Ruxandra begged. "You'll kill her. Stop."

"No, I won't." Ishtar smiled down at the princess. "But she'll wish I had."

She knelt on Princess Khilkoff's chest and started on her face. *Goddammit. I must stop her.*

Ishtar aimed her fists to do the most damage possible. The princess's nose broke with a crunch, spraying blood. Her eyes swelled and closed. Her cheekbones and eyebrows split, leaking more blood.

"HELP THE PRINCESS!" Ruxandra screamed the command. *"EVERYONE COME HERE AND HELP! NOW!"*

For one second Ishtar fixed Ruxandra with a gaze so angry that Ruxandra felt her stomach curl in on itself. Then she rose to her feet and strode out of the alley. Ruxandra ran after her.

"Make yourself visible," Ishtar snapped. "I won't talk to a ghost."

Ruxandra turned noticeable and walked beside her, mouth closed tight.

"I don't understand your anger." Ishtar walked around the corner and headed for Kade's house. "Do you think I should have killed her like that scum you dispatched three nights ago?"

"How did you—"

"The secret police follow you, Ruxandra. They report to the empress, and she tells me. So explain, Ruxandra, how is that any different than what I did?"

"I killed him," Ruxandra said. "He died in less than a minute. What you were doing to her—"

Ishtar's head tilted. "Do you not understand what happened, Ruxandra? She is a *traitor*. She tried to *murder* me so she could secure her claim to the throne if Anna is assassinated, solely by virtue of having the right man's cock between her thighs."

"Why not kill her, then?" Ruxandra demanded. "And don't tell me your promise to Delfino prevented you."

"I did better than kill her." Self-satisfaction oozed out of Ishtar's words. "I *cowed* her. What I did will give her nightmares for the rest of her life. I made it so she doesn't trust herself and doesn't trust Delfino. I've put fractures into their alliance and weakened their attempt to destroy Anna. If she is still stupid enough to ally herself with Delfino after that, then she will die on the scaffold beside him."

Ishtar put a hand on Ruxandra's shoulder and turned her so they were face-to-face. "Things are coming to a head, Ruxandra. You need to either leave or pick a side: mine or theirs."

Yours? Not Anna's?

Ishtar stepped around Ruxandra. "Now, I believe Kade's house is nearby. I want to wash the blood off."

She didn't get a chance.

A black carriage stood outside Kade's house, pulled by four black horses. A driver in black sat on the seat. Alexi leaned against the doorframe, talking to Kade's manservant, Ivan.

When Ivan's eyes grew wide, he turned. If the sight of Ishtar, covered head to foot in blood, with bruised, bloody knuckles, made an impression on Alexi, he didn't show it.

"There you are." Alexi stepped to the carriage and opened it. "The empress requests your presence."

"May I wash first?" Ishtar asked.

"She said it was urgent." Alexi's tone was bland, but he didn't move from the carriage door and clearly expected Ishtar to get in. "Something to do with the Metropolitan and his continuing riling up of the peasantry against Her Majesty and your lack of success in stopping it."

"Of course." Ishtar stepped into the carriage. "Ruxandra, think on what I said."

Alexi climbed in behind her, and they drove off, leaving Ruxandra alone in the streets.

"The master will not be home today," Ivan said as the carriage left. "He hopes to see you tonight."

"Thank you."

Ruxandra sat in the chair in her room, staring at the empty fireplace. Nika came in, curtsied, and started a fire. Ruxandra nodded to her but didn't move.

Am I truly no better than Ishtar?

She'd killed the man in the alley as a gut response to what had happened to the Alchemist. She'd been angry and hungry and had given her fury free rein.

So how am I different from Ishtar?

Well, she probably wasn't hungry . . .

It was ridiculous thing to giggle at one's own jokes, especially after such a night. She still couldn't stop, which told her she wasn't thinking clearly at all.

Ishtar planned it.

The thought stopped Ruxandra's giggles.

She said she read the minds of everyone in the Kremlin before she changed, which means she knew how Khilkoff would react. She slept with Delfino to goad her into attacking.

Ruxandra took off her clothes, climbed into bed, and stared at the ceiling.

She never planned on killing the princess. She wanted to humiliate and disfigure her . . . why? To make their coup come apart?

Or to make it happen faster?

She found no answers and turned over to sleep, hoping to talk to Kade the next night. But when evening came, he had still not returned.

Ruxandra was getting hungry, and could feel the Beast grumbling. She dressed and walked to the outer city, looking for someone to eat. To her surprise the streets glowed with torchlight. Men stood in groups, carrying knives or clubs or shovels—anything they could use as a weapon. The kabaks did a brisk business, but no one stayed for a second drink. Houses were shut tight, and reaching out with her mind, she felt fear radiating from the adults, and confusion from the children still awake.

The churches shone like beacons, the warm yellow light of their candles spilling out their open doors. Ruxandra drifted closer to one and looked. The priest shared communion with a long line of men.

"Is it true?" one man asked another. "The *vampir* are in the city?"

"They've killed a dozen people already. Remember Yazon Washko?"

"That beast who liked to rape women in the alley with a crowd watching? Death was too good for him."

"His blood was drained, they say. And he was not the first. Kirill's grandmother, too."

"Kirill's grandmother was older than the North Star," a third man said. "A strong wind could have killed her."

"Yes, but her blood was drained, too. And now the priests know where it is hiding. That old church that the empress doesn't allow anyone to use. It's in there."

Ruxandra sprinted across the city and ran straight into a company of the empress's army.

Fifty men in uniform stood in front of the door, muskets at the ready, bayonets fixed. Torches, jammed into the surrounding earth, lit them red and yellow, hollowing out their eyes and cheekbones, making them look like standing corpses.

Alexi was at the top of the church steps, looking at Ruxandra.

She circled the men and joined him.

"They cannot see you, I take it?" he said under his breath, nodding at the men.

"Not unless they have the same magic you do."

"They do not. Is the church's mob coming?"

"Not yet, but soon. Are they inside?"

"The Alchemist. Not the others."

"I should get her out."

"You should stay with her," Alexi said. "No one has discovered the passage for three hundred years. I doubt anyone will tonight, but we have the empress's orders to keep them from going inside and looking."

Ruxandra looked at the grim, scared men in their neat ranks. "People are going to die."

"I know." Alexi looked out into the night, searching the street for rioters. "I suggest you go below. We cannot have the Alchemist coming up in the middle of things, can we?"

Ruxandra smelled something burning the moment she started down the stairs. She ran, fear for the Alchemist driving her faster than any human could move.

A thin layer of smoke floated in the library air. The Alchemist's crucible, charred and split, sat in the center of the destroyed chalk circle. Water and footprints had smeared the neatly drawn lines and obscured the writing. Three empty buckets lay on their sides outside the circle.

The Alchemist sat on the floor, weeping.

Her clothes were burned and her hands red and swollen. Tears tracked gray trails through the soot and burns on her face. Ruxandra reached out for her emotions and found a dark pit of anger, despair, and misery.

The Alchemist saw her and put on a small, fake smile. "Good evening, Princess. How are you?"

"What happened?" Ruxandra asked. "It didn't work?"

"Oh, even worse than not working," the Alchemist said. "My tiny, beautiful crucible melted. It split and the lead spilled onto the floor. I had to douse the flames with water, which, of course, ruined everything."

"I am so sorry."

"No need." The Alchemist sounded brittle, as if the slightest blow would shatter her. "Nothing has changed. I am still the same. I have no gold, I have no hope, and I am doomed to serve the bitch empress until she decides she no longer has a use for me, after which she will torture me to death. Everything is fine."

"Come," Ruxandra said. "We need to clean you up."

"Why? A burned slave works just as well."

Ruxandra scooped the Alchemist up in her arms, holding her gently to not make her pain any worse. Up close, the scent of her made Ruxandra's stomach and the Beast in her skull growl with anticipation.

Shut up, both of you. We have other things to deal with first.

She carried the Alchemist to the baths and put her on the bench.

"Stay here," Ruxandra said. "I will return in a moment."

Ruxandra left at top speed, fetched a change of clothing from the Alchemist's room, and sprinted back. The Alchemist hadn't moved. Ruxandra filled a bucket of water and took up a cloth. Then she undressed the Alchemist. The skin on the Alchemist's breasts and ribs had turned purple and green from her beating. The welts on her back had gone down, but the bruises from the lashing still stood out against her pale skin.

"Stand up," Ruxandra said, "put your hands on the wall."

The Alchemist did. Ruxandra knelt at her feet. She cleaned each one, then started up the Alchemist's legs. She kept her touch gentle and smooth. The Alchemist didn't respond, not even when Ruxandra reached her backside. Ruxandra gently ran the cloth over her back. If the bruises still hurt, the Alchemist gave no sign.

Then, when Ruxandra's hands wrapped around the Alchemist's stomach, the woman leaned back against Ruxandra. Ruxandra kept her hand motions gentle as she worked up to the Alchemist's breasts. And when the Alchemist turned her head to kiss her, Ruxandra met her with an open, welcoming mouth.

When their lips parted, the Alchemist whispered, "I don't want to stay here anymore."

"Then we'll go," Ruxandra said. "Come, I'll take you to Kade's house." *And farther than that. When I leave Moscow, I'll take you with me.*

The Alchemist dressed, and they walked up the stairs. Noise, faint at first but growing louder, filled Ruxandra's ears. It grew loud enough that even the Alchemist, with her human hearing, stopped and listened.

"What is that?" she asked.

"Shouting," Ruxandra said. "A lot of it. The priests called on the people to march. They think a vampire lives in the church. At least there's no sound of battle yet."

"Yet?" The Alchemist's eyes went wide. "Are you expecting one?"

"The Metropolitan has stirred the peasants up, and there's a company of the empress's soldiers at the church door."

"We should go the other way."

"We can't." Ruxandra took the Alchemist's hand. "Anna warded the Kremlin against me. I can't enter it, even from the tunnel."

"What do we do?"

"Remember how I surprised you? When you hold my hand, I can make it so you aren't noticed, either."

"Really?" Despite her misery, the Alchemist sounded intrigued. "However did you learn that?"

"I once had to smuggle my servant out of a castle before they beat her to death."

Ruxandra could smell the Alchemist's fear and kept a tight grip on her as she led her up the stairs, through the church, and out the door.

The men Ruxandra had seen claiming the vampire lived here had come, led by a priest, with a hundred others beside them.

They shouted and jeered and demanded to be let inside. The soldiers' muskets pointed forward now, their bayonets gleaming in the torchlight. The crowd stayed back, kept at a distance by three priests who exhorted them to stay calm. They yelled and threw bottles instead.

Ruxandra led the Alchemist out the door. Alexi glanced at them once, nodded, and turned back to the crowd. It grew louder, but didn't advance. Together, both unnoticed, the women made their way through the streets crowded with peasants. Some marched, others talked, some stood around looking frightened. They blocked every major street corner and the bridges to the inner city.

"We'll get through," Ruxandra said before the Alchemist could open her mouth.

The Alchemist looked nervous but muttered her thanks. Ruxandra sniffed the air for Anna's men, but didn't catch any familiar scents.

Halfway across the road to the bridge, Ruxandra's feet stuck in place.

CHAPTER
TWENTY-ONE

N<small>O! NOT NOW!</small>

The Alchemist took two steps past and jerked to a halt, her hand still caught in Ruxandra's. She turned back, frowning. Her expression changed the moment she saw Ruxandra's face.

"Princess?" the Alchemist said, concern filling her voice. "What is wrong?"

"I can't move my feet," Ruxandra whispered. She glared around her, unable to see the magicians from the crowd. "Someone is attacking me."

"Who?" The Alchemist turned in a circle. "I can't see. There are too many people."

"Look for people not moving," Ruxandra said. "People chanting, maybe. I don't know what they do."

"How can you not know?"

"I can't see them!" Ruxandra bent down, the movement made awkward by her anchored feet. She extended the talons on both hands, dug deep into the earth, and pulled. She pulled up two handfuls of dirt and straightened. She clenched the dirt in her right hand, compressing it.

"What are you doing?"

"Getting ready to fight."

"Who?"

"Magicians. There's four of them—that's how many Alexi used—but I can't see them."

"Why can't you—" The Alchemist cut her own words short. "Magic, that's why."

Ruxandra breathed deep, taking in all the scents around her, and scanned the crowds. *They are here somewhere; I just have to find them.*

A gap in the crowd cleared the intersection. Ruxandra breathed deep, caught four scents still in place. Two more sniffs and she had a rough idea of where they stood. She also caught more scents not attached to bodies she could see, coming closer. Two men reeking of steel and gunpowder and fear.

"There is a man at each corner." The Alchemist whispered the words. "And two coming toward us."

"Stand behind me."

The Alchemist did. "What do we do?"

Ruxandra twisted in the direction of one of the four stationary scents and hurled the handful of dirt in her left hand. It smacked against a body, and for a moment outlined part of a man in its dust.

When Ruxandra had doused Alexi with water, she'd done it out of irritation. But doing so had shown her that, while she could not *touch* someone protected, that didn't mean she couldn't *hit* them.

The dirt she'd compressed with her right hand was hard as a rock, and she hurled it with all her strength. It smacked the center of the outline and Ruxandra heard bones crack. The dust-covered outline dropped to the ground, and Ruxandra was free.

She grabbed the Alchemist, tossed the woman over her shoulder, and ran.

The Alchemist bounced on her shoulder as Ruxandra weaved in and out of the crowd, moving fast and unnoticed. The Alchemist clung to her without a sound. Ruxandra jumped to the low roof of a house, used it to jump onto a taller one, slid down the other side, landed on a street free from the crowd, and ran to the city wall. She jumped it and kept going.

Ruxandra finally stopped at the far edge of the outer city, in the shadow of a barn. They were far away from the crowds, far away from the fires and the noise. She put the Alchemist down, and the woman promptly fell, her legs folding under her like paper. She sat on the ground gasping.

"That was amazing," the Alchemist gasped. "And I never want to do it again."

Ruxandra breathed deep. She could smell no one nearby. "Can you see anyone?"

The Alchemist looked around them. "No."

"Good."

"So." the Alchemist's voice sounded faint. "Now what?"

"I don't know." Ruxandra looked up at the sky. Midnight had not yet come. She closed her eyes and listened, catching the sound of chanting peasants, shouting soldiers, and horses snorting and whinnying. Ruxandra closed her eyes and waited.

The shooting started.

The peasants' shouts turned to screams as volley after volley of gunfire echoed through the city. Shovels and pitchforks and axes clashed with swords and pikes. Horses screamed as they were stabbed and lashed out with their hooves at their attackers.

People died, everywhere.

The Beast rumbled inside Ruxandra, sensing the blood she smelled, reminding her that it had been four days since she'd fed.

Shut up. We'll feed soon enough. Right now we have to get the Alchemist someplace safe and figure out how to stop this mess.

"Do you think the others are safe?" The Alchemist asked.

"I don't know." Ruxandra closed her eyes and reached out with her mind. She tried to find Kurkov and the others, but there were too many people screaming and fighting, too much terror and violence and hatred and pain to sort it all easily. She opened her eyes and slumped.

"At least they didn't catch us," the Alchemist said. "Thank you for that."

"They nearly did," Ruxandra said. "They knew we were going to be there and they laid a trap for us."

"Were they secret police?"

"I don't know. They didn't smell familiar, but that doesn't mean anything. They could have been police I haven't found yet; they could have been anyone."

"No," the Alchemist said. "They couldn't. They had to be magicians to trap you, and the secret police do not have that many."

Ruxandra frowned. "Then why can I never see them?"

"Talismans, probably. They don't need magicians to follow you, just to trap you."

So if they weren't the magicians I scented when Alexi trapped me, who were they?

The Alchemist leaned back, looking up at the sky. "Did you know the spell that summons Ishtar doesn't require any magicians?

The words themselves are magic and draw on the power of hell to open the gates."

"I didn't know," Ruxandra said. "But I'm not surprised. I don't think my father's men were magicians, and they summoned her."

"That's why we could do it using Eduard and Kurkov. We just needed five warm bodies to chant."

So easy to bring evil into the world.

More shots rang out, and the Alchemist cocked her head to listen. "What's happening?"

"People are dying."

"How much can you hear?"

"All of it."

The Alchemist's hand, light and warm and strong, landed on Ruxandra's shoulder. "I am sorry. You were right. We should have listened, no matter the risk to ourselves."

"We all want to stay alive," said Ruxandra. "You know I have forgiven you." She put her hand over the Alchemist's, feeling the woman's warmth against her skin. She felt cold inside, and scared. She did not know what had happened to the others; she did not know where Kade was, and she did not know how to stop any of it.

She reached out with her mind, searching for Kade, and discovered something else entirely. A moment later she heard them outside the wall. She stood up, cocked her head to hear better.

"What is it?" the Alchemist asked. "What do you hear?"

"Soldiers," Ruxandra whispered. "Horses. Coming from outside the wall. Hundreds of them."

The Alchemist stood, too. "Tatars? Do we need to run?"

"I don't know who it is. But yes, we should run." She reached out with her mind and felt a grim sense of purpose from the men beyond the walls. She turned her senses back to the city, feeling the conflicts there so she could plan a clear route through.

One presence blazed brighter than all the rest, and it was moving toward them.

"Wait," Ruxandra said. "Wait just a little longer."

"Why?" the Alchemist asked, fear in her voice. "What are we waiting for?"

"Kade."

And minutes later, wearing all black and smelling of blood and battle, Kade stepped out of the darkness to join them.

"You are both unhurt?" he asked.

"Yes," Ruxandra said. "Though not for lack of trying on their part."

"Magicians tried to catch her," the Alchemist said. "They tried to catch me."

"Not magicians," Kade said. "Priests. The magicians of the secret police are in the Kremlin, awaiting Anna's commands."

"You're sure?"

Kade smiled, but his face looked grim and angry. "I am still in Anna's good graces, and still in her service, for now. Though after today's events I am not sure how long that will last."

"You can't leave her service." Desperation tinged the Alchemist's words. "Not until we free our friends. She will kill them."

"She will not," Kade said. "Not while they still hold some use for her. And as long as there is chaos, they will still hold some use for her. But I was not referring to my leaving. Belosselsky escaped."

"What?" Ruxandra said. "How?"

"He was warned." Kade practically spat out the words. "He and Princess Khilkoff. Those are her troops out there. Belosselsky's men are already inside the city."

"Are they joining forces against the empress?" Ruxandra asked.

"More fighting," the Alchemist said. "More death."

Within, the Beast rumbled its rather gleeful opinion on that. Ruxandra ignored it.

"Much more," Kade said. "Now we must go. Ishtar needs us."

"Ishtar?"

"She sent me to fetch you, Ruxandra. She says now is the time for you to join her."

The sounds of fighting from inside the city had begun dying down. Ruxandra listened, heard the cries of the injured and the wailing of women over their dead. *All this for what?*

"Ruxandra." Impatience filled Kade's voice. "Now."

Ruxandra shook herself free of her thoughts. "We have to get the Alchemist to safety. Then we can talk to Ishtar."

"There is precious little safety in this city right now," Kade said. "It might be best if she just waits here."

"*She* is standing in front of you," the Alchemist said. "And *she* knows a safe place, if you two will take me."

"Of course," Ruxandra said.

Kade frowned. "Only if we carry her. We need to hurry."

"That's fine," the Alchemist said. "Just no jumping over buildings this time. I don't think I could survive it."

The place she had in mind turned out to be a small house near the north of the city proper. It was hemmed in by houses on both sides, and looked neither comfortable nor lived in. But it was also far away from the Kremlin, the library, and the rioting. The Alchemist pulled a key out and opened the door. The interior smelled musty, and there was no furniture.

"What is this place?" Ruxandra asked.

"A bolt-hole." She smiled. "They come for magicians sometimes, so it pays to have a place to run. Now go quick, then come back."

"We'll try," Kade said.

Ruxandra glared at him. "We will. Or at least I will."

"I'm glad." The Alchemist brushed a hand against Ruxandra's face. "Be careful."

She locked the door behind them.

Ruxandra and Kade ran through the streets, both listening to the sounds of the crowd. Kade led them toward the Kremlin, trying to see as much of the situation as possible before they went to Ishtar.

"Stay noticeable," he said as they moved closer to the crowds. "I don't think they can tell what we are just by looking. So if we act human, we may be able to slip by the church's guards."

"And if not?"

"Then run."

Soldiers now patrolled the streets around the Kremlin and the enclave. They had taken over the army camp near the walls and flew a flag Ruxandra didn't recognize.

"Belosselsky's family crest," Kade said. "I'm sure he has told Anna that they are there to help quell the peasant unrest. Not that either of them will believe it."

Farther on, a large crowd of peasants gathered in a square near one of the churches. Kade and Ruxandra slipped into the crowd, craning their necks to see like the others around them. In the middle of the square, a large post had been erected, bundles of sticks and firewood stacked around it.

Kurkov was chained to the post.

The man had been beaten bloody, his eyes mostly closed. Blood dripped from his lips and his nose, and his face was a swollen mass. His knuckles were bloody, too, suggesting that, whatever else had happened, he had not gone quietly.

Kade's lips pressed hard together in a white line. He started moving forward, pushing his way through the crowd. Ruxandra stayed on his heels. People complained, and some pushed back, but no one stopped them. They reached the front of the crowd and Kade turned to one of the peasants.

"Who is he?" Kade asked. "What has he done?"

"Where have you been?" the man demanded. "Hiding your head up your arse? That's one of the witches."

But he isn't. He's a librarian. Ruxandra looked over Kurkov with horror, knowing she would never convince his captors.

"They caught him at a kabak with his sodomite lover," the man said. "Apparently he fought like a demon. Anyway, they beat him, trussed him up, and set up the stake. Say they'll burn him tomorrow night."

Kade vanished from human notice and charged into the square, moving faster than Ruxandra had ever seen him. She went unnoticed herself and started forward, fangs and talons coming out. They would have to fight free of the crowd, but if they could get to him . . .

Ten feet from the post, Kade hit something he could not see and was slammed back to the ground. He hit hard, got up, and charged again. Ruxandra caught him as he bounced back the second time. He pushed her off and circled the post, trying again and again to break through.

"It's like the barrier around the Kremlin," Ruxandra said. "We can't get through it."

Kade swore in six languages, turned on his heel, and strode back through the crowd. "We need help. Come."

He led Ruxandra back through the city to the church above the library. Soldiers still stood in a double line before its door. Some had torn uniforms and bruises; others wore bandages. Alexi stood behind them, a saber in his hand. His blade had been cleaned, but not his uniform, which was spattered with blood. The street in front of the church was empty, save for puddled blood and scuffed, stained earth.

Kade strode forward. "Is Ishtar inside?"

"Yes. She's waiting for the two of you."

"Good," Kade said, walking past him into the church. "Kurkov has been arrested."

"What?" Alexi's surprise sounded genuine. "When?"

Kade had already gone in and didn't answer him.

"Earlier this evening," Ruxandra said. "They're going to burn him."

Alexi leaned over to one of his soldiers, spoke briefly in his ear, and headed inside. "I must speak to the empress."

Ruxandra followed him down into the library and found Kade leaning on the table in front of Ishtar. Ruxandra breathed deep, trying to see who else was in the library.

"It is Kurkov," Kade was saying, fury filling his voice. "He has been taken by the church. He will burn at the stake tomorrow."

"I know," Ishtar said.

"They have warded the place of execution so I cannot enter it."

"I know."

"I would not lose this man!" Kade's fist thumped the table hard enough that the sound echoed through the library. "I need soldiers to rescue him."

"There are no soldiers available, Kade," Ishtar said. "All the empress's troops are either inside the Kremlin or beyond the walls. She will not spare any to rescue a librarian."

"What about his men?" Kade's finger jabbed at Alexi. "Send them in."

"I do not have the authority to send them in."

"Then I will speak to the empress!" Kade took two steps and jumped up to the balcony above and the hallway to the Kremlin.

"As will I," Alexi said. "If you will excuse me."

"Foolish," Ishtar said. "To care about a human so much as that."

"Kurkov is a good man," Ruxandra protested.

"He's already dead," Ishtar said. "Even if Anna sends troops, the first order the defenders will have is to execute their prisoner. No, the man has no hope, and Kade should accept that."

He will not. He'll be hugely angry with the empress.

Angry enough to change sides, maybe?

And Ishtar would know it.

"Ishtar." Ruxandra spoke slowly, weighing the words as if they were gold. "How did the church find Kurkov?"

Ishtar frowned at her. "Do you not understand what is happening here?"

"I understand that more people are going to die. How did they find Kurkov?"

"Of *course* people are going to die, Ruxandra. That is the point!" Ishtar pushed up out of her chair and walked around the table. "This is about power, Ruxandra, nothing else. And only the one powerful enough to lead this country can help us."

"Us?"

"*Us.* I said that it would be time to choose sides, Ruxandra." She began pacing, and the excitement in her voice grew. "This is the time to seize the reins of power. The church needs to be crushed so the peasants will no longer trust its protection. Belosselsky's men need to be killed. And Anna needs to publicly execute him and put his head on a pike at the gates of the Kremlin."

She stopped pacing and closed in on Ruxandra. "And you, my child, you must help us. There is still time before sunrise. Go to the outer city, and open the gates for Princess Khilkoff's men. Then kill their leaders."

"Why?"

"Because an army without its leader is an armed, furious rabble. They will loot and rape and the people will be clamor to be saved." Ishtar's eyes flashed with joy and anticipation. "Then, and only then, can Anna seize true, unfettered power from the chaos."

Ruxandra nodded. "How did the church know where to find Kurkov?"

"What?" Ishtar stared at her as if she couldn't comprehend the words. "Ruxandra, pay attention."

"I have paid attention." The words came out as a growl. "You've set up everything so that the city will fall into chaos. People have died already, and thousands more will be killed if the armies clash. If the church executes Kurkov, Kade will be more than willing to kill whoever he thinks did it, and I'm sure you will give him a list."

"Fear is necessary—"

"No, it isn't!" The words echoed off the shelves around them. "None of this is necessary! Did you help Belosselsky and Khilkoff to escape? Did you tell the church where Kurkov was hiding? Did you set all of this up just so you could watch this city tear itself apart?"

Ishtar's face went cold. "I told you. Power comes from fear. Fear comes from chaos. From the chaos and fear we create now, we will lead them to something better."

"It isn't worth it."

Ishtar stepped back from her, eyes narrowing. Her lips pressed hard together, and her face went red with anger. "Are you standing against me?"

Ruxandra felt the power in the woman's eyes, and with it came the need to love and protect Ishtar that had plagued her from the very beginning. *This is the one who made me. An angel. A monster.*

She is just like Elizabeth—not as crazy and sadistic perhaps, but as heartless. I stayed with Elizabeth because of magic that I thought was love; this is no different.

There is nothing she can offer that is worth being around her. She remembered the screams of the dying and the blood on Alexi's clothes. She remembered Kurkov's swollen, bruised face and the fear in the Alchemist's voice as the priest had caught them. She felt her own grief and horror and rage.

"Yes," Ruxandra said. "I am."

Ishtar stared at her one moment longer, and then turned on her heel and left. Ruxandra stood where she was, listening to Ishtar's footsteps go up the stairs and into the tunnel to the Kremlin.

"I am glad," Michael said.

Ruxandra turned. He was standing nearby, watching them from the stacks of the library.

"I wish I could say I realized the truth from the moment she arrived." The old man stepped forward, a scroll in his hand. "I wish I could say I recognized the danger, but I did not. We were fools. And we are fools still."

He held out the scroll to her. "This is a copy of the ritual to banish the devil back to hell. It needs five magicians."

Ruxandra looked at it. "Could Kade be one of them, if I can convince him?"

"No. It is human magic, not vampire magic."

"Then have only three, if Derek is here."

"We have two with Derek," Michael said. "The Alchemist is missing. The others are still locked up in the Kremlin."

"I know where the Alchemist is," Ruxandra said. "I'll get her. As for the others . . ."

"We will need to rescue them," Michael said. "Derek and I will try to think of something. But it will take time. So come back tonight, after the sun has set. Hopefully, we will have a plan by then." The magician looked haunted, his eyes weary, his gray beard unkempt as cobwebs in an abandoned building. *My friend.*

What she felt for Michael and the other male magicians was not powerful, not passionate or exciting, but it was true. It lit up a corner of her heart that had been empty a long time.

Ruxandra nodded. "Thank you." She touched his cheek—he looked surprised—then turned and ran, up the stairs, out of the church, and through the city.

I feel better now. I know who I am and whom I value. And if Kade opposes me, too bad.

She made a pair of stops at two large, wealthy-looking houses before she went to the Alchemist's bolt-hole. She tapped the door with her knuckles, hoping against all odds that the Alchemist would be awake.

The Alchemist opened the door wide and stared in surprise at the load Ruxandra carried.

"Blankets," Ruxandra said. "And food. You must be starving and exhausted and—"

The Alchemist stepped forward, put her hand on the back of Ruxandra's head and pulled her in for a long, deep kiss. Then she pulled Ruxandra inside, shut the door and locked it. She kissed her again, her hands running up over Ruxandra's breasts.

"Alchemist."

"Shut up," the Alchemist whispered. "You are alive, and I am alive, and I need this now."

Ruxandra managed to spread the blankets on the floor while the Alchemist undressed her. She managed to kiss her back and caress her as they knelt together on the ground. The Alchemist brought her to climax first, with fingers inside her and her tongue caressing Ruxandra's breasts. Then Ruxandra knelt between the Alchemist's legs and stayed there until the other woman convulsed in passion. *Why must there be pain and death when there is this? What is wrong with human beings?* But that question led to questions of good and evil, of God and angels, and Ruxandra didn't want to go there. She cleared her mind and scooted up to the Alchemist's mouth. The woman shuddered, lips parting. Ruxandra bent to the task of pleasure.

Two hours later the Alchemist ate. The Beast inside Ruxandra was growling continuously now, demanding to be fed. Ruxandra forced it into silence and lay beside the Alchemist, watching over the other woman as she dozed.

"Ruxandra," the Alchemist whispered at one point. "Sleep."

Ruxandra shook her head. "I can't. The Beast might escape."

"The Beast?" The Alchemist's eyes came open. "What Beast?"

And so Ruxandra told her everything, from her time at the convent to Elizabeth to Venice to her last conversation with Ishtar.

The Alchemist listened to it all in silence, eyes never leaving Ruxandra's face, and, when the story was over, pulled Ruxandra down with her again. They made slow, gentle love this time, and at the end of it, the Alchemist wrapped her arms around Ruxandra's shoulders.

"Now sleep, my princess," the Alchemist said. "My brave and magnificent princess. You will not hurt me, I know it. Not even with a Beast inside you."

And so Ruxandra slept, and her dreams were sweet.

And when she woke, the world was on fire.

TWENTY-TWO

THE HOUSE WASN'T BURNING. No flames threatened them yet, but Ruxandra heard them crackling and smelled smoke. Outside, people cried in panic. Ruxandra went to the window and then jumped back with a yelp of pain as the sunlight touched her skin.

The gray-and-yellow haze of smoke that rolled through the streets dimmed the late-afternoon sun. The light smarted rather than burned—but it still hurt. Ruxandra peered out the window from the side, staying out of the sunlight's direct path. The light outside hurt her eyes but didn't burn. The buildings across the street were intact. Behind them huge columns of black smoke rose. She looked as far to the side as she could, then swore and ran for the Alchemist.

Ruxandra shook the Alchemist awake. "Get dressed, fast!"

The woman rolled to her feet even as she tried to blink the sleep from her eyes. "What's going on?"

"Fire. Everywhere." Ruxandra grabbed the top blanket, brought her talons out and shredded it into strips. A hundred twenty years before, she had done the same to fight Elizabeth in the daylight. The cloth would not completely protect her but would save her from the worst of the burns. She wrapped it over her arms, legs, and head, anywhere that her dress and stockings might not cover. She moved fast, finishing the strips and tying them off in the time it took the Alchemist to find her clothes. Then she put on her own clothes and her cloak on top.

"What do we do?" The Alchemist kept her voice steady, but there was panic in her eyes.

"We get away."

"To where?"

"I don't know."

Ruxandra opened the door and peered out, squinting against the sun. Flames, twenty feet high, rose up at either end of the street, three blocks from the house. Ruxandra jumped to the roof of a two-story house across the street.

They had set fire to the entire neighborhood.

Houses all around blazed, their wooden frames catching and burning like so many funeral pyres. The heat was growing unbearable, even though the fires were still a block away on all sides.

Who would do this? Not the church or the secret police. They would have sent the magicians to trap me, not burned the city.

Ruxandra jumped straight up as high as she could to look beyond the flames. She spun in the air, taking in everything as she reached the apex of her jump. Lines of men with buckets ran from the Neglinka, but they weren't trying to quench the flames. Instead they were wetting down the buildings outside the neighborhood, trying to keep the flames from engulfing them as well. Beyond them soldiers stood in ranks, muskets ready, on every street and intersection. Some wore the uniforms she'd seen on Belosselsky's men the night before. Others wore different uniforms.

Khilkoff's men, maybe. Belosselsky could have let them in.

Ruxandra landed on the roof and jumped down to the ground. "Any good news?"

"It wasn't the church or Anna," Ruxandra said.

The Alchemist's mouth twisted. "If that is all the good news, we are in trouble."

"We are." Ruxandra took her hand. "Cover your mouth and come with me. Try not to breathe too deep. We have to find a way past the flames."

There wasn't one.

The streets had been lined with hay and wagons and left to burn. Flames engulfed the buildings on all sides and had spread to others. It moved closer as they searched, like a relentless, starving animal, feeding on everything it could see.

I might be able to get out by myself. Ruxandra looked at the height and width of the fires, trying to calculate if she could escape with the Alchemist on her shoulder or back. *But I don't think I can break free with her, too.*

"I take it we are in trouble?" The Alchemist attempted a light tone, but her voice shook.

"Yes," Ruxandra said. "We need to get past the flames."

The Alchemist pursed her lips and looked at the flaming mess in the streets. "How strong are you, Ruxandra?"

"Not strong enough to jump the flames with you on my back."

"Not what I was asking." The Alchemist broke into a coughing fit. When it stopped, she wiped her mouth. "This smoke will kill me before the flames. If I gave you instructions, could you rip the side off a building?"

Ruxandra's mouth fell open.

The Alchemist grinned. "I am a genius, remember? We need to get over the flames, so we'll build our own bridge. Now, find the place where the flames are thinnest. I'll wait here."

Ruxandra raced through the neighborhood and back to the Alchemist. "In the direction of the Neglinka. There are two streets where the flames are only ten feet high and thirty feet deep."

As she said the words she heard the crash of a building coming down, and the roar of the flames grew louder.

"One now," Ruxandra said.

"One is enough. Now take me there and listen."

Ruxandra listened as she led the way. The roar of the fire was deafening, and the heat so great that Ruxandra's skin blistered where it wasn't covered by cloth. The Alchemist chose a three-story house right beside the flaming street and then retreated, unable to stand the heat. Ruxandra ran inside the house.

The wooden houses had been built around a solid frame of thick beams and posts, their cladding put on the outside. Inside, a second layer of wall protected against the cold of the winter.

Ruxandra's talons ripped through the inner walls as if they were paper. They tore through the support beams in a series of vicious swipes. She cut through the bottom supports first, smashing wood planks with fists and boots, and hacking through the supports with her talons. On each floor above she did the same, leaving intact only a few supports on the side nearest the flames.

When she was done, the entire front of the house leaned and swayed, ripping and popping as the frame began to buckle.

Not yet. Please, not yet.

Ruxandra ran back to the middle floor, grabbed the beam across the front of the building, and pushed hard.

Nails screeched, and wood protested and twisted. For a moment Ruxandra thought the wall was going to come crashing down.

It held together and swung wide, like a giant door, into the street.

Yes!

Ruxandra leaped up, hacked her talons through the nails that still held, and kicked the top of the wall. Slowly, ponderously, the wall fell forward, smashing onto the flaming wreckage in the street. Even over the noise of the fire, Ruxandra heard the Alchemist's cheer, cut short by a coughing fit. Ruxandra ran to her, grabbed her, and tossed her over her shoulder.

"Take a deep breath!" Ruxandra shouted.

Soldiers converged around the falling building. Ruxandra turned unnoticed. Smoke rose from under the fallen wall as it began to smolder. The flames beyond it still rose high and wide but were no longer insurmountable. Ruxandra raced to the end of the building, bent her knees and jumped.

She landed just short of their bayonets.

She went through the soldiers, scattering them like leaves. Several shots followed her as she ran, but the men could not see their target. She turned a corner and went another dozen blocks before she let the Alchemist off her shoulder.

"Where to now?" the Alchemist gasped.

"The library," Ruxandra said. "Michael has a spell to get rid of Ishtar."

She held tight to the Alchemist's hand as they walked through the streets, keeping them both unnoticed. The sun beat down on her, heating her body though the cloak and the cloth strips. The spots blistered by the fire burned and itched like fresh wasp stings.

The troops were gone from the library, the streets around it empty. Ruxandra and the Alchemist dashed down the steps and into the library proper.

"We should wash," the Alchemist said. "Get the stink of smoke off us before anything else."

"A lovely idea," said Alexi. "Unfortunately, there is no time."

Ruxandra pulled the Alchemist behind her. She breathed deep, smelling for other secret police.

"I'm alone," Alexi said. "You don't have to be afraid of me. In fact, you need to help me."

"No." Ruxandra looked around for something to throw. "I don't."

"Here." Alexi tossed a heavy bag toward her. It hit the ground with a clang rather than a thud. "Open it."

Ruxandra glared at him. She could not feel his emotions, nor read any deception in the expression on his face. She knelt and opened the bag. Inside were fifteen lead shot, each two inches across.

"I heard what you did to the priest," Alexi said. "I thought these would be better for throwing, next time."

Ruxandra's eyes went from the shot to Alexi. "Why?"

"Because we have a common enemy. And I don't think I can defeat her without your help."

Ruxandra rose. "Ishtar?"

"Ishtar." Alexi looked around. "Michael! Derek! Come out!"

The two magicians emerged from the stacks, watching him with wary eyes.

"I told you earlier that I have spies everywhere," Alexi said. "I have spies in the church and the court, and here I had Eduard."

"What?" The Alchemist's voice rose so high it became a screech. "Eduard?"

"In exchange for not arresting Kurkov and charging them both with sodomy—punishable by death, by the way—Eduard agreed to be my eyes and ears in the library. That was how we knew about the ritual and all your other plans."

"That bastard," Derek growled. "I will end him. With a knife in his bowels."

"You don't need to. He died fighting for Kurkov. Stabbed three guards before they shot him. The two were together in a kabak in a room that I understand is one of their favorites. And do you know why they were there?"

Ruxandra felt her blood heating up with rage. "Ishtar told them to go someplace safe."

"Exactly. She suggested they go well away from the riots before they started. Eduard left a note with one of my men saying this and where they would be."

"Wait." Michael frowned. "How did Ishtar know when the riots were going to start?"

"That is the question, isn't it?"

"She started them." Ruxandra closed her eyes, trying to calm her mind even as it filled with the sounds of gunshots and the screams of the wounded and dying. "She tipped off the church about what was going to happen."

"And Prince Belosselsky and Princess Khilkoff, I suspect," Alexi said. "Everyone was prepared except the empress. The attacks forced Anna's troops back to the Kremlin, and now Ishtar is helping her plan a counterattack which, while it appears to be a stroke of brilliance, will result in a great deal of destruction and loss of life."

"To sow chaos and fear," Michael said, his eyes now beyond weary. He looked at Ruxandra. "To make humans kneel in terror and to ravage the world. That's what you told us."

"We were starry-eyed fools," Derek said heavily. "And so was your empress."

"Yes," Ruxandra said, wishing she could take more joy in their realization. "You were."

"As in Moscow, so in the rest of Russia," Alexi said. "We must stop the insurrection before it grows worse, and that starts with getting rid of Ishtar."

"Will Anna support us?"

"No, nor will she give me my magicians. Ishtar came to her last night saying that you had become unstable and wanted to kill her, so Anna keeps the magicians with her at all times."

Ruxandra frowned, thinking. "What about Kade?"

"He has been sent out to an army camp, fifty miles from the city. Anna has decided that a show of force, rather than diplomacy, is the order of the day. Kade should have reached the camp early this morning. They will bring troops to reinforce Anna and drive away Khilkoff's army from the walls."

"I think Khilkoff's army is inside the walls," Ruxandra said. "We saw soldiers in different uniforms beside Belosselsky's troops."

Alexi's expression went from anxious to grim. "This will be bad. Can you command them to put down their weapons?"

"Probably," Ruxandra said. "If I can get close enough."

Alexi nodded. "Right. We remove Ishtar and disperse the rebel armies before the counterattack. You and I will get the other magicians. Michael, Derek and the Alchemist will make copies of the scroll for them."

"It will be done," Michael said. "They will be ready when you return."

"You forget," Ruxandra said. "I can't get into the Kremlin."

"I did not forget," Alexi said. "There is another way in."

Ruxandra's eyebrows rose.

One side of Alexi's mouth quirked up. "You didn't think I shared all my secrets, did you? Now come. We must go quickly."

"What about Kurkov?" Derek asked. "Can we not help him?"

"Anna won't risk the troops to save him," Alexi said. "Even if he wasn't surrounded by a mob and priests. His only hope would be if our armies can take the church before they kill him."

"What are the chances of that?" the Alchemist asked, her voice trembling.

"None," Alexi said gently. "There is no hope for him."

The Alchemist bit her lip. "Ruxandra, you cannot get near him?"

Ruxandra shook her head. The Alchemist looked to Michael and Derek. Both men had tears in their eyes. They saw the Alchemist's expression and went white. Then they nodded. The Alchemist went to her knees and wrapped her arms around Ruxandra's legs.

"Please," she begged. "Do not let him burn."

Ruxandra put her hands on the Alchemist's shoulders. "I can't get near him. I cannot help him."

"I know." The Alchemist clung tighter to her legs. She looked up, tears gleaming on her face, dripping off her chin. "But please, don't let him burn. Can you do that?"

Ruxandra's heart lurched at the grief in the Alchemist's face. She thought of Kurkov's cheerful laugh and rough, ribald manner. She remembered his knowledge, deep and wide and always available to her. She remembered the love between him and Eduard, and the way he had begged her to rescue the Alchemist. Then she remembered his bloody, swollen face, and the chains on the post cutting into his arms.

"Yes," Ruxandra said. "I can do that."

The Alchemist pressed her face into Ruxandra's legs, tears soaking the fabric of her dress. "Thank you."

"Start copying the scroll," Alexi said. "We will return as soon as we can."

They left at once.

"Kurkov first," Ruxandra said, her voice bleak.

"Of course." Alexi walked in silence beside her for a time. "For what it is worth, I am sorry."

"You would have tortured him if you could," Ruxandra snarled, letting out some of her rage on him. "If it were not for you, none of this would have happened."

"I did torture him," Alexi said, his voice calm in the face of her rage. "I ordered him beaten and I made him watch his lover being beaten. And I would do it again if I thought it best for the country."

"It is never best for the country!" Ruxandra said. "Why don't any of you understand that? You're a bastard, Alexi."

"Yes."

"So stay out of my way."

The crowd around the church was smaller, but still large enough that no one could easily disperse it. Guards still surrounded Kurkov. His face was even more swollen, his eyes nearly shut. Two soldiers took turns poking him with the tips of their bayonets, to the amusement of the crowd. Kurkov swore and raged at them, his voice weak, but still carrying.

"The priests are here," Alexi said. "Two beside the pyre. Can you see them?"

"No." Ruxandra stared at Kurkov. She wanted to shout to him, wanted to pull him off the post and bring him back to the library, to heal him and tell him that all would be well again. Or, at the least, let him die with those who loved him. Not like this. Not alone.

A bayonet jabbed a little deeper, and he groaned.

She reached into the pouch and pulled out a lead shot.

"Can you hit him from here?" Alexi asked.

I am so sorry, my friend.

She pulled her arm back and threw with all her might.

Kurkov's head exploded in a blast of red and gray and white. His body convulsed once and went limp, sagging on its chains. Guards shouted and swore, searching the crowd for the source of the rock.

Ruxandra and Alexi were already gone.

Ruxandra didn't say anything at all as he led her through the city. Tears flowed down her face and she did nothing to stop them. Alexi kept silent as he led her to the warehouse where, weeks before, Kade had destroyed the carriage. The remains of the carriage still decorated the walls and floor, like a scattered toy broken by an enraged, giant child. Alexi walked through the debris and knelt in the middle of the room, prying at something with his knife.

Ruxandra could see nothing there, but she heard something pop. Alexi lifted his hand, showing her a metal disk surrounded by wax. At the same moment, Ruxandra saw the trapdoor Alexi knelt on.

"That's how," she whispered. "I wondered."

"This leads below Terem Palace," Alexi said. "It will take us to the dungeons."

The tunnel was long and clear and easily passible. Alexi brought out a key and opened the door at the end. A set of steps took them up to the dungeon and a pair of men on watch at the door. Ruxandra tensed to attack. Inside her the Beast howled, sensing her intent.

"Stand down," Alexi said to the men. "Anna's orders. The magicians must come with me. Now."

The soldiers saluted and opened the door. The Beast snarled in frustration but didn't attack.

The men were in bad shape. Bruises covered their bodies, and they had trouble walking. They saw Alexi and began to shake. Alexi ordered them out of the cell and down the tunnel. He explained in short, terse sentences what was going to happen. The men didn't ask any questions. They were cowed—their wills nearly destroyed by beatings and lack of food. They stumbled forward; their steps were slow and painful. They leaned on each other and Ruxandra, though none would let Alexi touch them. He brought them back to the warehouse, helped them up the ladder, and led them, squinting at the sunlight, to the old church above the library.

Two secret policemen stood inside, waiting.

"Ishtar is down below," one said. "We are to take your sword, Alexi, and lead you all to her."

"I see," Alexi said. "Do you trust me more than her?"

Before either of the men could reply, Ruxandra killed them.

A single swipe of her talons took both men's throats. They dropped to the ground. Alexi stared in shock as his men's blood spurted across the floor. One of the magicians whimpered.

"I don't have the luxury of mercy anymore, Alexi. Do not think I will forgive you that. You made this happen, and I'm ending it," Ruxandra said. "Come. Now."

Face hard, he nodded. She led the way down, the magicians behind and Alexi taking up the rear, his sword in his hand. Ruxandra pushed open the library door and stepped in.

The Alchemist, Michael, and Derek knelt on the floor, each with a secret policeman behind them and a knife at their throat. Their faces were bleak and frozen in terror. Beside them, fury radiating off him in waves, knelt Kade. A dozen more secret police stood behind them, and Ruxandra smelled four more that she couldn't see.

And above them, on the balcony, stood Ishtar, light gleaming off her hair red as fire.

"Really, Ruxandra," she said. "You didn't think you could win this, did you?"

TWENTY-THREE

RUXANDRA'S FEET FROZE in place, magic holding her feet as surely as if they had bonded with the marble beneath them. She reached into her pouch for the shot. She knew she couldn't touch Ishtar, but if she could get the secret police off the magicians, she could take out the others.

"If you throw anything, my men will kill your magicians," Ishtar said. "So don't be foolish."

"Why?" Ruxandra demanded, not taking her hand from the pouch. "Why kill them? Why do any of this?"

"I told you. From chaos comes order, from fear one gains power, and from proper subjugation, mankind learns to obey." She smiled. "As you can see."

"You could have helped Anna, could have built up the city—"

"That never works, Ruxandra." Ishtar leaned her elbows on the balcony, as relaxed as if she lounged in a drawing room. "I have watched humans for thousands of years. If you build up one group, another just comes along and takes what they have. You build that one up, and the next group does the same thing. No, the only way to make people obey is to tear them down so far that they cannot even *dream* of rising up again. Which is why Anna needs to put down this rebellion in the most brutal manner possible. Only after that will people properly fear her."

"Stupid," Kade said. "This entire mess is stupid. I had Belosselsky contained. I had Khilkoff and Delfino listening to me, and you—"

"Exposed them for what they were and gave them the rage needed to begin their insurrection," Ishtar said, her voice strong and certain. "An insurrection that will be brutally crushed, showing the rest of the nobles that Anna is to be obeyed."

"And the church?" Ruxandra fingered the shot in her bag. Even at top speed, she couldn't get off three before one of the magicians died. She needed to *think*. "Why stir them up?"

"Because they are God's." Ishtar's mood turned; she spat the last word from her mouth like foul, rotten flesh. "He abandoned all these people, and they need to realize it. Otherwise they will have hope, which will stand in the way of their subjugation."

"Enough of this," Alexi said. "Ishtar, I am arresting you for crimes against the empress and Russia. Men, take her."

No one moved.

"The empress rescinded your authority, Alexi," Ishtar said. "I told her you were working with Ruxandra, and she stripped you of your command. You are nothing."

Alexi shrugged. "I thought as much. Pity."

Then he drew a pistol and shot one of the secret policemen.

Kade moved in a blur of speed, jumping to his feet and charging at the men who were confining the magicians. Ruxandra hurled a shot at the man holding the Alchemist. His head exploded and he dropped.

Kade's talons lashed at the policeman holding Derek, but the magic that protected the policeman made Kade's hands skid away, like stones thrown on ice. Kade stumbled, blocking Ruxandra's view of Michael. She switched her aim and threw the second shot at the one holding Derek, taking off the top of his skull.

The third man shoved his knife into Michael's throat and ripped it out. Ruxandra's third shot scattered the policeman's brains.

The Alchemist and Derek scrambled toward their friends. Swords clashed as Alexi fought a man Ruxandra couldn't see. The other secret police rushed forward, swords out.

"Protect them!" Ruxandra screamed at Kade as she dodged the policemen's swords. She swung at them, but the magic that had protected Alexi on the bridge protected them, too. She pulled two more shot out and jumped to the balcony. Kade put his body between the men's swords and the magicians. He spread his arms wide.

"Get back!" Ruxandra shouted as she hurled her first shot. It went into a policeman's back, tore through the blood and bone, and exited his chest. "Get into the stacks!"

The Alchemist and Derek grabbed the other magicians, hauling them out of sight. Ruxandra threw a second shot, killing another man. Six broke off from the fight and ran for the stairs. Ruxandra jumped down, spun, and threw again. The shot blew through two men's legs, dropping them.

Pain, so sharp it was exquisite, tore through her body. The point of a sword drove into her back, sliced flesh and organs, and ripped out her stomach. Ruxandra screamed and spun, taking the blade with her as she slashed her talons at an attacker she couldn't see or touch. She howled her rage and threw two more shot at men she could see. One slammed into a man's chest. The other mashed through a skull. Both fell.

Another sword slashed through the tendons in the back of one knee, sending her to the ground. The surviving men from the stairs charged. Ruxandra used her one working leg to jump forward. Two leaps took her across the room and over the big table. The men ran after her.

Ruxandra picked up the table and hurled it at them. Two scrambled out of the way. Four weren't so lucky. Bones broke, and men fell to the ground, screaming. Ruxandra threw more shot, killing the other two.

Someone shouted in pain and fell to the floor. Alexi leaned over an invisible body. He came up with a pistol and fired. Another body Ruxandra couldn't see hit the floor. She sniffed the air, searching for the last one.

A shot rang out, and smoke hung in the air where the unseen pistol had fired. Ruxandra threw at the shape it outlined. Blood spurted. Alexi stumbled past her, sword in hand. His left arm hung down, limp and covered in blood. He drove the blade into something twice.

"That is all of them," he said. "Where is Ishtar?"

Ruxandra reached out with her mind. "Upstairs. She hasn't gone back to the Kremlin."

"Find her. Kade! Bring the others!"

Ruxandra pulled the sword from her body and flexed her knees. The wounded one had already healed. She jumped back to the balcony. Ishtar was out of sight, but Ruxandra could smell her easily enough. She followed the scent away from all the bedrooms to the door at the end of the corridor. Ruxandra shouted back to let Kade know where she was and waited.

Kade appeared first, the magicians behind him, lanterns and scrolls in their hands. Alexi, grimacing with pain, brought up the rear.

"She's inside," Ruxandra said.

"That's a closet," said Derek.

"Not just." Ruxandra opened it, closed it, and opened it again as she had seen Ishtar do days before. Machinery ground against other machinery, and the back of the closet moved aside. Ruxandra went up the stairs and found Ishtar sitting in the middle of the room, a lantern in her hand. She looked up at the glowing stars above her.

"And here you are," she said. "Did you have fun killing the policemen?"

"Spread out," the Alchemist said. "Surround her. Begin."

The magicians spread around the room, holding up their scrolls. They began chanting in Latin, the words echoing in the chamber.

"Really?" Ishtar rose from her seat. "This is your plan?"

"Don't move." Alexi raised his sword. "Unlike the vampires, I have no compunction about hurting you."

"Nor I about hurting you." Ishtar smiled. "But I will tell you what. If you all agree to leave the city, I will not kill your magicians where they stand."

"You will not kill anyone," Kade said. "I cannot touch you, but I can keep you from touching them. We both can."

Ishtar nodded. "True, but then, you would have to be able to see me. *Vanish.*"

"You gave her a talisman?" Ruxandra yelled at Alexi.

"Not me," he protested. "It must have been Anna."

"Ruxandra!" Kade shouted. "Where?"

"There!" Alexi shouted, pointing at Derek. Ruxandra jumped in front of him just in time to take a knife to the stomach. She winced and grabbed for it, but could not touch it.

"Oh, dear, that must have hurt." Ishtar's voice floated in the air. Ruxandra sniffed the air, and even as Alexi pointed, jumped in front of Dmitri. This time the knife drove into her shoulder.

"How irritating." Ishtar's scent moved back, and Ruxandra followed it. "Did you know they need to read the entire invocation to make it work?"

"The Alchemist," Alexi said, but Ruxandra was already there. The knife jammed into one of her breasts, tearing through her bodice and hacking open the flesh below.

"I did wonder how you found the priests without help," Ishtar said. "I suspected you used scent, but now I know."

She retreated to the benches and the lantern in the middle of the room.

"She's taking something out of her pocket," Alexi said.

The lantern door swung open.

"The protection spell blocks a person from a vampire's sight and hearing." Ishtar's voice was conversational. "I don't think anyone thought to block scent. But then, most vampires don't develop their noses the way you did."

Something flared into bright flame. Black smoke, thick and viscous and stinking, billowed out from a suddenly flaming bag on the ground. The stench was terrible—sulfur and vomit and ammonia and death. The humans in the room gagged and coughed, and Victor vomited. Ruxandra breathed hard out of her nose, trying to drive away the stench. Smoke filled the room, making it impossible to see.

Blades clashed, and Alexi shouted in pain. He stumbled back, blood oozing from the gash across his stomach. Ruxandra ran toward him, sniffing the toxic stench in the hopes of finding Ishtar. Smoke moved and billowed as Kade rushed over.

Air whooshed out of the Alchemist's body.

Ruxandra spun and jumped. She caught the Alchemist around the waist before the other woman hit the ground. Blood poured from her back, covering Ruxandra's arm.

"That way!" shouted Derek, running for the door. Terror made the obese man move faster than one would have thought possible. Sasha and Dmitri stumbled after, coughing and wheezing. Victor stayed where he was, retching and throwing up bile. Ruxandra picked up the Alchemist and carried her from the stinking room.

Halfway down the stairs, she heard a scream of pain, cut short.

She stumbled out into the library and saw Derek's body, his hands against the wound that had killed him. Beyond him Dmitri and Sasha lay unmoving in spreading puddles of blood. Ruxandra put the Alchemist on the floor, wrapping her arms tight around the woman.

"Dammit," the Alchemist whispered. "It hurts."

"You'll be all right," Ruxandra began.

"Not the time for lies." The Alchemist gasped in a wheezing, pain-filled breath. "She hit my kidney. I'm dying."

Tears welled up in Ruxandra's eyes. Through them she saw a blur of movement as Kade ran past, stepping over the bodies of the magicians.

"No," Ruxandra said. "You can't die. I won't let you die. I won't."

"You can't stop me," the Alchemist whispered. "It's unfortunate, you know."

"No . . ."

"I really wanted to see China."

"No!" Ruxandra shouted it. "Listen to me."

The Alchemist's eyes began to close. Ruxandra shook her hard, making her cry out.

"Listen!" Ruxandra hissed. "I can save you. I can change you. I can make you like me, and we can go to China together!"

Ruxandra raised her hand and ripped the fabric around it with her teeth, baring the skin.

"No."

It was a whisper, barely audible. Ruxandra stared down at the Alchemist. Her narrow face had gone pale, her breathing labored, but her eyes were clear and on Ruxandra.

"No." The word seemed to make the Alchemist's voice stronger. "I have lied and stolen for my research. I have done things I am not proud of to survive. But I have never killed anyone."

She gasped in a breath and whispered, "Please, don't take that from me."

Ruxandra's tears blinded her. She brought down her arm and wrapped it around the Alchemist's body, holding her close.

"Promise me?" the Alchemist whispered.

"I promise." Ruxandra's voice came out broken, tears running down her face and dripping on the Alchemist. "I promise. Just rest. I've got you. I'll hold you until—"

But the Alchemist was gone before Ruxandra could finish the sentence.

Ruxandra wailed. She held the Alchemist's body tight, rocking her back and forth like a sleeping child as her grief poured out.

At some point Alexi stumbled past. Victor crawled out of the stinking room to collapse on the ground, rise, and make his way to the stairs on unsteady feet. Ruxandra didn't move.

It wasn't until Kade came back and sank to the ground beside her that Ruxandra looked up. Kade took a handkerchief from his pocket and wiped Ruxandra's face. He took his time, cleaning all the tears from her face. When he finished, Ruxandra lay the Alchemist's body down on the floor, then crossed the woman's arms and closed her eyes. Kade pulled two gold coins from his pocket and lay them over her lids.

"I couldn't stop her," Kade whispered. "I couldn't get near her. She walked down the tunnel to the armory like she didn't have a care in the world. I wanted to tear her throat out, but . . ."

He fell silent, looking at the Alchemist's body.

"What do we do?" Ruxandra could barely speak the words. "We can't hurt her, Anna won't go against her, and the church won't listen to us if we go to them."

"Leave?" The word came out as a question. "I don't know what good we can do here. I don't know if there's *anything* we can do here."

Ruxandra shook her head, feeling fresh tears start. "There has to be a way."

"How?" Kade demanded. "Anna won't listen to us now; we have no allies that can reach her, and we can't even touch her."

"My dear one, none of my children can hurt me, once they've looked on me."

Ruxandra still remembered the smile on her face when she'd said it: self-satisfied and certain, secure in the knowledge that she could not be touched.

Inside her mind the Beast snarled its hunger and fury. It knew that blood had been spilled, that there were lives it could have taken, had Ruxandra allowed it.

Four days? Or five? Ruxandra shook her head. "I need to hunt."

"As do I," Kade said. "The armies will attack soon, and we can hunt among the victims of the battle. And then . . ."

No child of hers can touch her once they've seen her.

"I will go to the house after dark," Kade said. "They will not be patrolling the enclave. I can get the money I have there and clothes for both of us. Then we can leave this city."

Ruxandra nodded, though she didn't look at him. "Where will we meet?"

"Outside the north gate."

"All right."

Ruxandra stepped over the bodies of the magicians and headed for the stairs to the surface.

The streets were still near the church. No one marched, and few people wandered the streets. The fire still burned, its black smoke cloaking the city thickly enough to hide the sun. Ruxandra, cloak over her head, skin covered with cloth, moved like a gray wraith through the streets. She didn't bother turning unnoticed. She had no need of it.

She went by the Kremlin and the enclave. Belosselsky's and Khilkoff's troops marched together, or huddled behind barricades. Cannons stood in the streets, their barrels pointed at the Kremlin walls. Horses whinnied and stomped, sensing their riders' nervousness.

There were fewer troops than before. Ruxandra expanded her mind and discovered more men frantically shoring up barricades and manning the outer city gates against the Imperial Army on the other side.

She found Delfino, hanging from a hook on the side of the bridge. His plump body sagged limply, his face frozen in a scream of agony. A bloody patch of open flesh sat between his legs where his genitals used to hang. The last of his blood dripped down his body, over his face and arms, to fall into the water below.

Princess Khilkoff got her revenge, then.

Ruxandra walked past the Kremlin, past the enclave, to Alexi's warehouse. The trapdoor stood open. She shed her clothes and cut away the cloths covering her body and then descended into the darkness.

Naked, she walked the length of the tunnel, her bare feet making no sound. She listened as she went, reaching out with her mind. The radius of her ability underground was much shorter than above, but it was enough. There was no one in the tunnel, and only the two guards on the other side.

She turned unnoticed and picked up her pace.

By the time she reached the end of the tunnel, she was moving at full speed. She hit the door with the full force of her body, smashing it from its hinges. It slammed against the wall and bounced off the steps. Ruxandra jumped and raced up the stairs.

The guards were still drawing their swords when she killed them, her talons tearing out their bellies. The Beast howled in anticipation, then snarled in fury when Ruxandra left them to die where they lay. She bounded up more stairs until she stood in Terem Palace.

She extended her mind. She found Anna at once, in a room full of nervous men. She found dozens of others—servants, cooks, guards, and housekeepers going about their duties.

Then she felt Ishtar.

The woman was practically glowing with anticipation and blood-lust. She was in a room at the rear of Terem Palace. She felt relaxed and happy, as if she did not have a care in the world. She also had company, and judging from the lust radiating off him, both were going to be distracted, at least for the next few minutes.

It was more than enough time.

Ruxandra slipped up the stairs and through the halls, dodging the occasional patches of sunlight and moving unnoticed past the few courtiers she saw. Ishtar's room was unlocked when Ruxandra reached it. She turned the handle and pushed on the door. It swung open silently.

The room on the other side was huge, easily twice the size of Prince Belosselsky's study. Pale-yellow wallpaper with a hand-printed pattern of green and white flowers covered the walls. Yellow curtains covered the windows, hiding the black smoke outside. A white couch and two white chairs stood before the ornately decorated fireplace. A fire blazed, heating the cold room.

An oversize bed with white sheets and furs and a white cloth canopy dominated the far end of the room. Ishtar lay on it, mouth open, eyes shut and knees spread wide as a man moved between her thighs. Ishtar gasped her breaths in rhythm to his hard thrusts. Ruxandra didn't recognize the man, though judging from the uniform pieces spread over the floor, he was one of Anna's soldiers.

Ishtar's dress lay on the floor as well. Four round silver disks had been sewn onto the front of it. The sight of them set Ruxandra's hackles on end and threatened to make her snarl. She stifled it and slipped across the floor in silence. The man inside Ishtar increased his pace, grunting with the effort and making the bed shake.

Ruxandra grabbed his ankle and threw him across the room.

The man's sudden withdrawal brought Ishtar's eyes open. The crash and his shout of pain as he hit the far wall made her sit up. Ruxandra didn't watch. She grabbed Ishtar's dress and threw it in the fire. One of the silver medallions touched her skin, raising a blister and making her swear.

"What the fuck are you doing?" the man on the floor shouted. "I'll kill you!"

Ruxandra brought out her fangs and talons and snarled. Inside her the Beast screamed, wanting to tear his throat out. The man went whiter than the sheets he'd been on a moment before.

"Get out," Ruxandra said. "Now."

He crawled out the door, dragging one leg behind him.

"I assume you are going to offer to take his place," Ishtar said, "since he will be useless for the rest of the day."

"You should have let us send you back." Ruxandra kept her voice calm, despite the fear she felt and the snarling Beast inside her. "You shouldn't have killed them."

"Why not?" Ishtar scooted across the bed, reaching for a robe. "Did the skinny woman mean that much to you?"

"Did I ever tell you what I was like when Elizabeth found me?"

"An animal." Ishtar stepped out of the bed and pulled the robe onto her shoulders. "Incapable of controlling yourself. Starving to death. Killing anything that moves. I saw, my dear. I watched the way you butchered those girls. Very amusing."

"The Beast," Ruxandra said. "To survive, I created the Beast—a wild, hungry animal that lives inside me and is completely separate from me. When I become too hungry, it breaks free and kills whatever it can."

"I know." Ishtar walked across the room, took up a chair near the fireplace. "Though why you think I should care is beyond me."

"Because it is still here." Ruxandra followed her, stood before her. "And I am very, very hungry."

Ishtar leaned forward in her chair. "Whether or not it is separate from you, whether or not you are starving, the Beast is as much my child as you are, and once it meets me, it will not be able to harm me."

"No." Ruxandra brought the tips of her fingers and her thumb together on each hand, making spikes with her needle-pointed talons. "It won't be able to harm you if it *sees* you."

Ishtar frowned.

It was the last thing Ruxandra saw before she plunged her talons into her eyes.

Then she set the Beast free.

TWENTY-FOUR

THE BEAST SCREAMED AGONY into the darkness. Its body contorted and changed, the arms growing longer, the legs shortening, the spine shifting. It was free—free from the dark prison of Ruxandra's mind—only to be thrust into a different sort of darkness. It dropped to all fours and howled.

Something in the room moved.

The Beast froze. It heard harsh breathing, sensed warmth in the cool air of the room, and smelled the scent of desperation.

Human.

It felt the beat of a pulse, the vibration of blood flowing through veins, sweet and warm.

Food.

The Beast leaped.

The human twisted, its feet skidding on the floor. The Beast's talons grazed it but did not catch it. A blade slashed into the Beast's leg. It snarled and swung its claws, but the human was already moving, running toward the lit fireplace.

The Beast spun, leaped, and this time smashed into the human, taking them both to the ground. The human screamed. The blade slammed again and again into the Beast's stomach. The Beast roared in pain and reared up, swiping with its talons. It ripped into flesh, caught on bone, and tore free. The human screamed.

Then it hooked a leg over the Beast's and twisted, reversing their positions. The blade stabbed down a dozen times into the Beast's face, its neck and its chest, faster than any human the Beast had ever hunted.

But not fast enough.

The Beast felt the air vibrate as the knife plunged. And when it pierced the Beast's flesh again, the Beast grabbed the arm that held it. Its talons dug into flesh, twisting and ripping until it found the elbow joint. It drove its claws into the spaces between the bones. The human screamed again, pain and rage together. It shifted, and the Beast smelled something—flesh burning.

A flaming log struck the Beast full in the face.

Now the Beast was the one to scream. It twisted its talons and ripped. Flesh parted as the human's arm tore in two. The human fell away, and the Beast rolled and rolled, batting at its hair and face until the flames died.

"You animal!" The words meant nothing to the Beast, but Ruxandra, trapped inside it, heard Ishtar screaming them. "What have you done?"

The Beast smothered the last of the flames and rose to its feet. It growled, the vibrations coming from deep in its chest and filling the room. The Beast hurt. It no longer cared about just feeding. It wanted to destroy.

"Stay away," Ishtar said. "I mean it, stay away!"

Kill her, Ruxandra told the Beast. *Kill her and drink her.*

"I will end you." Ishtar's voice held no fear, only pain and fury.

The Beast roared its fury and charged. Ishtar swung the burning log, but the Beast felt it coming and ducked under. Its talons lashed out, sinking into Ishtar's leg. The Beast used the grip to pull itself up her body, wrapping its legs and arms around Ishtar in a vicious parody of an embrace and bringing them both to the ground. The flaming log burned into the Beast's back. It dug the talons into Ishtar's shoulder, twisting and ripping.

Ishtar's teeth sank into its neck.

It didn't stop the Beast from tearing her arm off.

The Beast howled in victory, pulled its neck free, and slammed its forehead down, hearing bones break.

The human tried to bite again. The Beast twisted away, drove its talons into the human's rib cage, and used them to push itself down the length of the human's body. It wrapped its arms around the human's thighs, pulling them apart. It could smell the human's sex, freshly used and still wet, in front of its face.

The Beast turned its head, opened its mouth wide, and sank its fangs deep into the artery buried in the human's thigh. Blood exploded into the Beast's mouth.

It wasn't human blood.

It smelled like human blood, felt like human blood as it burst into the Beast's mouth, but the taste was different. It was sweeter, stronger. It poured down the beast's throat, filling it with power. The Beast gripped the thigh tighter and pushed its face against the human's leg, sucking as much as it could. It could feel its injuries healing; feel its eyes growing back. The black turned gray, and it began to see shapes.

"That is ENOUGH!"

The voice roared loud enough to burst the Beast's eardrums. A hand grabbed it by the neck, threw it across the room. The Beast smashed through the wall, plaster and wood giving way, and landed in the hallway. One of its arms broke and it screamed.

Ruxandra surged forward in her mind, shoving the Beast aside and taking over. The Beast, sated on blood if not on life, sank back into the depths of her mind.

Ruxandra's eyes cleared just as Ishtar fell on her.

The fallen angel stood eight feet tall. Its white skin was covered in black leathery armor that clung tight to its flesh, covering everything but hiding nothing. Her wings spread wide, filling the hallway. A wickedly curved sword hung from one hand, and from the other dangled a three-headed scourge, razor-sharp stones woven into its twisted ropes. Ishtar's eyes burned bright red, and her open mouth showed row after row of razor-sharp teeth.

"Your turn," the angel said.

Ruxandra rose to her feet. She knew she could not attack, no matter how much she wanted to, not even to defend herself.

Ruxandra turned and ran.

Ishtar's scourge lashed out, wrapped around one of Ruxandra's legs and hauled her back. Ishtar flicked her arm and Ruxandra went flying again, through the wall, through Ishtar's room, and out the window. Glass shattered and wood splintered, and all of it embedded itself in Ruxandra's flesh. Sunlight, dim in the smoke-filled air, blistered her skin. She twisted in the air, landed on all fours, and jumped to the shade of the nearest building.

Wings flapped, and the whip hissed through the air, smashing her sideways against the wall. Ruxandra gritted her teeth from the pain, rose to run away.

The Angel's blade sliced through the air, and Ruxandra's feet came off.

She toppled face-forward to the earth. The wounds burned as if acid were being poured into the freshly opened flesh. Ruxandra screamed in agony. She tried to pull her body forward, digging talons into the cobblestone square.

The sword chopped down and her hands came off.

Ishtar's foot, wrapped in black armor and tipped with a gleaming black point, slammed into Ruxandra's body, rupturing her organs, splitting her open and sending her across the square to slam against the Kremlin wall.

Ruxandra was vaguely aware of guards running from the parapets, of men and women screaming. But her attention was collapsing, focusing only on the pain.

Ishtar grabbed her by her head, hauled her into the air, and dangled her there like a doll.

"Happy now?" Ishtar asked. "Thrilled with your victory?"

Ruxandra couldn't answer. Ishtar's sword sliced twice and Ruxandra's forearms flew away from her body. Ruxandra howled with pain.

"I gave you power, you stupid bitch," Ishtar shouted over Ruxandra's screams. "I gave you the strength to rule this world. And what do you do? You go to the *opera*. You buy *pretty dresses*. You dress in drag to hunt in the streets like a common murderer. You act like humans are your friends instead of your playthings. You are a stunning disappointment."

Her blade hacked sideways, taking off Ruxandra's legs at the knees.

"I am going to kill you," Ishtar said. "I am going to rip your body to shreds, and then I am going to send your soul down to hell, where I will spend *eternity* torturing you in ways that will make *this* feel like pleasure."

She shook Ruxandra, hard enough to grab her attention. "Do you hear me?"

Ruxandra heard. And she remembered, in a vision as clear as if it were happening, a day hundreds of years ago. Adela and Valeria and she were in the convent barn, and Adela said something to make them blush and giggle. The vision faded, and Ruxandra stared into Ishtar's furious face.

"Menj be a szájába nyitott csapások erdejébe," Ruxandra said. *Go walk into a forest of cocks with your mouth open.*

Ishtar threw her at the ground.

Ruxandra hit and the world went white. Ishtar's scourge whistled through the air and slashed Ruxandra's flesh, rising and falling faster than even Ruxandra could see. The skin peeled from her flesh, the muscle from her bone. The pain was so great that Ruxandra could not see, could not hear, could not feel anything except the agony in her flesh.

Then light.

White light, pure and blinding, streamed down from above.

The whipping stopped. Ruxandra managed to open an eye and squint against the brightness. She saw Ishtar stumbling back, her arms across her eyes.

"I am forbidden to stay on this plane," Ishtar had said when she was first summoned. *"As Ruxandra told you, this circle does not contain me, only summon me. But while summoned, heaven cannot detect me, save if I use my powers."*

A terrible noise, like stone tearing itself apart, filled the air. The air turned so cold that it froze and burned at the same time. A smell of smoke and sulfur filled the air.

"*No!*" Ishtar screamed, the word nearly lost in the sound of the black hole opening in the air beside her. "No! Not yet!"

Wind hit her, and only her, a furious gale battering her flesh. Ishtar braced herself, dug her shoes into the earth. Her wings flapped, and her hair flew. She screamed fury and defiance.

Her feet flew out from under her. She clawed at the ground, slowing but not stopping her inexorable fall into the black hole. She glared at Ruxandra, hatred on her face.

"I win," Ruxandra whispered.

Ishtar's scourge lashed out and wrapped around Ruxandra's leg. It burned into her flesh as it hauled her toward the black hole. Ruxandra tried to dig into the earth but had no hands, no feet. The stumps of her arms and legs left a trail of silver blood on the ground. The open flesh of her stomach and breasts, peeled by the same scourge that now dragged her to hell, blazed with agony as she slid.

"Come to me!" Ishtar taunted, yelling to be heard over the noise of the wind. "Come with me forever, Daughter!"

Ishtar stopped resisting and let the wind pull her into the darkness. Ruxandra picked up speed, the cobbles of the square tearing at her ruined flesh as the scourge pulled her to the dark portal and hell beyond it.

The white light blazed again, so bright that Ruxandra could see nothing at all.

And when it vanished, she was lying broken in the sun, before the Cathedral of the Archangel Michael.

She should have died. Had it been a bright, clear day, she would have died. But the smoke from the fires still dimmed the sun, and the last of the afternoon was already fading away. Her body broke out in blisters, but it was nothing compared to the pain she already felt.

A soldier stepped into the square, his weapon at the ready.

"Come here!" Ruxandra commanded. *"Now!"*

Kade found her three days later, in the dirt cellar of a kabak in the outer city.

She had drunk the first soldier dry after he dragged her out of the sun, and a second soldier who had come looking for him. The third and fourth she made smuggle her out the Kremlin through Alexi's tunnel and to the outer city.

She drank them and six more men before the wounds on her stomach closed up.

Now Kade watched, eyes wide with surprise, as hands and feet grew slowly off her stumps.

"Was there a battle?" Ruxandra asked.

"No," Kade said. "I found Belosselsky and gutted him like an animal in front of his troops. I told them if they left immediately, Anna would not be able to chase them. They listened."

"And Khilkoff?"

"Anna's army surrounded hers, offered her men a pardon, and offered the princess the choice between killing herself or spending the remainder of her days as a whore, beginning with a week of nonstop service to the Imperial Army. The princess shot herself."

Ruxandra took a moment to pity the woman, but only a moment.

"The Metropolitan witnessed your battle against Ishtar," Kade said. "He saw her dragged to hell. He has declared Moscow free of the taint of supernatural evil and ordered all true Christians to follow Anna faithfully."

"And so she wins." Ruxandra did not know how to feel about that.

"And Alexi her secret policeman still lives and protects her. And both have made it quite clear that, despite our service to Russia, we should not stay here longer than necessary."

"After all that?" Ruxandra shook her head. "How ungrateful."

"One should never count on the gratitude of princes," Kade said. "It tends to be fleeting. So once you are healed, we shall leave."

It took two weeks for her legs and arms to return to full size, another for her hands and feet. Kade kept her supplied with a steady stream of the mortally injured, the deathly ill, and the old. Ruxandra drank far more than usual, but by the end of it, she was whole again.

She spent three nights hunting, testing her strength and her speed. And she spent three days in Kade's bed, letting pleasure fill in the spaces made by loss.

And when those days ended, she shouldered a bag holding her boots, two dresses, two suits of men's clothes, and underwear for both, and walked out the gate.

Kade walked with her, his own bag on his shoulder.

"It will be good to go back to Europe," Kade said. "I think France would be an excellent place for us to start over. The French court is most intriguing."

"For you," Ruxandra said. "Not for me. I'm not going back to Europe."

"No?" Kade's face fell. "I had hoped . . ."

"China." Ruxandra turned to the east. "The Alchemist said that she always wanted to go to China. She even said she would take me with her."

"And now you'll go in her place?"

"It's new." Ruxandra remembered how the Alchemist, half-asleep in her arms, had spoken of getting away. "And since she can't go, yes, I'll go in her stead."

"And us?" Kade asked softly. "Will we be together again?"

For a reply Ruxandra turned back and kissed him long and hard on the mouth. Kade held her tight, one hand pressing against her backside, the other crushing her body to his. Their tongues played and danced in each other's mouths.

When they finally broke apart, Kade smiled. "I'll take that as a yes."

"I don't know when," Ruxandra said, "but yes, we will see each other again."

"Send me a letter when you've found a place to stay," Kade said. "Send it to the Cathédrale de Notre-Dame, addressed to Father Le Loup. I will ensure that they know to expect them."

"It might be years," Ruxandra said. "I have no idea how well the post works from China."

Kade shrugged. "We have years."

"Yes." Ruxandra looked east and smiled. "We do."

And then she ran, without looking back, into the darkness.

YINCHUAN, CHINA, 1824

R UXANDRA SPUN, the blade in her hand whistling as it cut through the air. The courtyard was empty, save for herself and the woman who watched her. Ruxandra twisted and turned through the steps of the form, from mountain to horse, from bow and arrow to girl, and with one final spin and cut she sat cross-legged on the ground, the sword straight in front of her.

"Very good!" Mai Chu called, clapping her hands together in excitement. "You have learned so much!"

"Does that mean I get a reward?" Ruxandra asked, looking at the other woman through lowered lashes.

"Yes!" Chu Mai held out a letter. "You got this! From South America!"

Ruxandra jumped to her feet and took the letter. Its postmark was a year old, the paper stained. But it was addressed to her.

She opened it and began reading.

Dear Ruxandra,

I hope all is well with you and that the years have been kind. I am surprised to say that I have run into a very old acquaintance of ours in Spain, and she and

I have embarked on a new adventure together. We have moved to Brazil, to make our home in the great city that is growing up here near the jungle.

I know you have been fascinated with the Orient and that it still holds great pleasure for you, but I do hope you might think of joining us. Elizabeth misses you and asks after you. Even Dorotyas mentions you from time to time.

So if you grow tired of the East, come join us in the West. There are new adventures to be had and new opportunities for us all.

With deepest respect,
Kade

Ruxandra stared at it, shaking her head.

Of all the people to end up with, he's back with Elizabeth.

She put the letter back in its envelope and went inside the house.

"Well," Mai asked, "who was it from?"

"An old friend." Ruxandra put the sword into its rack. She walked through the house, admiring again the bright colors of the interior, so different from the gray stone outside.

"And?"

"And he wants me to go with him," Ruxandra said. "To South America."

"South America?" Mei shook her head. "That's too far away! It would take years."

"It would," Ruxandra said. "If I were going."

She put the letter on the brazier in her room, watching it catch fire and blaze into ashes. Then she turned and, with a quick move, caught Mei in her arms.

"What do you think you are doing, foreign devil?" Mei asked, though her eyes glowed and her heart sped up with anticipation.

"Corrupting a pure and virtuous Chinese woman." Ruxandra picked her up and carried her to the bed.

"I don't know," Mei teased her. "I think maybe you should answer your friend's letter first."

"I'll answer him later." Ruxandra undid the sash on Mei's robe. "We have all the time in the world."

Thank you for reading Mother of Chaos!

Dear Reader,

I hope you enjoyed Mother of Chaos. It was my honor and pleasure to write for you. Of course I was only relaying the information that my Ruxandra was providing, but I hope I did so with clarity and wonder. Thanks for joining me on this fun and wild ride!

Get ready for many more adventures.

Also, if you're so inclined, I'd love a review of Mother of Chaos. Without your support, and feedback my books would be lost under an avalanche of other books. While appreciated, there's only so much praise one can take seriously from family and friends. If you have the time, please visit my author page on both Amazon.com and goodreads.com.

twitter.com/JohnPatKennedy
www.facebook.com/
AuthorJohnPatrickKennedy/
johnpatrickkennedy.net

Made in the USA
San Bernardino, CA
22 January 2019